Lady Rosamund And The Poison Pen

A Rosie and McBrae Regency Mystery

LADY ROSAMUND AND THE POISON PEN

A Rosie and McBrae Regency Mystery

By Barbara Monajem

First published by Level Best Books 21 April 2020

Copyright © 21 April 2020 by Barbara Monajem

This novel is entirely a work of fiction. The names, characters and incidents portrayed in it are the work of the author's imagination. Any resemblance to actual persons, living or dead, events or localities is entirely coincidental.

Barbara Monajem asserts the moral right to be identified as the author of this work.

First edition

ISBN: 978-1-9479-1527-5

This book was professionally typeset on Reedsy.
Find out more at reedsy.com

Praise for Lady Rosamund and the Poison Pen

Barbara Monajem's *Lady Rosamund and the Poison Pen* is a delightfully spicy mystery, peppered with sharp wit and memorable characters, especially the titular Lady Rosamund. Rosie is a woman who seems to know her own mind…or does she? Battling her greatest fear, Rosie must discover the true identity of the mysterious caricaturist Corvus, and outsmart the author of the poison pen letters before it's too late. Indifferent to the tongue-clucking of her peers, Rosie is full of surprises. Fans of historical mystery are in for an entertaining treat. – Kelly Oliver, Award-winning, bestselling author of the Fiona Figg Mysteries

Chapter One

S *he is too lovely, too flawless to be real.*
　—From the diary of Corvus

My husband, Albert Phipps, spends most nights with his mistress and slinks home just before dawn. The whole world knows about his liaison with Cynthia Benson, so why this peculiar behavior? An open secret is no secret at all.

I certainly have no objection to his continued relations with Cynthia. She is a dear friend of mine, and their liaison is one of the conditions of our marriage, along with his promise to spare me the physical intimacy which is usually required. This arrangement—a private matter to which the world is not privy—works well for both of us. He is enamored of Cynthia, but I am the daughter of an earl, the granddaughter of a marquis, and the cousin of a duke, and therefore my connections are to his advantage. He is a politician, you see.

Perhaps that explains it, for a polite fiction such as our marital bliss is an accepted method of appearing respectable—and in politics, appearance is all.

But that doesn't explain why *I* would agree to such an arrangement. If you must know, it's because I am far more peculiar than Albert. For one thing, I have no interest in carnal pleasures. But that's not the only reason. I don't intend to explain myself now—perhaps I never shall—but suffice it to say that by marrying me, Albert Phipps saved me from a fate worse than death. Yes, I daresay that sounds overly dramatic, but it is nevertheless true.

1

On the night I found the dead footman on the stairs, Albert came home unusually early, a little after two a.m. Thank heaven for that, as he found me on the landing, trying to decide what to do about the unfortunate man's corpse.

I was alone, tired but wakeful in the wee hours of the morning, and had started to creep down to the kitchen for a cup of warm milk. In the flickering light of my candle, I almost failed to see him lying there, blocking my path.

Although nausea stirred in the pit of my stomach, I knelt beside the footman, who was sprawled on the stairs with his neck at a ghastly angle, and checked his pulse—or rather, lack of it—not only once, but twice.

I am ashamed to admit it now, but my first thought was, *how inconvenient.* For me, I mean, which was horrid of me, for it was far more inconvenient for him. He was a young man, and last night he'd been hale and hearty, with most of his life ahead of him. The thing is, we aristocrats are taught to consider servants of no account, and although I strive to be compassionate to one and all, my upbringing comes to the surface at times, like a nasty slop of mud from the bottom of a pond.

Poor man, his body was still warm, but he must have been dead a little while. I'm a light sleeper, I think by choice—I adore solitude and darkness—and would have noticed if the sound of his tragic tumble had wakened me.

"Rosie, is that you? Good Lord, what the deuce is going on?"

I gave an undignified squeak and spied the pale face of my husband, with its prow of a nose, peering over the bannister above. "Heavens, Albert, you startled me! I thought you were still with Cynthia."

"Not tonight," he said. "I've an early morning meeting. Who *is* that on the stairs?"

"One of the footmen," I said, wishing I could identify him by name, but we call all our footmen James. "The tall, handsome one who's always flirting with the maids. He's dead!"

"Dead, you say?" Albert came down, attired only in his nightshirt. Since I do not have intimate relations with my husband, I rarely see him in dishabille—a most distressing sight, believe me. Fortunately, the light cast by his candle didn't reveal much uncovered flesh.

2

"He must have fallen down the stairs and broken his neck," I said.

"How bloody inconvenient." Do you see what I mean about upbringing? Albert is not an aristocrat, but the gentry are often just as bad.

He crouched to examine the poor man. I averted my eyes to avoid the sight of Albert's bare, rather scrawny legs as he bent. I am not precisely a prude, but I believe in respecting another's dignity.

"He had no business being upstairs at this time of night," Albert said.

This was true. The footmen sleep next to the kitchen. The maids' rooms are in the attics.

"He must have been trysting with one of the maids," Albert said severely. "Serves him right."

Coming from Albert, this seemed a trifle unfair. However, what is tolerated in a rich man is forbidden to a poor one. That is, quite simply, the way of the world.

Death seems an excessive punishment for disobeying the rules by which an orderly household runs, but the footman should have known better, and as for the maid, she would doubtless prove to be with child, which would cause no end of inconvenience. No better than they should be, these foolish girls, and—

Oh, drat! I sound like my mother again. Worse, it means I am *thinking* like her. If there is one thing I have sworn to avoid, it is becoming in any way a copy of her. Apart from physically, that is. I can't help but share her features, but I promise you the resemblance is superficial.

I'm not an unsympathetic person. Unlike Mother, I wouldn't dismiss a pregnant maid, but instead would do my best to find her a husband. I understand—in a detached, intellectual sort of way—that most human beings, particularly males, cannot resist carnal pleasures. I admit this to be necessary, for how else could the human race survive and prosper?

Albert straightened, eyeing me solicitously. "Are you all right, my dear? But I need not ask. You're not one to have the vapors."

It's true that I have very little sensibility, and a relief that Albert doesn't treat me like a delicate flower. My mother's idea of a lady is a weak creature in constant need of cossetting, and Mrs. Cropp, our housekeeper, agrees.

This attitude causes me no end of annoyance.

"What were you doing out here in the first place—competing with the maids for that unfortunate fellow?" He laughed.

"Ha, ha," I said. He knows how unlikely *that* is. Nevertheless, he jests about my frigid nature from time to time. I get the impression that he believes, deep down, that I wish I were stirred by the baser passions. Nothing could be further from the truth! Still, in most respects Albert is an admirable husband.

"I was going to the kitchen to warm myself some milk," I confessed. I loathe being caught out. It's absurd—a grown woman should be able to do as she chooses—but it's not that simple for one of aristocratic birth.

"Tsk," he said. "Why didn't you ring for a maid?"

Because I revel in solitude. Because I enjoy warming my own milk. Now, Mrs. Cropp would find out what I'd been up to and scold me. She disapproves of ladies who descend by way of the service stairs and heat their own milk in the wee hours. Like my mother, she is a model of propriety. Everyone in his or her proper place, she says, doing his or her proper job.

"I must say, this body is a dashed nuisance," Albert said. "Parliament frowns upon such things."

Surely everyone frowns on mishaps such as the one suffered by the footman, but Albert invariably thinks in terms of political advantage. Through my influence, combined with his clever machinations, Albert became a Member of Parliament, but that's not enough. He intends to be Prime Minister one day.

Politics is *such* a bore, but to each his own.

"I shall have to call in the authorities," he grumbled. "Word will get out. What if the broadsheets get ahold of it?" He was whining now. He has a horror of the caricaturists and their relentless mockery of those in power.

My mind was a few sentences back. "The authorities? Why? He's only a servant who took a tumble."

Albert stomped past me up the stairs. "Come now, Rosie. Surely you know that all suspicious deaths must be reported to the coroner."

I followed him. "Suspicious? In what way?"

4

"Why would a perfectly able footman fall down the stairs? It seems highly unlikely. What if someone pushed him?"

"Why would anyone…? Oh." I saw what he was getting at. "You think he was visiting one of the maids, they had a falling out, and she *pushed* him?" I found that hard to believe—none of our housemaids show signs of a violent temper—and yet other possibilities popped into my mind. "Or that two of them were competing for him"—I knew this to be true—"and the one he *wasn't* trysting with found out and took her revenge? Or the other footman, lusting after the same girl, decided to get rid of him?"

How horrid—both my gruesome thoughts and the fact that I seem to possess a vulgar streak. Luckily, my mother doesn't know.

"Precisely." Albert strode into his bedchamber to pull the bell rope. "In any event, as a sudden, unexpected death, it must be reported."

Hovering in the doorway of his chamber (a room I would shudder to enter), I gave Albert a dubious frown. I couldn't help dreaming up lurid possibilities, but I didn't take any of them seriously.

"I can't afford to let it pass, but it must be hushed up," he said.

That sounded like a contradiction to me. However, out of the mouth of a politician…need I say more?

"But I have an early appointment, an important one, and—" He tugged the bell again several times. Its clang echoed up from below. "I have it! You can take care of it."

"I?"

"Of course, darling." He only darlings me 1) when we are in public, or 2) when he needs me to help him. The first is part of our façade of mutual affection and thus entirely acceptable to me. The second is mildly annoying. Since we married for our mutual benefit, he needn't butter me up when he asks my help.

"I'll run off to my meeting, and you'll get in touch with Sir Edwin." At my blank look, he added, "The magistrate. Tell him you interviewed the maids so as to assure yourself—and him—that none of them are guilty. He won't want to contradict you, because of your connections."

True, but he also wouldn't approve of a woman assuming such a function.

"He'll have the coroner and a jury in immediately, they'll dismiss it as an accident, and it will be swept under the carpet before it has a chance to get out," Albert said.

It seemed to me that no sweeping of anything was required. No one was guilty of anything but carnal folly, and in any event, an accidental death in our household wasn't fodder for the caricaturists. But Albert was looking mulish, and judging by the heavy footsteps from below, Stevenson, our butler, was on his way up.

"Very well." Come to think of it, I rather liked being given a responsible role, and if I plied Sir Edwin Walters with brandy-laced tea, macaroons, and society gossip, he might not mind.

***

Several hours and a horrific amount of fuss later, I sat down to breakfast at last. By the time I finished with the three maids who sleep in the attics, I felt as wrung out as the handkerchiefs—particularly Joan's. She is the downstairs maid and has a tendency to weep at the slightest thing, and a beloved footman with a broken neck could hardly be considered slight. I had Mary Jane (my personal maid) dress me, and breakfasted on coddled eggs served by a grim-faced footman—the remaining James whose real name, I learned when I questioned him in turn, is Maurice. The body was in the scullery, which was awkward, since the kitchen maid understandably refused to scrub pots and pans alongside a corpse.

Instead of sending for Sir Edwin, I opted to visit him instead. It was a fine spring day, I wished to see him before he left home for the court at which he presides, and I was dying to get out of the house and into the relatively fresh air (the best one can ever say of London).

The hackney soon dropped me at Sir Edwin's door, and a surprised servant let me in. It's not usual for a lady, married or otherwise, to accost a magistrate at his residence, but my standing and reputation put me far above the usual. I was shown into a library crammed with bookshelves—a heavenly place—as well as various tables and chairs and a large desk at which Sir Edwin sat

6

writing.

He laid down his pen and stood as I entered, his florid countenance beaming. "My dear Lady Rosamund, what a charming—and unexpected—surprise. Do have a seat."

"Good day, Sir Edwin," I said, choosing a lyre-backed chair. It would have been a pretty chair but for the lurid stripes of the cushion. Covering the cushion with my derriere seemed the best way to avoid eyeing it aghast. "I have come at my dear husband's request. There has been an unfortunate accident in our household, and he felt it should be reported to the proper authorities."

"An accident." Sir Edwin plumped his sizeable bulk back into his chair. "What sort of accident?"

I told him. "We believe he tripped and fell down the stairs, as the flight used by the servants is quite treacherously steep. It seems he broke his neck and died instantly. I found him in the wee hours this morning."

"And Mr. Phipps sent you here to tell me?" Sir Edwin demanded. "Good God, what is wrong with the man? You must be well-nigh prostrate with shock."

"I admit to being a little tired," I said, "but that was from consoling the maids. Albert had an important meeting today and asked me to be his deputy."

"Humph," Sir Edwin said, "most inappropriate. I shall have a word with him." He rang the bell, and the servant, who had just closed the door behind me, reopened it. "Bring tea for Lady Rosamund, and some of those macaroons Cook made yesterday."

I smiled. "That is precisely what I would have offered you, Sir Edwin, had you come to my house. With a little brandy, of course."

"An excellent notion—it will help you compose yourself."

I was perfectly composed. I have made a thorough study of composure and how to achieve it. It's not something I care to discuss—I never mention it to anyone—but it was a matter of necessity. Almost life and death, and I'm *not* being hysterical. However, there was nothing to be achieved by contradicting Sir Edwin.

"I would have been entirely happy to call at your home, Lady Rosamund," Sir Edwin said. "It's proper of Phipps to inform me—any unexpected death should be reported, and I shall pass on your information to the coroner—but on such an unimportant matter, a brief note would have sufficed."

"That's what I thought," I told him, "but you know Albert. He is terrified of gossip and the broadsheets, and since James—whose real name, I gather, is Harold—was young, handsome, not given to clumsiness, and beloved of two of the three maids who sleep in the attics, he felt it behooved him to take the matter seriously." Or at least to make it appear that he had done so, but of course I didn't say that. "He asked me to interview the maids."

"Entirely unnecessary," Sir Edwin said, "as I shall explain to Mr. Phipps. A lady of your delicate sensibilities must be sheltered from an inquiry, even such a trifling one as this. I shall ensure that your evidence, if required, is read to the jury, so you need not fear being called to testify." He rubbed his hands together. "Nevertheless, a delight to see you all the same, and to share the latest scandals."

I couldn't help but be indignant—I'm as competent to testify as most men—but far more annoying was the fact that all he wanted to hear was gossip.

I tried again. "He wished me to question them and watch their reactions." Very well, I was embroidering a little. Albert hadn't expected me to do more than inform the maids and get on with my breakfast. I would have preferred to give myself credit where it was due, but while Albert's initiative might be seen as undue concern, mine would be construed as foolish feminine imaginings. "So that I might reassure you that the footman's death was indeed accidental."

"And was it?" said a voice out of nowhere.

I started—most annoying, as I loathe being taken by surprise. A man emerged from the shadows at the far end of the bookshelves, a slim volume in his hand.

"An accident, that is," he said. "Was it?"

How dare this—this *person* address me directly? And with such insolence of manner, I might add. I gave him my frostiest stare. "I don't believe we've

8

met."

"Tsk," Sir Edwin said. "I'd forgotten all about you, McBrae. You bury yourself amongst the books and don't make a sound. Lady Rosamund, allow me to present Mr. Gilroy McBrae of Scotland; McBrae—Lady Rosamund Phipps."

McBrae bowed. "A pleasure, Lady Rosamund." Did I detect a smirk on his otherwise unremarkable features? He was of medium height, solidly built (but with no suggestion of fat), dark-haired, and dressed for comfort rather than fashion. All in all, unworthy of comment. I gave him a curt nod in return.

"*Was* it an accident?" he asked again.

Sir Edwin waved a hand. "Of course it was, my dear fellow; why are you harping upon it?"

"Because Lady Rosamund is dying to tell you all about it." Good God, he *was* smirking. How dare he presume to know what I wished to do?

"Not at all," I retorted. The gall of the man. Dying to tell, indeed. Only the vulgar express themselves in such dramatic terms—and he, despite his Eton-and-Oxford accent (not the common thing in a Scotsman), was definitely a vulgar sort. "There was nothing to it. The maids were hysterical, needless to say."

"Only to be expected, dear lady," said Sir Edwin.

"But each in her own way," Mr. McBrae said, adding after a pause, "Needless to say."

He was mocking me, although I couldn't quite see why—how irritating. If someone mocks me, I prefer to know the reason.

I raised my brows.

The corner of his lip curled. "From shock, from anguish, from grief, from fear........." His voice drifted contemplatively. "Despite being mere servants, they *are* individuals."

Believe it or not, I almost rolled my eyes at this stupid comment. (I never roll my eyes, as it's frightfully ill-bred.) Before I had a chance to compose a more appropriate response, he asked, "Do you have other footmen, my lady? Did you question them as well?"

"Only one," I said, nettled now. I should have known better than to think raising my brows would depress the pretensions of a Scotsman. "Yes, I questioned him. As for other male servants, our butler is too old for the sort of intrigue you imply."

He snorted. (Can you imagine?) "No one is too old. Passion afflicts us all and ends only at death."

Thank God, I thought, that I am not so afflicted. Imagine suffering from such a lifelong inconvenience! However, if I had expostulated, he would have taken it as proof, horrid man.

Sir Edwin chuckled, and he and Mr. McBrae exchanged patronizing male glances. The servant arrived bearing a tea tray. There were three cups—a pity, as this meant Mr. McBrae was likely to remain.

Don't mistake me—I do my best to remain unbiased against the Scots, the Irish, the Americans, et cetera. It's ridiculous to characterize an entire population as all stupid, all dishonest, all vulgar and obnoxious, or what have you. However, Mr. McBrae, by a mere curl of the lips, woke within me an array of prejudices I never dreamed I possessed.

Sir Edwin asked me to pour, and soon we were drinking excellent tea with generous dollops, not of brandy, but of an obscure Scottish beverage called whisky, the gift, Sir Edwin said, of Mr. McBrae's father, the Laird of Loch Something-or-other. I was prepared to turn my nose up at it—a substance brewed in the highlands in illegal stills, dear *God*—but whatever else is said about the Scots, they have the manufacture of whisky down to an exquisite art.

"Do tell us about it, Lady Rosamund, if that will make you feel better," Sir Edwin said, making me wonder if perhaps my current annoyance had to do with men in general, not McBrae in particular.

I sipped my tea and pondered the choices set before me. 1) State that I felt perfectly well, which would obviate the necessity of telling them anything. 2) Get on with my story, thus reinforcing their stupid prejudices about women. 3)—

Ah. Of course. "My feelings hardly matter," I said sweetly. "What about that poor footman, cut off in his prime?" I bit into a macaroon, closing my eyes to savor both it and life itself.

"Indeed, indeed." Sir Edwin shook his head and tut-tutted. "However, if he was upstairs at that time of night, it's, er, regrettably plain what he was about."

"Alas, yes. One tries to inculcate proper behavior in one's servants, but—" I sighed in a helpless, feminine manner. "Often they prove to be little better than animals."

Did I detect a flash of annoyance in Mr. McBrae's eyes? I hoped so, although I wasn't quite sure I understood it. His gaze went dark in a mysterious, almost dangerous sort of way.

Heavens, how fanciful of me. He wasn't a prepossessing man—quite ordinary-looking—and his eyes were nothing out of the common, as a second glance assured me.

"And did you conclude with whom he had been slaking his animal urges?" asked McBrae.

"Oh, yes, quite easily," I said. "Henny, the upstairs maid, was the most frightened of the three. She is pretty in a blowsy way and a dreadful flirt. I fear she led poor James on—not the dead James, whose name is Harold and didn't need leading on, but the living one, Maurice."

"Perhaps we might call them by their given names," McBrae suggested.

"Do you know," I said, "I haven't the slightest notion why one addresses all one's footmen by the same name. It's not difficult to learn their real names, and far more efficient than crying out "James!" and getting the wrong footman or perhaps both at once. During my childhood, there were four Charleses—utterly absurd." Why, I wondered, had I become sufficiently distracted from my dislike of McBrae to speak to him frankly, as if I valued his opinions or thought he might be interested in mine?

Oh, get on with it, I told myself. "In any event, I expect Henny and Harold were lovers, but I doubt they had a falling-out. Quite the contrary, judging by her bemused and dreamy expression when I wakened her this morning. Henny is frightened not because she pushed her lover down the stairs—she didn't—but because she fears she is with child. One cannot force a dead lover into marriage."

McBrae shrugged. "She has but to seduce Maurice, and her problem will be solved."

"Heavens, I hope Maurice is not such a fool," I said. "Her flirtations and his resulting jealousy would make the household a most unpleasant place."

"That would never do," McBrae murmured. "And the other maids?"

"Joan, the downstairs maid, truly loved Ja—Harold, so she is grief-stricken. She isn't the sort to murder the man she loved, no matter how jealous. The third is my personal maid, Mary Jane."

"And?"

"And nothing. She's my personal maid."

"And therefore above suspicion?"

"Yes, if there were anything to be suspicious about, which there isn't." I was beginning to wish I'd taken option one, but once on this road I had to continue to the end. "Lastly we come to Maurice, who clammed up and became even more morose than usual when I questioned him."

"And that proves him innocent?"

"I believe so. He's a man and would find a surer way to kill his rival than pushing him down the stairs. That's much more the work of a woman in a fit of temper."

"Which brings us back to the maids."

How exasperating of the man. Scotsmen have a reputation for backwardness, but this one wasn't living up—or rather, down—to it. "No, because if there had been an altercation in the corridor, I should have heard it. I'm a light sleeper." The instant the words were out, I knew what he would reply: that in that case I should have been wakened by the commotion of a fall down the stairs. Unfortunately, I had already made it clear that I'd heard no such sounds.

An immediate diversion was called for. "Tell me, what are you reading, Mr. McBrae?" I indicated the book he had set on the table.

"The poetry of John Donne," he said.

I almost pouted, so great was my dismay. Generally, I feel a delightful connection with those who adore Donne's work.

"So," he said, "neither Henny nor Joan show signs of guilt. Nor do Mary

Jane and Maurice."

"Precisely," I said, relieved that he hadn't challenged me about not hearing this or that.

"Nor anyone else in the household," he said with an air of pondering an intriguing mystery.

"There isn't anyone else."

"No cook? No scullery maid? No kitchen boy?"

"The cook is too old and fat to walk up all those stairs, the scullery maid lives out, and we don't have a kitchen boy." I stood, before he suggested the housekeeper. If Mrs. Cropp wanted to get rid of a footman, she would find a more conventional way of doing so, such as having him sacked for immoral behavior. But I had the feeling that if I remained much longer, Mr. McBrae's nosy questions would stir Sir Edwin to genuine suspicion, and what a pickle we would find ourselves in then!

Both men rose, and we parted with the customary expressions of cordiality. I was immensely thankful to leave Sir Edwin's house, and although I took the hackney for appearance's sake, I had the jarvey drop me at the closest hackney stand—for his convenience, nothing to do with mine—and went the rest of the way home on foot. I needed a brisk walk to get my temper under control.

I had never taken such a dislike to anyone as to Mr. Gilroy McBrae.

Chapter Two

*W*e were introduced entirely by chance. She is steeped in the typical prejudices but rather clever, and in spite of myself, I quite liked her. A pity, because I shan't allow that to change what I'm about to do.
—From the diary of Corvus

Nothing gets in the way of an enjoyable meal quite as much as a tantrum.

A few days later, I had just finished a sustaining breakfast of ham, eggs, and plum cake when the front door slammed, its echo reaching all the way to the breakfast parlor. Albert stormed into the room. "Who the bloody hell is responsible for this?" He snapped a rolled up sheet of paper against his palm. His beak of a nose twitched in fury.

"Albert! What a surprise," I said brightly, recognizing the warning signs of a fit of temper. "I thought you were at a meeting."

"At which some kind soul presented me with this…" He snarled, words evidently failing him, and threw the offending paper down. "The broadsheets will make a laughingstock of me."

The lugubrious countenance of Stevenson appeared in the doorway; no doubt the remaining James and assorted maids hovered right behind. I shot Stevenson a look suggesting that they all make themselves scarce, but Albert caught my glance and turned, roaring, "Go!" He kicked the door shut.

Albert in a tantrum is such a bore. However, as I said before, in other ways he is a satisfactory spouse.

I unrolled the paper and spread it on the table, setting various cups and bowls on the corners to hold them down. It was a caricature which featured not so much Albert, but me! I stood at the top of a staircase, a scowl on my face, in the act of pushing a tall, handsome footman down the stairs. "What in heaven's name?"

"By God, I'll make whoever did this pay!" Albert raged.

The caption read: *The Desperate Wife Scorned*. The doomed footman was saying, "Sorry, mum, just can't bring meself to do it." His words faded to a scream, while I said (to quote the caricaturist—let me make myself clear), "I can't even pay the help to t__ me!"

I burst into laughter. I couldn't help it. The entire notion was absurd, although the portrait of Albert, off to the side with his monstrous nose in Cynthia's magnificent bosom, was delightfully accurate. Apart from the scowl and the lewd implication, the portrait of me was quite flattering. No one had chosen to mock me before. I suppose, being so ordinary, that I'm difficult to caricature.

Even more interesting, this portrait was by no ordinary caricaturist, but by the artist who had taken London by storm a year or so before. He signed himself Corvus (which is Latin for 'crow') and so far no one had unmasked him. Whoever he was, he knew a great deal of what went on in society, often behind closed doors, and commented upon it most wittily. It was no small honor—and rather fun—to be mocked by this mysterious man, or so I saw it.

"It's not funny!" yelled Albert. "How dare this—this Corvus person make a fool of me?"

I controlled my whoops, since Albert was practically foaming at the mouth. I didn't see why. "It's me he's making fun of, not you." Or at least not much. "If I don't mind, why should you?"

"You don't mind being accused of murder?"

"When you look at it like that, I suppose it might be annoying, but it's utterly absurd. Cynthia and I are the best of friends. I encouraged her to continue to be your mistress. I'm not the least bit desperate or scorned, as everyone knows—everyone who matters, that is. As for those who don't matter, who cares what they believe?"

"It looks bad," Albert said. "It makes me look like a neglectful husband,

and you an unstable wife."

By ordinary standards, I suppose he is a neglectful husband, but I wouldn't have it any other way. As for unstable… Uneasiness prickled between my shoulders, but I dismissed it as irrelevant; this caricature was not aimed at character flaws of which only my family is aware. "No one will believe this nonsense. We're both well-respected, and no one faults you for having a mistress. Most well-off men of our class do."

"I have ambitions," Albert said. "I can't afford to be a figure of fun."

I sighed my exasperation. "All politicians are made figures of fun sooner or later." Even my own father, a rather innocuous peer who now lives secluded in the North, was singled out from time to time when he spoke up in the House of Lords. "One must take it with a good grace and get on with life."

He ran his hands through his hair. Albert is proud of his thick head of hair, but what with all the raving, it stuck out every which way. What a good thing the caricaturist hadn't seen him like this.

Who, I wondered suddenly, was Corvus, and how did he know about James falling down the stairs?

Albert echoed my thoughts. "The story about the footman shouldn't have got out. I wish I hadn't sent you to that damned magistrate."

With difficulty, I refrained from rolling my eyes. Men are supposed to be rational creatures, but Albert, however clever in the political arena, is lacking in that regard. Much as I wish to be supportive, I hope his greatest ambition remains unfulfilled. With Albert and his tantrums at the helm of government, England would be doomed.

"You sent me there so that everything would be right and proper," I reminded him. "Besides, Sir Edwin didn't care about the footman. The news was probably spread by the servants—those who live on our street, those who heard about it in the tavern last evening, et cetera, et cetera."

His gaze narrowed. "By God, if Stevenson—"

This time I did cast my eyes heavenward. "No, of course not. Stevenson would never gossip about his betters." I don't believe this for a minute, but I thought Albert might. I didn't want his wrath to fall on our longsuffering butler. "It might be any servant who lives nearby. They couldn't help but hear the gossip, see the body carried out, and so on. Everyone knows caricaturists get their juiciest stories from servants."

Albert's cheek twitched. He snorted down his nose like a bull.

"For heaven's sake, you're fussing like a fishwife," I said. "Over nothing!"

Albert shot me a furious glare and stalked out. Evidently the servants didn't scatter quickly enough, for he threatened to sack them all before storming upstairs.

Stevenson stuck his head in the doorway. The poor man did his best to keep his eyes on me rather than on the drawing spread out on the table. I didn't blame him for being eaten up by curiosity, but class differences and enraged husbands being what they are, I couldn't invite him over to take a look.

"Some fresh coffee, please," I said.

***

Albert burned the caricature.

"Why?" I demanded when he told me.

"Because it's an abomination. What else would I do with it?"

"I rather liked it," I said, almost pouting. "I thought I might have it framed."

"Good God, Rosamund," he said. "Sometimes I wonder if you're a little bit mad."

I froze, inside and out. I cannot, simply cannot tolerate even the slightest suggestion of madness. "Don't be ridiculous," I managed to say.

"I want you to stay home this evening—perhaps for several days. You must keep your head down until the gossip blows over."

Honestly, for a man who can be quite adept at political strategy, he is sometimes surprisingly dense.

"That's the worst possible response to this sort of thing," I said. "It will appear as if I'm embarrassed by it, or worse, as if there is some truth to the story."

"But there *is* some truth to it," he said. "I *am* neglectful of you."

"Because I prefer it that way," I said. "And so do you. I refuse to let some

17

fool of a caricaturist and a bunch of tattle-mongers dictate my behavior."

It was his turn to pout. "Very well, but I should accompany you more often at least for a while."

This solution from the man who campaigns ceaselessly to increase the penalties for thieves, footpads, highwaymen and the like. Albert is most accomplished at arousing people's fears. Every time the Lords, the Commons and the general public become complacent, he reminds them of the rash of outlawry that will inevitably follow once the war is over. He is utterly relentless, and yet when the tables are turned he trembles like a worm. (Do worms tremble? Perhaps I'm being unfair to them.)

"Heavens, no," I told him. "Again, that would seem to substantiate what the caricaturist is suggesting. We must behave exactly as usual. Brazen things out. It's the only way."

I'm not as courageous as I led him to believe. I knew what sort of chaff to expect for the next few days, and so I prepared a number of appropriate responses. Fortunately, I didn't have to worry that Cynthia would be upset. She is tranquil by nature, which is one reason I enjoy her friendship. Although I appear composed, I am seldom truly calm. I find her presence soothing.

Which meant I was particularly thankful for the note she sent me that afternoon. *Will you be at the Baffleton ball tonight? Delabole pleads mortification and refuses to come.* I could almost see her rolling her eyes. (Not that she would do so in public, of course. She is very well-bred.) I answered with a resounding *Of course!!! It will be fun for once.*

I suppose I must introduce Mrs. Delabole, who is Cynthia's elderly companion. She was foisted upon Cynthia by her cicisbeo, Sir Roderick Frockmartin, for the sake of propriety—or so he claims. It's really because he wants Cynthia for himself. Mrs. Delabole is prim and extremely proper, so he expected her presence in the house to drive Albert away—after which, I assume, he would send the old lady away as well—but of course it didn't work. Nothing gets between Albert and his goals, whether it's the passage of a bill in Parliament or another frolic in bed. For a well-off widow like Cynthia, it is quite *de rigueur* to have a lover, so Mrs. Delabole has no choice but to turn a blind eye to the goings-on. I quite understand that she finds the current scandal embarrassing, but how craven of her to hide as if she were the one being caricatured.

In order to reach Cynthia's side, I had to run the gauntlet of my host, hostess, and various acquaintances who demanded if I'd seen *it*. Needless to say, I laughed each time and said *Yes, wasn't it hilarious?* But one can only laugh at the same thing so many times, and my laughter became forced, which I fear made it seem as if I truly were upset.

Miss Tubbs, a gaunt spinster of about my age and one of my least favorite busybodies, accosted me with a languishing sigh and asked the same question as most of the women I'd encountered. "Was he very good-looking, your footman?"

"Yes, we called him Handsome James—as opposed to Morose James, the other footman. (This wasn't strictly true, as it was merely how I thought of them.) The maids adored him."

The paper flowers on her turban quivered coyly. "But their mistress did not?"

If I were able to do so, I would have arched an incredulous brow. But although I know a great deal about composure, my eyebrows insist on working in tandem. I shrugged—elegantly, I hope. "My dear Miss Tubbs, he was a mere servant."

She snickered. "True, but it does make a juicy story." For an unmarried woman, she has an extremely vulgar mind.

I continued down the room, fending off jests about my attire ('Shouldn't you be wearing your blacks?') and my temper ('Stay away from the stairs, fellas, she's dangerous!'). Just before reaching Cynthia, I encountered Lady Danby, one of the elderly tabbies and quite a dear friend. She is as short and plump as Miss Tubbs is tall and thin, and her taste in clothing is preposterous. This evening, her gown was a violent purple, and the ostrich feathers in her turban nearly doubled her height! She asked me the standard question and I returned the stock answer about Handsome and Morose. I made a droll face. "As it chances, Morose James's real name is Maurice, so he's Morose Maurice."

She chuckled obligingly but peered at me, her eyes moist and sympathetic. "You're a brave girl. I had a *tendre* for a groom once."

Damn the woman! Did she seriously believe I'd been enamored of Handsome James? "My dear Lady Danby, even if I were the sort to indulge in a clandestine affair—which you know very well I'm notI would *not* do it with a servant." How dare she?

Lady Danby tipped her head to one side. "Not even if you were in love?"

I broke into horrified laughter. "With a *footman?*"

Someone jostled me, but by the time I caught myself and turned, there was no one but a servant with a few strands of black hair poking from beneath his wig, weaving his way through the crowd with a tray of wine.

"Footman!" cried my companion. "You jostled this lady. Come here and apologize!"

I put up my hand. "Don't make a fuss, Lady Danby. No harm done." I certainly didn't care about being jostled—or perhaps it's that I didn't care to be embarrassed. I had come perilously near to sounding like my mother again. One is taught from childhood that servants are lesser beings. Some people deem them little better than animals, but I'm not that sort. (They may behave like animals, but so do their betters, Albert being a case in point.) But even though I can't consider them my equals, I try not to insult them to their faces. Or backs. There was absolutely no excuse for my behavior. Annoyance at an old lady's assumption shouldn't make me lose my awareness of those about me.

"Nonsense," Lady Danby cried. "Footman! Come back at once or I'll see that you're dismissed."

The servant, slippery as a snake, vanished into the crowd. Lady Danby said, "Excuse me, but I must report the man's misbehavior to Lady Baffleton."

Thankfully, I escaped to Cynthia.

My husband's mistress has golden curls and a voluptuous figure, and her tranquility lends her an air of mystery. It is a strange and dangerous combination which is irresistible to men. Consequently, many women dislike her and are ravenous for an opportunity to vent their spite.

She is very good at concealing her emotions—assuming she experiences any strong ones, for if so I have never seen them. Most of the time she seems mildly amused. I expect that is part of her mysteriousness; that faint smile on her rosy lips makes people wonder what she is thinking about them. Tonight, there wasn't much doubt about her opinion of the ladies gathered about her. She looked painfully bored—and perhaps the tiniest bit queasy, although it was hard to tell for certain. I'm sure I didn't blame her; gossips make me sick. The world would be a better place if someone pushed *them* down some stairs.

"Dearest, how lovely to see you," I said, elbowing one of the witches aside. I'm sure they'd been doing their best to get a rise out of her. They should have known they hadn't a chance of success. "We have so much to laugh about tonight. Can you imagine—*me* falling in love with a footman? Corvus is usually sharper-witted than that."

She tittered. "Indeed, it's completely absurd. I don't know *what* he was thinking."

I took over the conversation, doing my best to engage them all in speculation about who Corvus could be, and whom he might caricature next. Eventually the gossips drifted away to greener pastures, but it seemed like eons before we got a few moments alone.

"Good God, what a bunch of crows," I said. "I've said the word *hilarious* so often tonight that I doubt I shall ever use it again. I feel as though I've used up my allotted quota of that particular word—rather unfair, I think, as it's a good one."

She snickered, which turned into a yawn. "So tedious, darling." She cocked her head at me. "Are you really as amused as you seem?"

"Of course! I laughed and laughed, but to tell the truth, I really don't understand what the gossips find so fascinating. Everyone knows you're Albert's mistress, and plenty of widows have affairs with married men—including some of those we've spoken to tonight."

Cynthia is only a few years older than I, but she is far more worldly wise. "Yes, but one maintains a polite fiction about one's respectability. Now Corvus has laid it out for everyone to see and comment upon." She made a moue of distaste. "As if that wasn't bad enough, it's not usually Albert's nose that gets shoved between my breasts, but now everyone is making warm jests about what *does*."

That had me stymied. After a sip of wine and a long moment of thought, I said, "You're not serious." But she was. "Heavens, why?" I wailed. I simply can't understand carnal behavior.

"I haven't the slightest idea. It's one way to avoid conceiving a child." A faint shadow crossed her face, which I couldn't interpret. She is barren, but she shows no sign of wanting children any more than I do. "Not that men care much about that," she added. "But how did the artist know?"

"Maybe it's a commonplace act, and he guessed because of your large bosom. Or maybe he didn't intend that at all and was merely making game of Albert's big nose."

She gave one of her languid shrugs that drive men to slaver like dogs. At the moment, one of those very men was headed toward us. What a bore.

"Regardless, it makes me look like a slut and a marriage-breaker," Cynthia said. "Would you believe, they're all saying you will cut my acquaintance now."

"Such nonsense. You are my dearest friend in the world." I hugged her—although I suspect I needed the hug more than she did. "Like every scandal, it will soon blow over."

"There wouldn't *be* a scandal if it weren't for you," Sir Roderick Frock-martin said in a voice of ice. He is tall and broad, with a distinguishing touch of silver to his hair, and would, I think, be quite pleasant-looking if he smiled. I can't say for sure, for he never treats me to anything but a baleful stare.

I raised my brows in feigned astonishment. "I? But my dear Sir Roderick, I didn't *really* push the footman down the stairs. Why in heaven's name would I put myself to such inconvenience? The house has been at sixes and sevens, thanks to coroners, juries, grieving servants, the footman's bereaved relations, et cetera. If I'd wanted to get rid of him, I would merely have asked the butler to replace him."

Cynthia stifled a laugh, but Sir Roderick ignored this sally in his typically starchy way. "If you kept your husband at home where he belongs," he snarled in an under voice, "he would leave Lady Benson be." He shook his finger at me. "It is *your* fault she is subject to the mortification of that caricature."

Since Mrs. Delabole proved useless as a chaperone, he blames his lack of success with Cynthia on me. I was seriously tempted to say so, but it might have annoyed her. For some reason which I simply cannot comprehend, she is invariably polite and considerate with Sir Roderick. She allowed him to foist Mrs. Delabole onto her (for God's sake, why?), and he never ceases to attempt to woo her away from Albert. Surely he must know by now that he won't succeed.

"Thank heavens you're finally here, Sir Roderick," I said. "Who better to comfort her than her ever-faithful cicisbeo?"

So catty of me, but he deserved it.

***

A letter sealed with black wax brings news of a death, or at the very least it is related to mourning.

That explained Stevenson's somber expression—more somber than his usual, at least—as he set the salver with the morning's post on the breakfast table some days later. If I'd thought about it, I would have ascribed his excessive gloominess to grief at the loss of the footman—or more likely, dismay at the prospect of interviewing several dozen applicants before finding a suitable replacement. As it happened, I didn't think about his expression or the post until after I'd finished my kippers and was well into the toast with butter and marmalade—a lucky chance.

I glanced through the pile of correspondence—mostly invitations, as well as a crossed and re-crossed and therefore largely undecipherable letter from my mother. Not that I care much for her letters, all admonishments and advice, but filial piety obliges me to read them. I came upon the missive sealed in black quite near the bottom. Dear Stevenson! He'd assumed bad news and wished me to enjoy my meal before learning of it.

I frowned at the unfamiliar handwriting. If any near relative had died, I would have received the news by express. Nobody was likely to send me condolences on the death of my footman, unless it was another stupid jest.

With only the mildest trepidation, I broke the seal and unfolded it—a half sheet of foolscap, which indicated a fairly lengthy letter.

I KNOW EVERYTHING ABOUT YOU.

That's all it said, in firm capital letters. There was no signature.

Everything about me? Puzzled, I turned the sheet over but learned nothing new, except that it had been posted at the Chief Post Office in Lombard Street. There wasn't really much about me that wasn't already known by anyone to whom it mattered. Twenty-four years old, a little on the tall side, and rather ordinary in appearance. I wish I could say I had striking auburn hair and flashing green eyes, like the heroine in a dreadful novel, but no such luck—my hair is a darkish brown and my eyes a greyish blue. My countenance probably deserves another adjective with *ish* on the end, but I can't think of one. My provenance and situation you already know.

So what did that enigmatic sentence mean? And why the black sealing wax?

I folded the missive and set it under the rest of the correspondence, finished my breakfast, and brought it all upstairs to my boudoir—the little room next to my bedchamber where I take care of letter-writing and such. I have a lovely little *secrétaire* decorated with old-fashioned marquetry, in which I keep all my correspondence, writing paper, and so on.

Oh, very well, I wasn't quite truthful just now. I do have a secret, but no one knows about it except my family. However, they've seen no sign of it for years.

Except for Mary Jane, who isn't family but may as well be, as she knows more about me than anyone else. However, I try to conceal my little foible even from her.

So, as I'd concluded by then, this bizarre missive had nothing to do with my secret. My family do their best to forget that my foible exists, so they wouldn't send me such a thing, and Mary Jane is extremely loyal, not to mention entirely above such folly as anonymous letters.

So what the devil did the letter mean? (I do know how to mind my language, by the way, but I don't see why men are free to curse and swear while amongst their contemporaries, while we ladies must adhere to prim propriety at all times.)

It meant nothing at all. I was tempted to throw it on the fire, but something forestalled me—my natural curiosity, perhaps. I hadn't the slightest notion how to go about finding out who'd sent it, for it was a sheet of paper like any other.

No, actually, it wasn't. It was good quality foolscap. Not only that, a half sheet, when a quarter, or even an eighth sheet would have been appropriate for a brief note. A relatively well-off—and wasteful—anonymous letter-writer, it seemed. (Or a servant in a well-off household who enjoyed wasting his master's paper.) The lettering itself was tidy and precise, suggesting an educated individual.

The seal proved more interesting: a poorly-made representation of a cow, for it had excessively long horns and over-abundant hair. The cow had a rather friendly face—what portion of it one could see despite the hair. Poor creature, I thought, forced to seal such an unpleasant communication. (But don't tell anyone I said that; only children are allowed to attach anthropomorphic significance to inanimate objects). Two features made it unpleasant. 1) It was anonymous, and 2) it purported to know more about me than I wanted anyone to know. This combination rendered it vaguely threatening, more so the longer I dwelt on it.

So I shouldn't dwell on it. I stowed the letter away—not in my desk, because I wouldn't put it past Stevenson to poke about out of curiosity, once Mary Jane and I were out of the house. Instead, I concealed it between the pages of the second volume of *The Mysteries of Udolpho* and put the seal in the secret compartment at the back of my *secrétaire*. Then I got on with the usual business of the day.

But not quite. I took the letter out to make sure it was still there. Yes, I knew it was there, but I had to verify its whereabouts anyway. And then I verified it again. Then I decided it wasn't a good enough hiding-place—or at least that was my excuse to myself for checking on it twice. But it really *wasn't* a good place, for a half sheet of foolscap, folded small enough to fit in a book, takes up quite a bit of space. If anyone took that book off the shelf, the letter would fall right into his or her hands. Not that anyone was likely to do so, but…

Perhaps I should choose a slightly larger book, I decided, something I (or Mary Jane or even Stevenson) would be unlikely to read. There were quite a few larger volumes in Albert's study, but the thought of leaving my letter there, where anyone might come upon it, made me frankly queasy. The only larger volume in my bedchamber, where I could check on it anytime I wanted, was a treatise on knot gardens. It was larger in every way, with plenty of room to conceal a half sheet of foolscap, folded once. No one in my household has shown the remotest interest in gardens, especially outmoded ones. I stowed the paper there with a sigh of relief.

(But I checked it once more before leaving the room. I would have checked the seal as well, but opening the secret drawer was too much bother. Or so I told myself, but since I was considering checking it when Mary Jane came into the room to help me change clothes, this may be untrue.)

On to the business of the day. One of the most trying aspects of the life of a lady of fashion is just that—fashion. Not that I object to dressing well—one wants to look one's best—but shopping bores me. Unfortunately, remaining in the forefront of fashion requires a great deal of time and attention.

Clothing, to me, is largely utilitarian—it covers our nakedness, protects us from cold or sun or rain, et cetera. Naturally, one chooses fabrics which drape well in colors which become one, but that seems sufficient to me. I am a great admirer of Mr. Brummell's fashion sense (apart from the overly complex cravats) and wish females would adopt a similar simplicity of style. Unfortunately, feminine taste seems to run to more and more frills and furbelows.

Fortunately, Mary Jane adores fashion and is more than willing to make up for my lack of interest. I take her shopping with me, but truthfully, she does the shopping and I merely pretend. If she chooses some styles and fashions which are better suited to her than to me, I don't object. Once the clothing is made and fitted and paid for, I feign a dislike for some article which I didn't care for from the start. She therefore acquires something practically new which, with a few alterations, will suit her very well, and we're both content.

It would be simpler if we didn't have to go through this charade, but on the one occasion when I suggested just having something made for her, she spoke in nothing but monosyllables for days. Evidently I had injured her pride. What, I ask you, is the use of pride to a servant?

She bustled into the room, hurried me into a walking dress, pelisse, and half boots, and soon we were in New Bond Street. I tried my best to appear interested in sketches, fabrics, trims, and so on, but my mind kept wandering back to the anonymous letter. I wasn't afraid, precisely—there was no cause for concern—but I was definitely unsettled, and that irritated me. How dare some unnamed person unsettle me, daughter of an earl, relation of a marquis and a duke, et cetera?

"How about this one, my lady?" Mary Jane showed me a simpering female with rosebud lips in the latest number of *La Belle Assemblée*. "With several extra sets of ribbons and frills, needless to say."

It was a testament to my uneasy mind that I agreed without the slightest shudder. Even if I consented to wear such an excrescence, I wouldn't seek to vary its appearance with alternative frills. Thank God I needn't economize on clothing. But Mary Jane would certainly make the most of such a gown.

Eventually we escaped the *modiste's* establishment. We took the long way back, window-shopping along the way, and soon found ourselves on Oxford Street in front of Hartley's, my favorite stationery shop.

A crowd of illiterates gawked at the shop window while someone equally ill-dressed and malodorous, but somewhat literate, read aloud the captions on the caricatures displayed there. Mine wasn't amongst them. Evidently my day of notoriety was over.

Or maybe not. "That's 'er!" cried an ill-bred voice. "The one in the print what got took down!"

A glance at the window showed that there was indeed a conspicuously empty space amongst the prints. A clerk was visible through the window, preparing to fill it. I put my nose in the air and swanned past the crowd, ignoring the stares, guffaws, and vulgar remarks, whilst Mary Jane followed, hissing and brandishing her parasol at anyone within reach.

"Oh, dearie me," Mr. Hartley, the owner, a cheerful, rosy-cheeked man, muttered to himself as I entered, waving his hand frantically at someone off to the side—the clerk in the window, I thought. He bowed and greeted me, but without his usual smile. "You honor us, Lady Rosamund, but I fear I cannot do more than I have already done."

"About what?" I asked. It was kind of him to remove the print. I hadn't even expected him to do that. A brilliant thought occurred—why not buy another copy? I would have to hide it from Albert, but that was better than not owning it at all.

He wrung his hands. "Mr. Phipps bought every remaining copy of that infamous caricature. He left not five minutes ago."

Damn! "Good heavens, why?"

He blinked at me, evidently trying to think what to say. "For the, er, sake of your peace of mind, my lady."

"*My* peace of mind?"

Mr. Hartley paled. "He, er, said you were frightfully overset, my lady—practically on the verge of a decline." His eyes flicked toward the window and back.

"As you can see perfectly well," I retorted, "I am no such thing." I fumed. I try to appear supportive of Albert, but this was too much. He was protecting himself, but knowing that buying up the prints made him look ridiculous, he blamed it on me. People would think I had pleaded with him to purchase all the prints and destroy them.

I followed the direction of his furtive glance. The clerk was backing away inch by supposedly stealthy inch, a rolled paper in his hand.

"It seems he didn't buy quite *all* the copies," I said, tapping my foot irritably. I don't like being lied to.

Mr. Hartley paled even more and started stammering I know not what. I beckoned him closer. His eyes widened as if I were about to strike him. I know many women who would behave in such an unladylike fashion, but I'm not one.

I glanced about me, but no one was near enough to hear. "I don't mind if you put it back in the window," I muttered. "But..." I paused, glancing behind. Mary Jane was several feet away, looking at a case of penknives, but still I lowered my voice even more and walked toward the rear of the shop, where we could speak privately. "You must save that copy for me. I want my own copy, and I'm sure my husband will burn all the rest."

He let out a sigh. His rosy color returned. He took out a handkerchief and dabbed his brow. "You're most forgiving, my lady."

"Not at all," I said at my most magnanimous. "Why shouldn't the lower orders have some amusement at my expense?"

His expression indicated that he thought me eccentric, but so what? Eccentricity is expected of the wealthy. So are declines, I suppose, but it infuriated me that someone would believe me so spineless.

"I shall do my best," Mr. Hartley went on, "but if Mr. Phipps returns, I may find myself obliged to sell it to him."

I waved this objection away. "As long as you get me a copy, I don't care what he does with the rest. I suppose he has gone to various other stationers on the same ludicrous mission."

"So he indicated, my lady," Mr. Hartley said. "As I told him, he cannot possibly buy up every copy. It has already gone to several provincial towns. It's an extremely popular print."

"I never imagined myself the focus of such attention," I said. "However, one does better to ignore such things." I wouldn't be able to ignore my mother and eldest brother (my two nosiest, most annoying relatives) when they wrote to me, but nothing could be done about that.

Mr. Hartley snapped his fingers, and the clerk approached. "Run and purchase a few more copies of the Corvus print wherever you can find one." He mentioned the names of several stationers the clerk should try. "Hurry, before Mr. Phipps gets them all. On your return, put one on display in the window again." The clerk bustled away.

"Surely more can be printed," I said.

"If Corvus permits," he replied. "Alas, since no one knows who he is, we cannot request them directly."

"Not even from the printer?"

He sighed and shook his head. "The printer, Mr. Charles, denies all knowledge of the artist's identity."

Once again, I wished I had control over my eyebrows, but it seems raising both at once conveys my disbelief reasonably well.

Mr. Hartley nodded deprecatingly. "I too have difficulty believing that, my lady, but Mr. Charles insists that the artist contacts him through an intermediary."

"Corvus seems very determined to keep his identity a secret," I mused, feeling a delightful surge of curiosity.

"So he does. Mr. Phipps announced his intention of demanding the original plate from Mr. Charles, but I doubt he will get it." Mr. Hartley spread his hands in a gesture of resignation. "And what would be the point? Corvus could produce the same etching again if he chooses."

"Or draw a new caricature mocking my husband," I sighed. Or me, I thought, picturing a drawing of me languishing on a sofa, at death's door due to mortification. But I could do nothing to stop him, so I put that thought out of my mind and went home.

Needless to stay, his next effort was far, far worse.

Chapter Three

She wasn't supposed to be amused.
—From the diary of Corvus

The next letter arrived the following day. How tiresome, I thought. Stevenson had definitely taken note of the first one. He, and perhaps the remaining James who often sorted the post, would be doubly curious about a second. It was none of their business, but it's devilishly hard keeping secrets from servants.

Doggedly, I finished my plate of kippers. I refused to let an anonymous letter-writer affect my appetite. I left my coffee unfinished and took my correspondence upstairs to my boudoir.

The letter was a little longer this time. *I MEANT WHAT I SAID*, it read nastily. *I KNOW EVERYTHING THERE IS TO KNOW ABOUT YOU.* The word 'everything' was heavily underscored.

I crushed it into a ball and threw it toward the fireplace. Unfortunately, I missed, and the letter sat before the hearth like some horrid little demon, making tiny snickering sounds as it uncrumpled itself.

I ignored it and opened my other correspondence. As expected, my mother had learned of the caricature. Her writing was as illegible as always, but since what I managed to decipher was a combination of scolding and lamentation, I didn't waste my time. I dashed off a quick response indicating that I wasn't the slightest bit upset, and that the less said, soonest mended (wishing she would take the hint, which she wouldn't). I accepted a few invitations and declined another.

31

The anonymous letter still squatted evilly before the fireplace. I couldn't leave it there, for one of the maids would most likely read it if I did. I got up with a sigh, opened it, spread it flat, and read it again. I forced myself to examine the paper dispassionately. Everything was as before: the same half sheet of foolscap posted at Lombard Street, and the same seal with a cow in need of a haircut.

I was wondering what to do about it—if anything—when Stevenson scratched on my door and announced that Lady Benson urgently requested to see me. "Are you at home to visitors, my lady?"

"I'm always home to Lady Benson," I said crossly, for he knows that perfectly well. After he left, I folded the letter as small as possible and slipped it into the very bottom of the pocket of one of the cloaks hanging on the back of the boudoir door. I didn't think Stevenson would think to snoop there, nor had Mary Jane any reason to touch it. Later, I would hide the letter properly.

I made my way downstairs to find Cynthia standing before the fireplace in the drawing room, looking—would you believe it—quite annoyed. "Bring wine," I snapped to the curious Stevenson.

Cynthia flapped a hand. "No wine, thank you, for I mustn't stay."

"Bring it anyway," I told the butler, who bowed and shut the door behind him.

Cynthia put down her reticule and pulled me into her arms. She hugged me tight, then retreated to the sofa. Such a gesture of affection was as unprecedented as her annoyance.

Not unappreciated, though. I don't get a lot of hugs. My father is an affectionate man, given to regular embraces, but he lives far away in the North. Sometimes I wonder if I should get a lapdog or a cat. "What is it, Cynthia dear?"

"I'm so sorry, Rosie." She looked pale and tired, which was unlike her.

"Sorry about what?"

She reached into her reticule for a large sheet of folded paper. "I came to show you this. I shall leave immediately afterward. It would be unwise for me to be seen here if you have morning callers."

Impatiently, I unfolded the paper. No need to look at the signature to recognize Corvus's style of drawing. The print featured Cynthia and me, half undressed and flushed becomingly pink, in a passionate embrace. Her large naked breasts were smashed against my smaller ones, and our lips were locked together. The caption queried unpleasantly, "Close friends...or even closer?"

"Oh, for God's sake," I exploded, "what a load of rubbish."

"I know, but people will believe it."

"So what? Without even trying, I can think of three other pairs of ladies who are almost certainly more than close friends." I huffed. "Needless to say, I understand it even less than carnal relationships between men and women. What, I ask you, is the point? It doesn't even result in children."

"To some extent, that probably *is* the point."

I pondered what she'd said and recognized the justice of it. By what I've seen, carrying and birthing children is an unpleasant, not to mention life-threatening, process. One would think men would have a little more consideration for the burdens they place on their womenfolk—but no, physical desire trumps all.

"But no one knows for sure about those other ladies," she said, "and as long as their close friendship doesn't become a cause for open discussion, it doesn't matter." She shrugged, not her languid sort of shrug, but almost pettish. "I shall go now. Until some more interesting scandal supplants this one, we must cease to be friends."

"What?" I gasped. "We shall always be friends!"

"Yes, Rosie darling, but we must *pretend* to be at outs. We must make people believe that we are not close. You won't see me at any social occasions for quite some time."

"We can't just—just give in to that horrid caricaturist!"

"We have no choice," she said. "For the sake of your good name, you must treat me as the merest acquaintance for the foreseeable future."

"But it makes no sense," I cried. "Everyone knows you are Albert's mistress. How could you be my lover as well?"

"It's not unheard of," she said wearily.

33

LADY ROSAMUND AND THE POISON PEN

Usually, I would exclaim at such a bizarre notion, and she would share some of her worldly wisdom, but today all I could think was how much I would miss my dearest friend. I protested, but she remained adamant. She straightened her bonnet and left the room, descending the stairs just as Stevenson toiled up them with the wine.

"I'll show Lady Benson out," I told him. "We shan't need the wine." I hurried down after her. I was almost in tears. "It will blow over, love. Don't desert me like this."

"I'm sorry, but I have no choice." She trod quickly out the front door and into her carriage. After glancing about to make sure no one was watching, she blew me a kiss through the window and drove away.

That brought on the threatened tears. I sucked them back inside, willing them to cease. I do not allow myself to weep, as it is a sign of weakness. I hurried back upstairs to hide both the second anonymous letter and the new caricature. I certainly didn't want to frame it, like the other one—in fact, I wanted to burn it—but I intended to show it to Albert first. Perhaps he could convince Cynthia to ignore the gossip and go on as usual.

"Impossible," he said as we dined together that evening, after which he was to go to a card party whilst I attended a musicale. He had already seen the print and had visited Cynthia that afternoon. "She is prostrate with anguish over this development."

Ordinarily, I would have laughed at such an absurdity. Albert likes to think of Cynthia as a fragile little thing, which is nonsense. Look at how calmly she decided to avoid me for God only knew how long! She has a core of steel—far more than I have. I try to emulate her composure, although in this instance, it hurt too much to do so. How *could* she drop me so easily?

"Now will you heed my suggestion that you absent yourself from society for a while?" he said.

"And give in to Corvus?" I cried. "Never! Which reminds me, I have a bone to pick with you. Not only did you unnecessarily buy up and burn dozens of copies of the other print, but why did you announce to several stationers that you did so because I was going into a decline?"

"I don't know what else I could have said." Albert helped himself to an after-dinner brandy. "Although you've been very courageous, Rosie, I know the print upset you, especially on top of finding the dead footman. I wanted to—to stamp it out as completely as I could."

I blew out a sigh. Albert does like to think of himself as a chivalrous sort.

"I visited the same stationers today and have already burned every copy I could find of the second print."

"Thank you," I said. "But don't you dare tell anyone I'm overset, because it's not true."

Armed with righteous indignation, I dressed and went to the Logan musicale. The ladies didn't behave anywhere near as obnoxiously as I'd anticipated. Some, like Miss Tubbs, asked after Cynthia in sly voices, but that was easy to shrug off. Others, whom I will not name for fear of damaging their reputations, said that if what the print implied was true, they completely understood and sympathized with me. Far worse were the gentlemen, who seemed to find the subject matter stimulating, leering at me most offensively and making lewd comments when they thought I couldn't hear. Or perhaps they hoped I heard them; regardless, they disgusted me.

Lady Danby, bless her, commiserated with me and also asked after Cynthia.

"She's prostrate with anguish," I said, quoting Albert. It was untrue but what he would call politically expedient, and it drew a few murmurs of commiseration from nearby ladies—most likely insincere, but better than nothing.

I wished I knew Corvus' identity, so I could give him a piece of my mind. An image popped into my head—one so audacious that I couldn't help but chuckle.

"What?" Lady Danby asked.

"I was thinking that Corvus deserves a good birching." That evoked a medley of giggles from the same ladies. I may be innocent, but I'm not stupid; I realized at once that I'd said something risqué.

"What an excellent notion," Lady Danby said, chuckling with the rest. I stared at my shoes, embarrassed at my ignorance but determined not to show it. From what I remembered of being birched as a child, it was painful and mortifying. How I missed Cynthia already! She was the one person I could safely ask about such matters. Perhaps I could write and ask her.

My reverie was interrupted by a crisp, male voice. "Well met, Lady Rosamund."

I looked up to find Mr. McBrae regarding me with a twinkle in his eye. Odious man, he'd doubtless heard my comment about birching. A flush traveled from my breast to my eyebrows. I was glad I couldn't see myself in a mirror; I would have been even more embarrassed. It was bad enough that a gaggle of gossips thought I'd meant something risqué. That this smug, tiresome Scot did so infuriated me.

I put up my chin. "Good evening, Mr. McBrae. I never thought to see *you* at an exclusive musicale." Yes, that was rude, but something about him brought out the worst in me.

"Life is full of the unexpected," he said, but his eyes showed that he had registered the insult and despised me for it. Unsurprisingly, he didn't explain his presence.

My companion nudged me, reminding me of my manners. "Lady Danby, allow me to present Mr. Gilroy McBrae from Scotland. Mr. McBrae, Lady Danby."

They exchanged compliments, and he passed on to join a group which included our host. Judging by the familiarity with which Lord Logan clapped him on the back, they were well acquainted.

"He doesn't sound like a Scot," Lady Danby said, her eyes narrowed. "He's rather underdressed for the occasion, but I suppose we shall be obliged to recognize him. Wherever did you meet him?"

"Sir Edwin Walters introduced him. He's the son of the Laird of Loch-Something-or-other."

She sniffed disdainfully. Our hostess asked us to take our seats, the music began, and I promptly forgot about Gilroy McBrae.

***

The third letter came the next morning. Unfortunately, Albert was at the breakfast table with me, and even more unfortunately, he noticed the black seal.

"Someone died?" he asked. "I hope not a family member."

"No, it's a meaningless little note, written by someone who wasted a half sheet of foolscap on a single sentence."

He frowned. "By someone…meaning whom?"

"I don't know," I said crossly, tossing it across the table. "Have a look at it yourself."

"*I KNOW HOW VERY UNWORTHY YOU ARE,*" he read. "Unworthy of what?"

"How should I know?" I buttered my toast and spread it lavishly with last summer's strawberry jam.

"No signature." He turned the sheet over. "It's certainly addressed to you, Rosie, but who can have sent it?"

"Someone in London, judging by the postmark," I said.

"And why a black seal?"

Again, I had no idea and said so.

"Well, it doesn't matter," he said. "Burn it." He flung it in the general direction of the fire, missing by several feet. James—as Albert still called him, although I had begun to think of him as Maurice—was in the act of bringing in a fresh pot of coffee. He set the coffee on the table, retrieved the note and put it on the fire. I would have preferred to keep it, but I could hardly say so without cumbersome explanations. I wouldn't forget what it said.

But to make sure, I would record it. In code.

Code, you ask? Yes, code. More on this later; for now, Albert was speaking.

"If you receive any more like it, let me know," he said.

What would be the point of that, if his only advice was to burn them? "I received two others, but they were equally ludicrous. Whoever wrote them says he or she knows everything about me, which seems highly unlikely, but even if it's true, what does it matter?" Yes, I was a little afraid it *did* matter, but I wasn't about to say so.

"I hope you burned them, too."

"I did," I lied.

"First those horrid prints, and now these anonymous letters. Most unsettling, but don't let such nonsense worry you."

"I shan't," I said.

"Everything will be fine."

"Of course it will," I said.

The melancholy truth is, I *am* unworthy. I have a substantial character flaw. I do a good job of hiding it, but that doesn't mean it's not there, lurking to take me unawares and make a fool of me. Or worse.

I shook off these thoughts. As long as I maintained my composure, I would be perfectly fine. I'd been perfectly fine for years; I couldn't allow a few letters to rattle me. I should just ignore them. Sooner or later my anonymous correspondent would tire of writing them.

In the meantime, perhaps Albert was right; I *should* burn them.

But later, when I went upstairs, I couldn't bring myself to do so. Not only that, I took a quarter sheet of foolscap and wrote the third message on it so I would remember the exact words. The night before, I'd hidden the first two letters behind the headboard of my bed. I added my transcription of the third.

Yes, I realize this gave me an opportunity to verify the whereabouts of the other two. But I didn't. I could have opened them, folded them and tucked them away, given in to the compulsion to open them again and again, but I didn't. I simply tucked the third piece of paper in with the others and returned to my boudoir.

Where I recorded the contents of all three letters in code. My code is quite simple, based upon a phrase from the Bible. I supposed a clever decoder, such as those who work for the Home Office, could work it out, but what was the likelihood of that?

At this thought, I laughed at myself, but it wasn't a cheerful laugh. I can imagine almost anything happening, particularly if it's dreadful or makes me look unbalanced. Oh, very well—mad.

Fortunately, no one is likely to care about my code, much less waste time deciphering it—or even realize what it is. I add an extra layer to my code so it looks rather like someone's faithful practice at perfecting her copperplate.

If Mother found it, she might even praise my diligence. She carps about almost everything I do, but she has actually praised my handwriting once or twice.

I couldn't stop wondering who had sent the letters, and also about Corvus, and the more I thought, the more I hated feeling so powerless against both my persecutors. I wished I could find out who Corvus was, but others had tried to identify him without success. However, I realized suddenly that I did have several clues about the identity of the letter-writer.

First, he (or she; there are plenty of spiteful women out there) lived in London, judging by the postmark. Second, he or she knew something about me (or thought so). Third, he or she used a most unusual seal. Neither clue number one nor two was much use to me yet, but I could certainly do a little investigating of number three.

Since it was Mary Jane's afternoon off, I brought Morose Maurice with me. Needless to say, I tried Hartley's first.

"I'm not here about the second Corvus print," I told Mr. Hartley. I hadn't glanced at the window and refused to care whether the print was there. "I don't want a copy of *that* one—it's far too horrid. I'm thinking of having a new seal made, but I'm not sure what I'd like to put on it. Can you perhaps show me some samples?"

"Delighted," Mr. Hartley said, rubbing his hands together, but none of the samples he showed me had a cow (no surprise) or even a creature in a style resembling that of the seal on my letters. I told him I would think about it, perhaps make a few sketches, and then return to discuss them with him. (Not likely—I can't draw worth beans.)

So much for that, but there are plenty of stationers in London. Fortunately, I have a good memory and easily recalled the names of the stationers to which Mr. Hartley had sent his errand boy a few days earlier. I had Maurice fetch a hackney, and we set off to visit the others.

First we went to the closest, Wilkes's, at the very bottom of Old Bond Street. The second print was amongst the others in his window. I was willing to bet all the stationers had made a profit on my husband's folly whilst keeping at least one or two copies for themselves.

I'd never been to this shop before, but the proprietor recognized me at once and had the grace to show his chagrin.

"I'm not here to complain about those silly prints," I told him, waving away his feeble attempt to excuse himself. "Buying them up was my husband's idea, not mine. I'm here to order a seal." My experience with Mr. Wilkes echoed that of Mr. Hartley—plenty of good ideas if I really wanted a seal, but nothing even faintly like the impression on the anonymous letters. I fed him the same story about bringing some sketches and took another hack to the next one, which was in Piccadilly. More prints of me and no luck there either. I left, pondering.

Two concerns had raised their pesky heads: 1) Much as I enjoy the deference accorded me by shopkeepers, I was tired of being recognized, and 2) I had a better chance of getting results if I showed the shopkeepers the impression left in the black wax.

This meant taking another hack home and changing into my oldest, most outmoded clothing. Since Mary Jane wasn't there, I didn't have to listen to her squawks of protest. My appearance is a matter of pride with her. She would have told me the gown I had on was suitable only for picking blackberries from a hedgerow (precisely the reason I'd kept it), and that the ribbon on the bonnet was faded and worn, and would I please let her replace it first.

"I'd rather not be recognized," I told James (no, Maurice, drat it) as the hack pulled up in front of B.P. Charles and Co. in the Strand. "It embarrasses the stationers, especially if that print is still in their windows. Don't announce me or take umbrage if the shopkeeper is not as deferential as he should be."

"Yes, my lady," Maurice said.

"And don't address me as *my lady*," I added. "A simple *ma'am* will do."

Like many stationers, Mr. Charles is also a printer. The boy from Hartley's hadn't been sent here looking for copies, but I remembered the name from my discussion with Mr. H. So this was where the obnoxious Corvus had his etchings printed, I thought as I crossed the threshold. It was messier than the usual stationer's, but perhaps this was because of the cramped quarters and the unfashionable location. Clerks of all persuasions crammed the shop, noisily ordering paper, pens, pen knives, ink, et cetera. I'd never found myself in such a situation before, as usually a path was carved before me by a servant, and generally I was served first, as only rarely someone of higher precedence arrived at the same moment as I.

Just getting into the shop and looking about me involved quite a bit of jostling, and at first I wasn't sure I liked the anonymity. However, once I'd got past the crowd and could look about me at the various wares, I quite enjoyed myself. There were prints and playbills on all the walls, including Corvus's drawings of me. Further down on the walls were pinned samples of paper, but those didn't interest me. The kind of foolscap used for the anonymous letters was to be found in every other stationer's I'd visited.

Most of the goods on display in glass cabinets were utilitarian—ink bottles and stands, wax jacks and bougie boxes in cheap metal, meant no doubt for clerks in various offices. But I spied a few silver items and a very pretty porcelain set—irises on the white background of a tray, pen and knife holder, ink bottle and pounce box. There were wafers to seal letters, such as those in inferior circumstances are obliged to use. Ah—a number of seals on display in a cabinet, but in a gloomy shop crowded with customers, I couldn't see them at all well.

I must say, there are distinct advantages to wealth and social status, such as not having to wait forever for service. But since I had chosen to shop incognito, I mustered my patience and waited my turn. At last a harried clerk approached me. "May I help you with something, ma'am?"

I raised my eyes from the cabinet. "I should like that porcelain desk set," I said, pointing.

My potential as a customer rose visibly in his estimation. "Yes, ma'am," he said, bustling over to the cabinet, unlocking it and extracting the set. "Shall I have it delivered, or…"

"My footman will carry it." I beckoned to Maurice, who hovered just inside the door.

My status rose even higher. He unlocked the cabinet and carried the set to the counter, where he ordered the only other clerk—even more harried—to package it. "Might I interest you in something else, ma'am? A sketchbook, perhaps, or some water-colors?"

I suppressed the temptation to roll my eyes. (A pity, because indulging in such a vulgarity was permissible, since he didn't know who I was.) He would naturally expect such ladylike pastimes to interest me. My needlework is passable, but my water-colors are as bad as my sketches. "Some other time," I said. "Today I'm looking for a seal. I should like to see what you have ready-made, as well as some samples of what might be custom-made for me. And I should like a silver wax jack to go with it, if you please."

"I should be delighted to show you some, ma'am," he said. "Perhaps you might like to step into the back, where we can put the boxes and seals out on a table. The light is better in there."

This was much more like what I am accustomed to. On our way, I encountered the scowls of several customers who had just entered the store and would have to wait their turns. We passed into a large room where several colorists were at work. An open door to the rear showed where the printing press, silent for now, was kept. The clerk escorted me to a table next to a window, through which sunshine poured in. The clerk pulled out a chair, set several seals on the table before me, and bustled away to bring more.

I glanced at the seals, but I must say, watching the colorists was far more interesting than looking at seals I didn't intend to buy. What fun it must be getting to see the scandalous prints before everyone else.

Voices came from outside the room. "I'm sorry, sir. Mr. Charles is out, although he should return soon." The clerk sounded out of breath. "I've a customer in the back looking at seals. Perhaps I could help when I'm done with her?"

"Thank you, but I must speak to Mr. Charles. I'll wait." That clipped voice sounded familiar. I turned to see Gilroy McBrae in the doorway, just as he spied me.

"Well met, my lady," he said with his obnoxious grin.

Damn! I scowled at him, but I couldn't undo what he'd said. The clerk, who was even more impressed than before, would doubtless learn my identity.

He did so immediately, thanks to the horrid Scotsman. "Tell you what,

Jenkins," said McBrae. "I'm acquainted with Lady Rosamund. I'll help her with the seals while you take care of that crowd up front."

The clerk's eyes went round. He gulped. I don't suppose many of the *haut ton* shopped there. "That's—that's most kind of you, Mr. McBrae." He set two wax jacks and three boxes of seals on the table. "If that's all right with you, my lady?"

I assented with my most regal nod. The clerk bowed and scurried away.

McBrae pulled up a chair and sat next to me—rather too close for propriety, but it wasn't a big table. "Why the frown? I was trying to be helpful. The poor man is overrun with customers."

How typical of him to assume the worst of me. "Commendable of you," I muttered, "but I didn't wish my identity to be known."

"Ah," he said, his smile rueful now. "Sorry, but that cat's out of the bag."

"Indeed," I said frostily, refusing to be placated. I watched his hands as he examined the seals and set them in groups. He had square, competent-looking hands.

"Why hide your identity?" he asked. "Surely you get better, faster service that way."

I let out a huff. "Yes, along with attention I would rather do without. If you must know, it's because my husband has been going about town buying up those Corvus prints." I paused. "Which is stupidly wasteful, seeing as he burns them all. What does it matter if there are a hundred or a thousand remaining? Everyone who cares has seen them, and it will soon blow over. But the worst is that he blames his folly on me! He tells everyone it's because the prints upset me so much that I'm going into a decline."

McBrae snorted, which was vulgar but entirely apt.

"Precisely," I said. "I'm not the sort to be overset so easily. The first one didn't upset me at all; in fact it made me laugh. I ordered another copy for myself, which I will have to hide from him instead of framing it, as I would prefer."

He stared. "You want to *frame* it?"

"You needn't look at me like that," I retorted. "It's a skillfully executed drawing. Why shouldn't I frame it?"

"Because you were supposed to dislike it. You were supposed to be upset or enraged or something of the sort—not amused."

"Perhaps that is what the artist intended, but evidently he doesn't know the first thing about me." A little shudder passed through me, as I thought once again of the letter-writer who claimed he or she did.

"He definitely knows *something*," McBrae said.

"That the footmen fell down the stairs?" I shrugged. "Why wouldn't he know that? I expect all the servants in the street gossiped about it."

"True, but I was thinking of your husband's relationship with Lady Benson."

"That's common knowledge," I said. "So?"

"So by rights you should be upset by it. You should feel slighted by an inattentive husband. Jealous of Lady Benson, perhaps."

I burst into laughter—uncontrollable laughter, the sort of which Mother so strongly disapproves.

When at last I stopped whooping and wiped my streaming eyes, I realized that everyone in the room was staring at me, including McBrae. I didn't care about the others, but the Scotsman's expression unnerved me, perhaps because I couldn't read it.

"I beg your pardon," I said icily.

"For what?"

"Immoderate laughter," I snapped.

Now he let out a guffaw. "You have a lovely, joyful laugh."

Flabbergasted, I couldn't get a word out. I didn't like McBrae—didn't *want* to like him, either—but I couldn't help being affected by such an unexpected compliment and the smile that came with it. It made me warm to him, which in turn made me uncomfortable, although I couldn't have said why.

I returned to the topic at hand. "Joyful or not, I couldn't help it. Jealous of Lady Benson? Why, it's utterly absurd."

"Evidently the artist didn't think so," he said. "Nor does society."

"Society is peopled with idiots," I said. "They are just as willing to believe that Lady Benson and I are carrying on an illicit relationship. Not that I care what they think, but poor Lady Benson was quite upset by that second print—which I definitely *don't* want to frame, no matter how well executed it may be."

He was watching me with that quizzical expression again, but now he turned to the seals and grimaced. "Nothing wrong with these, but they're not the best quality. Why not have a family crest made?"

"Boring," I said, examining the seals. There were quite a number with flowers on them—roses, daffodils, irises, et cetera.

"Those are usually purchased by the wives of prosperous tradesmen," McBrae said, "to show that they don't have to use wafers."

"I already have one with a rose on it," I said, turning the others over in my hands. One box contained every letter of the alphabet in various plain or decorative styles. Another group McBrae had put together contained crosses, circles, circles containing crosses, and so on. A third group included a duck, a goose, a pig, even a skull. I rather liked that one. It would go perfectly with black wax, if one were of a macabre frame of mind, but imagine the horrified reaction of the recipient!

"Schoolboys and pirates," McBrae said.

I rolled my eyes. How strange—I forgot not to be vulgar. "Pirates don't have seals."

"How do you know?" he asked. "Have you ever met one?"

He had me there.

"So do smugglers. I knew a brandy smuggler once whose seal was a keg," he said.

It so happens that I *have* met smugglers. "I could imagine Black Johnny with a seal like that." I would never admit it to anyone, but I'd had a childish *tendre* for Johnny, a dashing fellow with a mischievous grin.

Rather like McBrae's, as a matter of fact. What a startling and unpalatable fact. My emphasis, mind you, was on childish. As I grew past girlhood, I became impervious to masculine charms. Even the most well-turned out dandies and the most beguiling rakes have no effect on me.

"He was the leader of the smuggling gang in Kent, near where I grew up," I explained. "At least half the village was involved in the brandy trade."

"We smuggle whisky where I come from," McBrae said, that twinkle back in his eye, as if he were daring me to ask if he'd been a smuggler himself.

It wouldn't have surprised me, but I refused to give him the satisfaction. Not only that, I didn't wish to know anything about the barbaric land of his birth. I examined the last few seals—a soldier on a cavalry mount and a set of scales. "No cows," I said at last, and then put a hand to my mouth. I hadn't intended to say that. Somehow, I'd progressed from freezing McBrae out to having a more or less civilized conversation with him, and now look what had happened.

"You want a seal with a *cow?*"

I didn't blame him for looking incredulous. "Yes," I said stoutly. "I adore cows." Could I trust him? I wondered.

What a stupid question to ask myself. Of course I couldn't trust him, but I needn't really confide anything in him. He knew next to nothing about me—I'd never even met him till a few days earlier—so he had no connection with the letter-writer. Safe as houses, I thought, and dug in my reticule. "I want one something like this, only a bit less untidy-looking."

He took the lump of wax and examined it in the light from the window. His lip curled a little. "It's supposed to look like that. It's a highland cow."

"A highland cow," I repeated, my mind working furiously.

"Aye, we have them in Scotland." Was that a bit of a brogue creeping into his speech? No, I was imagining things. "They need all that hair to keep warm."

"Oh," I said, my heart sinking. "Is this a common sort of seal for a Scot?"

He laughed. "Not that I know of. Perhaps it was made for a child in remembrance of a favorite animal."

I cursed inwardly. I knew very few people from Scotland, and those I did were peers and peeresses who would most likely seal letters with a family crest. I couldn't think of a single Scot who knew anything much about me, much less one who would send me anonymous letters saying he or she did.

"Who sent you this?" he asked—a prying question and none of his business.

"Oh, just a friend whose mother died," I lied. "She's not from Scotland. I wonder where she came by such a seal."

"Why not ask her?"

"I shall," I lied again, "not that it matters, since now that I know more about it, this is clearly not a suitable seal for me."

My day's quest had got me precisely nowhere. I was as much in the dark as before.

Chapter Four

C an it be that I am developing a conscience? Surely not.
—*From the diary of Corvus*

I arrived home quite defeated, but I cannot bear being in the doldrums, so although I felt like retiring to bed with a book, I went to Lady Danby's card party instead. A few people asked me solicitously if I was quite well. Perhaps I was paler than usual, but if so, I hadn't noticed it in my mirror. They were people I don't care for, such as my mother's arch enemy, Mrs. Brill, who can be counted upon to mean the opposite of what she says, and the wives of men Albert associates with in his clubs—acquaintances only, and not very interesting ones at that.

Far worse, though, I didn't play with my usual skill. I didn't lose much, but I'm accustomed to winning. Infuriatingly, my mind simply wasn't on it. Because of the prints? Because of the anonymous letters? Because of Mr. McBrae?

That last thought made no sense. Certainly I wasn't distracted because of McBrae, whom I disdained—but I disdained both Corvus and the anonymous letter-writer as well. Perhaps it was not knowing what might come next that disturbed me. Well, I had better get over it, and quickly. I refused to let either of them get to me.

The next day I received letter number four, saying I should be ashamed of myself—which I was, but only because I was letting such foolishness affect me. After transcribing its tedious contents and the date received onto another quarter sheet of foolscap—and also recording it in code—I forced myself to burn it.

Yes, I admit I had to force myself, but that was better than not burning it at all. I pondered destroying the first two as well but couldn't bring myself to do so. Maybe I would, I told myself, given a little time.

The following day no letter came, but rather something far worse. Albert had gone to Surrey the day before, so (thank heavens) he wasn't there when Cynthia burst in upon what I had hoped would be a tranquil day: reading a novel, cutting out a pattern for a reticule, drinking tea, and entertaining any morning callers who happened to stop by.

Perhaps *burst in* is not the right way to describe her entrance, for she glided as calmly as usual into the room, but what she brought with her certainly spoiled my day. At first I was delighted to see her, hoping she had seen sense and would allow herself to be my friend again. But the firm set of her mouth told me that this was not to be the case.

"Is something wrong, Cynthia-love?"

"I thought it my duty to get here before any morning callers," she said. "To warn you." She opened her reticule and pulled out a much-folded sheet of paper. She spread it upon the table.

For a third time, Corvus had chosen me as his subject matter. As before, the portrait was quite flattering. I was pink-cheeked and unrealistically pretty—even more so than in my first season, when I was young and fresh. As for what I was doing, I blush to mention it, so horrified was I.

"You're not going to faint, are you, darling?" asked Cynthia.

I shook myself. "No, of course not. Oh, how *dare* he?" For he had drawn me brandishing a birch rod, flogging a bare-bottomed man. The fellow was shown from behind, so couldn't be identified, but I knew perfectly well who it must be. "It's my own fault," I said numbly.

"Whatever do you mean?"

"At the musicale a few nights ago, I said Corvus deserved a good birching."

"Oh, dear," she said with a shadow of a laugh.

I felt myself redden. "Everyone there laughed, too, but I couldn't ask why without looking stupid."

"That's why I came here today. I thought you might need an explanation."

49

She made a face. "It's because some people find being birched erotically stimulating."

"You're not serious," I said, but of course she was. How charming—I had progressed from chasing footmen to birching caricaturists.

I have often wondered what her deceased husband was like, that she knows so much about carnal peculiarities, but she doesn't offer to tell me, and it would be impolite to ask.

But you're close friends, you might say. *Bosom bows know everything about one another.*

Ah, but I have a secret which I share with no one. There must be a reason for both Cynthia's unusual knowledge and her extreme reserve, and if I'm not willing to discuss my private matters, how can I expect her to divulge hers—particularly when she gives no sign of wishing to do so?

Another thought occurred to me. "I suppose you can also explain why so many gentlemen were leering at me after the second print came out."

She grimaced. "Yes, men tend to be stimulated by the thought of two women kissing one another."

You see what I mean? Carnal thoughts and behaviors make no sense at all.

"But Corvus isn't the sort of person who attends exclusive musicales," she said. "How could he have known what you said?"

"The same way he knew about the footman," I said. "Any number of people heard what I said and could have repeated it, including servants." The more I looked at the drawing, the more furious I became. "Oh, I could *kill* him."

"Quite rightly," Cynthia said. "But don't say so anyplace else but here, or he'll draw a picture of you knocking him on the head with a coal scuttle."

I couldn't even bring myself to laugh. "He's made it look as if I'm *enjoying* myself," I raged. Somehow he'd managed to infuse vigor and delight into my wielding of the rod.

"Yes, well, that's rather the point, isn't it?" she said.

"What do you mean?" I demanded. "I didn't mean I literally wanted to birch him! I just said he deserved it."

Stevenson scratched on the door. "What?" I snapped.

He stuck his head around the door. "Are you at home to morning callers,

50

my lady?" His eyes flickered to Cynthia and back to me. "None have arrived as yet. I only wished to ascertain…"

No, Stevenson was merely curious; he could have waited until someone had actually arrived before intruding on us. I sighed; he would learn about the caricature regardless. A few minutes sooner or later made no difference.

"Yes, of course," I said, refusing to be cowed by the gossips. "You may remove the tea things, but until Lady Benson leaves, show anyone who arrives into the blue saloon." This was not my normal practice; usually I would have them ushered into the drawing room, where we were now.

"Very good, my lady." Stevenson has his flaws, but in many ways he is an excellent servant. He understood perfectly well that Cynthia might wish to be smuggled out of the house. He came into the room, studiously avoiding looking directly at the print spread upon the table as he slowly retrieved the tea things and left.

"What do you mean, that's the point?" I repeated, almost whispering in case the butler was hovering outside the door. "How dare Corvus make me look so pretty and happy while I'm beating him? I remember being beaten as a child, and it was dreadful. I would never birch anyone." I eyed the offensive print. "I'm not a vain person. I don't think I was ever as good-looking as that."

She sighed. "Rosie, women tend to become more beautiful when they are aroused."

"I beg your pardon?"

Another sigh. "Physically aroused, I mean."

I gaped, disbelieving.

"A becoming flush, lips moist and red…"

"Do you mean to say that—that villain is suggesting that I would become *carnally aroused* by birching him?" I squeaked in my attempt to keep my voice under control. I wanted to scream.

"Well, yes," Cynthia said. "It's not unheard of. Punishing someone for pleasure, that is."

"Well!" I cried. "Never in my life have I imagined such a thing."

"I know, darling. You're such an innocent. And before you ask, no, Albert

51

shows no interest in birching. Clearly, Corvus is a man of the world and had no difficulty imagining such a scene." She hesitated, then said, "There's more."

"How can there possibly be more?"

The front door knocker sounded. Damnation! Morning callers, who might have already seen this abomination. Now that the crisis was upon me, how the devil should I behave?

"Drat," Cynthia said. "I'd better go."

"Must you?" I whimpered. (I cringe to admit it.) "Can't we be friends again?"

"We *are* friends, but no, not in public. I miss you, Rosie, but that's the way it must be." She heaved a sigh. "Before I go, please take another look at the man. Better to know the worst now than be mortified in company."

"What worst?" I snarled, disappointment getting the better of me. From behind, Corvus was an ordinary-looking fellow—dark hair, a nondescript partial profile that could belong to almost anyone, a set of muscled buttocks (unfortunately marred by a few red welts) and a broad back. I have seen statues before, and if I'd been in a mood to appreciate masculine beauty…but I wasn't.

Stevenson's measured footsteps passed along the corridor towards the front door.

"Look more closely." Cynthia picked up her reticule. "And hurry, for I really must fly."

I got the impression she would leave without explaining if I didn't do as she said, so I looked again. The man lay sprawled across a chaise, not quite flat on his belly, raised a little to one side. "What's that poking out from underneath him?" I asked. It looked as if he was lying on a mushroom. A deep pink one.

"His manhood." Cynthia let out a long sigh—exasperation at my dropped jaw and utter incomprehension, no doubt. "His, er, *aroused* manhood."

I was speechless.

"Usually, birching for pleasure is enjoyed by both parties," she said. "I'm sorry, darling, but do you know what I think this means?"

Numbly, I shook my head.

"I think Corvus took great pleasure in imagining this scene, seeing you in his mind's eye, flushed and aroused, and himself aroused as well. There is no doubt about it. Corvus is strongly attracted to you."

***

Well! I think you know me well enough by now to know that I took the bull by the horns in my own quiet way. First I folded the print and hid it under the sofa. Then I tossed the pattern for the reticule into the grate and watched it burn.

"What are you doing?" Cynthia asked.

"Providing evidence that I burned the print." I would have to draw the pattern all over again, but that was easily done.

"Then why not really burn it?"

"I shall, but later."

She chuckled. "You find it titillating?"

"No!" I said, appalled, but I didn't expect her to understand. She enjoys physical intimacy—she must, to stick with Albert—while I felt nothing but nausea at the thought of this creature lusting after me. And yet I—I had to somehow absorb and understand the print before I could destroy it. I know that makes no sense, but so it was. I wished Cynthia wasn't there, for she might tell Albert about my reluctance to burn it, and he might suspect that I'd kept a copy of the first one.

"I want Stevenson to think I destroyed it, but I may have to show it to Albert," I improvised. "Unless—do you suppose it may pass unnoticed? He *is* out of town for a day or so."

"No, for someone is sure to twit Albert about it upon his return."

At least I had time to get another copy for myself, or to pretend that I had burned it in a fit of rage. I kissed her goodbye and went to join my guests, motioning to Stevenson to show Cynthia to her carriage.

No hilarity this time, I told myself as I entered the blue saloon, but nor did I wish to reveal any of the shock and disgust that roiled within me. I chose bored indifference.

"Yet another print?" I asked with an amused smile.

That elicited a brisk nod from Lady Danby and a titter from Miss Tubbs, who had arrived at my house from different directions at precisely the same moment, each armed with a copy of the print. Miss Tubbs had already spread hers upon the table, while Lady Danby clutched hers with a glower.

"It appears I was right," I said, eyeing the drawing. "He *does* deserve a birching."

"I thought you might like to see it," Miss Tubbs gave as her excuse, "but think how embarrassing for you to ask to see one. Fortunately, my father has a subscription with Hartley's."

"That's most kind of you, Miss Tubbs," I lied, "since I don't suppose my dear husband would wish to show it to me."

"I should think not!" pronounced Lady Danby, shooting a glance at the window, where Cynthia was stepping into her carriage. She disapproves of my closeness with Cynthia, saying it is inappropriate under the circumstances. I have no idea why. A well-bred widow has every right to conduct an illicit affair. I know for a fact that Lady Danby has done the same—although, admittedly, not with the husband of her best friend. She is forever bringing up the example of Georgiana, the former Duchess of Devonshire, and Elizabeth, the present one, but my situation is quite, quite different. However, it's not one I can explain, so people will just have to think whatever they choose. It's a pity Cynthia is painted as an evil seductress, but I dislike being portrayed as a victim just as much.

"Where is Albert?" asked Lady Danby.

"Doing some of his endless political maneuvering," I said. "He's in Surrey today buttering someone up."

Lady Danby scowled. "That drawing is a gross insult, and if I were Albert, I would call the man out."

"Luckily no one knows Corvus's true identity, so there is no fear of that," I said. "Albert is a terrible shot, and both Cynthia and I prefer to have him alive and kicking."

Miss Tubbs tittered. "He must be quite a man."

"Oh, definitely," I said absently, pondering the drawing. I found that I was able to look at it dispassionately now. Unlike the print of a few days earlier, it had an unfinished look. My gown, for example, faded into a mere sketch at the bottom, and my feet were barely there. There was only the slightest hint of background, no caption, nor were there any speech balloons—but what was there to say but 'Ouch'? It had an almost dreamlike quality about it...

Because Corvus had been daydreaming about dallying with me? Again, a shudder of nausea rippled through me. The drawing didn't bother me anymore, but what had prompted it surely did.

I got myself under control. "Truly, it's not worth making a fuss about," I said in a light, indifferent voice. "Corvus has made me prettier than I am, so I suppose it's a compliment—in a vulgar, inappropriate way, but a compliment all the same." How *dare* he?

When I finally got rid of them, I retired to my bedchamber with two copies—Cynthia's and Lady Danby's. Miss Tubbs took hers away, ostensibly to return it to her unsuspecting father's collection, but no doubt to ogle the protruding tip of the man's member first. Which is entirely her business, but I cringed at the thought that she—and anyone else of a lascivious frame of mind—might feel tempted to do so with a print that also featured me.

I sat near my open bedchamber window, watching the breeze flutter the leaves of a nearby plane tree and enjoying the rare London sunshine on my face. Something had to be done. Albert might go the rounds of the stationers' shops again buying up the dratted things, but that would do more harm than good. The more attention Corvus got with his drawings, the more he would produce, the more money he would make, and so on ad infinitum. Well, perhaps not quite that long; sooner or later he would find another victim. But for the moment, he had every reason to continue to persecute me. He had to be stopped.

And it was up to me to do it.

I pondered. Just because no one else had discovered who he was, it didn't mean I couldn't do so. Have I ever given up when something truly matters to me? No, never, so I ordered coffee, which always helps me to think, and pondered some more. At last, a simply splendid idea popped into my mind. It was audacious and entirely improper, and I got up and twirled around the room, so pleased was I with it.

But the more I thought about it, the more I had to accept that I couldn't put it into practice. I have the misfortune to be a member of the ruling class of England. I know, I know: I have wealth, privilege, et cetera, and if I call that misfortune, there is indeed good reason to believe a mad streak runs through me. (And I don't wish to discuss it.)

The problem is that my wealth and status make me conspicuous. Recall what happened at B.P. Charles, printer! Even while dressed to look less well off, I garnered respect by both my manner and my possession of a footman—and then had the misfortune to run into McBrae.

To put my plan into action, I would have to pretend to be far, far lower on the social scale. I would have to go out alone—difficult, if not impossible, with servants hovering about all the time. I would have to dress in shabby clothing, which needless to say I don't possess. I would have to somehow render my face less recognizable, for who knew whom I might come across—possibly McBrae again, as he was acquainted with Mr. Charles.

What a pity, I thought. I have a talent for mimicry and can ape the speech of my inferiors reasonably well, and I enjoy play-acting. However, I know my limitations, and I simply can't look and act like a poor wretch. It's just not in me. Much as I would like to tackle this particular job myself, someone else would have to do it—someone less conspicuous with a lot of time on his hands.

None of our servants would do. We had only one footman at the moment, and frankly, I didn't trust anyone but Mary Jane. All the others are Albert's servants, and although they treat me with proper respect, they're not devoted to me the way Mary Jane is; and even for me, I doubt if she would consent to wear rags, hover on a street corner pretending to sell violets, and then pursue a printer's boy across what might be some rather grim areas of London. What I needed was a boy with nothing better to do. All the boys with whom I was familiar—the butcher's boy, baker's boy, and so on—might be hired for the occasional commission when no footman was available (for the shopkeepers naturally wish to oblige me), but not for a task which might take days.

What I needed was a penniless urchin. There are plenty of such urchins running about London, but I couldn't claim acquaintance with any of them.

Until now, I hadn't wanted to. Ragged urchins are an unpleasant reality that one is obliged to ignore, whilst keeping a tight grasp on one's reticule. Perhaps the boy who swept the crossing at nearby Oxford Street had a friend who might help me, I thought. Or the butcher's boy, if I could get a chance to speak to him without Mrs. Cropp or the scullery maid eavesdropping.

For that was another aspect of the problem: Albert would most certainly disapprove of what I intended to do. It would offend his notions of propriety, which are all very well, but if a man does nothing apart from ranting and buying up prints, what is a woman to do but take matters into her own hands?

"You little thief!" Mrs. Cropp's high-pitched voice, raised in anger, rose up from the back garden, disturbing my reverie. I stood and leaned out my window. The housekeeper had a thin, whimpering girl by the arm and was dragging her towards the house.

"I never!" cried the child. "I never stole nothing!" She launched into a string of curses, including several comments on Mrs. C's character, with some of which I agreed. Others were couched in terms far too vulgar for me to understand.

"Whatever are you doing, Mrs. Cropp?" I said. "You're hurting the poor child." I recognized the girl; she was perhaps eight or ten years old, and lived in a shed in the corner of Lady Beddoes' garden next door. Somehow she managed to occupy the shed undetected, except by me. Perhaps that was because I had the leisure to sit at my bedchamber window, watching everything from robins and squirrels to stray children, whilst the servants next door were kept busy with work. And rightly so, for the lower classes require constant occupation to keep their natural folly under control.

Or so my mother would say. The leisured classes seem as brimful of foolishness to me. In any event, I couldn't see that the girl was doing any harm, and I dislike Lady Beddoes, so I had said nothing about it. Unlike, may I add, what Mother would have done; a child living in a shed is much too irregular for her, so she would have put the girl on the parish.

"Caught her stealing eggs from the hen-house," Mrs. C shrieked. "I'll have her put in charge. She'll be transported for sure, the wretch—that, or hanged outright."

The child let out a wail that traveled all the way down my spine, but at the same time it struck me that here I beheld the solution to my problem. "Don't be foolish, Mrs. Cropp. She's hungry, poor thing. Bring her into the kitchen and give her something to eat. Better yet, she can eat in the breakfast parlor, and I'll sit with her and have tea."

Mrs. C gaped up at me. "But, my lady! She's a—a filthy, pest-ridden ragamuffin. You can't have tea with her. It wouldn't be right."

"Nonsense. I can have tea with whomever I please. Wash her hands and face and bring her to the breakfast parlor. I'll be down in a trice."

I shut the window and hurried downstairs. I wouldn't have put it past Mrs. C to let the girl go and claim she ran away, but I didn't reckon with the child, who quite sensibly believed me. She had every reason to do so. She knew I had seen her in the garden before, and I hadn't tattled on her then.

It wasn't quite comfortable to keep my mouth shut, mind you. I was brought up to revere law and order and to assume the worst of the lower orders, particularly the dirty, ragged sort. But I didn't care if she stole an egg now and then—it didn't affect me one way or another, so why make a fuss?

Once the table was set with a pork pie, some bread, and a wedge of cheese, I shooed Mrs. C out of the room and shut the door behind her.

The girl sat on the very edge of her chair and eyed me. "I weren't stealing nothing."

"No? It doesn't matter to me if you were."

"Weren't no eggs to steal," she said with a bit of a smirk.

I don't like being put in the wrong. Not that I really had been—I'd never said there *were* eggs, but I'd implied it. Most likely the child was right. I know very little about hens and eggs, but according to Mrs. C, our hens aren't good layers at the best of times, so we buy most of our eggs.

But it wasn't just that. A good servant never, ever smirks at her mistress. (She may do so behind her back, perhaps, but never to her face.) My mother would have thrown her out instantly (not that she would have invited her in in the first place). I must admit, that smirk and her know-it-all attitude got my back up. On the other hand, the girl wasn't a servant and perhaps didn't know the rules.

"Well then, let me put it this way: if you should be tempted to steal eggs, don't get caught. I might not be here to rescue you."

She continued to stare at me, not smirking anymore. It's hard to believe such an uneducated scrap capable of any but the most rudimentary thoughts, but I could have sworn she was analyzing me, would you believe. Sizing me up.

For theft, perhaps? If she wanted to steal from my house, shouldn't she furtively glance about her to see what she might find? Instead, her gaze never wavered from my face.

I served her a substantial helping of pie and set the plate before her, then poured her a cup of small beer. "Go ahead. Eat." I poured myself a cup of tea.

The girl had no table manners, but in all fairness, where would she have learned them? Studiously, I ignored that she used her hands rather than her fork, and chewed with her mouth open. She was precisely what I needed—dirty, fairly ragged, and much like a thousand other children on the streets—and best of all, female. I'd imagined hiring a boy, but this child and I had one thing in common—our gender. Better than nothing at all, I thought hopefully. A girl might be less likely to betray me.

I leaned across the table and spoke softly. "I should like to hire you to do something for me, but it must be a secret between us."

She said nothing, and only the slightest flicker of her eyes betrayed her surprise.

"Can you keep a secret?"

She rolled her eyes—proof positive that it's an inherently vulgar gesture. "'Course I can," she said, giving me an unlovely view of partly masticated pastry.

"Very good," I said, nauseated at the sight but bearing up bravely. "What is your name?"

"Jenny. Can I have more pie?"

I was beginning to tire of her lack of good manners. No please, no thank you, and she didn't even know how to address me properly. It felt awkward, just as it was uncomfortable to wait about in the stationer's for someone to serve me. "Very well, Jenny. I am Lady Rosamund."

Another eye roll. "I knows that."

"You may address me as 'my lady'."

Her nose twitched slightly, as if at a bad smell. "Right you are, milady," she said in a voice tinged with sarcasm. I didn't quite know what to think of that.

But it didn't matter right now. I served her another large piece of pie and went on. "Very well. Are you familiar with prints?" Blank face. "Caricatures, such as are found in print shop windows."

She managed an "Aye" whilst gobbling up the pie.

"Excellent. I wish to find the source of the original drawings by an artist who calls himself Corvus."

"Him what drew pictures of you," she said.

Good God, did everyone in London know about it? "That's the one."

Jenny cocked her head to one side. "Did you really snuff that there Harold?"

"No!" I retorted. "No, of course not."

"He were a handsome fella." She smacked her lips, reminding me startlingly of Miss Tubbs, which was absurd. Much as I dislike Miss Tubbs, she is of gentle birth, while this child was gutter scum. There could be no comparison.

"Yes, he was handsome," I said wearily. Perhaps it wasn't Miss Tubbs she reminded me of, but the inquisition of several nights earlier. "My maids adored him."

She winked and said, "So did all t'other females on the street, maids or not." She eyed the pork pie again.

Affronted (mostly because I couldn't tell whether or not she included me in the bevy of fools who'd loved Harold), I pushed the pie plate across the table. Let her serve herself.

She didn't bother, choosing to eat right out of the dish. I sipped silently at my tea, getting my annoyance under control. I watched a louse crawl through her filthy, matted hair. For some reason—a reason I didn't wish to examine—that helped me to not care what she thought of me, as long as she could be of use.

"I need someone to watch a certain print shop in the Strand and find out who delivers etchings there for printing," I explained. "They will arrive from various sources, possibly at various times of day."

She nodded, munching away. "Right you are." As if it was easy. No trouble at all.

I had to make her understand the importance of her mission. "The information I need is of vital importance, and I am willing to pay well for it," I admonished her. "I would far rather keep watch myself, but I would be conspicuous standing on a street corner." Not to mention all the other logistical difficulties involved.

The odious child chuckled. "Aye, that you would, milady."

Suddenly, I couldn't stand the sight of the louse. I reached out to pluck it from her hair, and she cringed—as if I'd meant to slap her! She leapt up from her chair, fear in her very blue eyes.

"Sit down," I said. "I wasn't going to hit you."

She stared at me and didn't move. What had I done to make her think I would harm her? I'd been kind to her, hadn't I?

"I merely wanted to squash that louse that's crawling through your hair," I said.

After a second's pause, she said, "What, me pal Larry? He's a good louse, he is. Best leave him be."

I laughed. What a plucky child she was. I gave up on the louse, for it suddenly occurred to me that the jest might be her way of telling me not to touch her. Such an abrupt rejection couldn't but pain me, but I understood all too well. I wouldn't want someone I scarcely knew to touch me, even in a friendly way, so why should she? I pushed the bread and cheese toward her.

She sat again and polished off the pie, using a spoon to scrape every last bit off the dish. She wiped her mouth with her napkin—surprisingly, not on her sleeve—and helped herself to bread and cheese.

"You have a much better chance of passing unnoticed," I said. "I want you to find out which delivery boy brings the original drawings by Corvus to the printer, and where he comes from."

"Follow him back, you mean?" She shrugged. "Why not? Got nothin' better to do."

Except thieving, I assumed, but I knew better than to say so. "I don't think it will be as simple as following him back. Corvus has published caricatures in London for a year now, and no one has been able to find out who he is. I assume whoever delivers the drawings…"

Or perhaps the etchings, I thought, but it would be much easier to deliver a sheet of paper unnoticed than a sheet of etched copper, wouldn't it? Most likely, the etching would be done by an employee of Mr. Charles. So for the moment, Jenny must look for rolled or folded paper.

"…must take a roundabout route, perhaps even passing them to someone else partway, or disguising them in some other sort of package." I had thought this through carefully, imagining how I might accomplish such subterfuge, and was proud of my conclusions.

"I can do that," she said, as if there was nothing to it.

"It's not that simple," I said. "How will you justify hovering about the print shop day after day?"

She frowned a question.

"Corvus doesn't provide a new caricature every day. Won't people get suspicious? Wonder what you're doing there, perhaps suspect you're a thief?

She scowled. "I ain't no thief."

"I didn't say you were, but nor do I want your presence to arouse suspicion."

"'Course not. If they twig me, the game is up."

"Precisely. Perhaps you could sell something at the corner—violets or some such."

"Nuts," she said, pointing at a bowl of walnuts and filberts which were past their best but still edible. "I could make like I'm selling nuts."

"An excellent notion." I offered her a shilling a day for expenses and five pounds when she got me the information I needed.

She opened her eyes wide at that. *Five quid?*

I nodded. She gave me a long, slow, suspicious look—an extremely impudent one, may I say.

She shook her head. "Naw. You won't pay me five quid."

"Indeed I shall." She wrinkled her nose, and I added, "Why wouldn't I?"

"Why would you? Nobs gets away without paying all the time." She picked up the napkin, wiped her mouth, and dropped it onto the table.

Shame pricked at me—not because of anything I had done, but on behalf of my peers. Still, the gall of the guttersnipe, questioning my honor. "Because I gave you my word." I thought about it and added, "I'm sorry if previous experience of your betters has been unpleasant, but when I purchase something, I pay for it."

She wrinkled her nose again, then shrugged and stood. "Like I said, nothin' better to do. I gets the first shilling now, right?"

"Three shillings for the first three days," I said, digging in my reticule. She snatched the money greedily. For all I knew, she would run off and never show her face again, but I was willing to trust her—a dirty little vermin-infested scamp. Surely she could find it in herself to trust me back. Isn't cleanliness next to godliness?

Perhaps not. I know plenty of clean, ungodly people.

I pondered as she polished off two slices of bread and half the wedge of cheese. I'd given her the three shillings for practical reasons. I couldn't require her to call on me every day to report, as that would arouse suspicion. As it was, Mrs. C might tattle about the little guttersnipe to Albert, who would wonder if I had run mad.

There it is again, that ghastly word. I fear I shall have to reveal why it bothers me so much—but not yet. In any event, I knew better than to let it disturb me then. All I needed was a reasonable explanation for my eccentric behavior.

Ah! As a gentlewoman of kindly disposition, I participated regularly in charitable acts, such as reading aloud to orphans or knitting socks for the poor. Why shouldn't I instead encourage enterprise? It's far better than to foster laziness by allowing the needy to expect handouts.

Or so my mother says, so there's probably something faulty in that last thought. But she would never encourage a grubby child to do anything but get out of her sight, so I felt doubly encouraged to help the little girl earn an honest income. Perhaps she would develop a taste for it and become a respectable citizen in due time.

"I wish you to return any time you have information for me," I said. "I shall tell Mrs. Cropp that I am helping you earn money by providing you with nuts or whatever else we can spare, and that you will pay me for them out of the proceeds." I hastened to add, "You won't really have to pay me, of course, but it may make Mrs. Cropp less suspicious."

Jenny wrinkled her nose skeptically. "Most likely she won't let me in to see you, the old witch."

I sighed at this accurate assessment of Mrs. C. Unfortunately, I wouldn't be able to dismiss her if she disobeyed me, as she is Albert's servant. Not that she would openly flout my orders, but she would tell the child I wasn't at home, or 'forget' to give me a message.

"I shall keep an eye out for you," I said. "I walk regularly in the square. In fact, the square is an excellent meeting place, for it's out of sight of the house. If my husband finds out that I'm supposedly helping you, he may try to put a stop to it."

"Your old man beats you, does he?" She burped, her eyes on the rest of the bread and cheese.

"No!" I exclaimed. "Definitely not." But I couldn't explain what I was afraid of. I never discuss it with anyone. "But he will be difficult about it, which would be *such* a bore. I shall try to walk in the square every morning and afternoon, and just before dusk as well if I get the chance. Unless you are hot on the trail of the delivery boy, you shall report to me there."

I instructed the disapproving Mrs. C to wrap the remaining bread and cheese, and put it, along with the nuts, in an old reticule. I sent the child on her way.

Now I had nothing to do but wait.

Chapter Five

I *t's my own damned fault, but I can't take it back.*
    —From the diary of Corvus

I'm not a patient person. Very well, I have two character flaws, but impatience doesn't get one thrown into Bedlam.

So now you know my greatest fear, as if you hadn't guessed it already.

It's not entirely my fault. I have a few peculiarities, but if it weren't for Great-Aunt Edna, the specter of madness would never have been evoked by my mother. In fact, I'm surprised she evoked it at all, for she's frightfully ashamed of it—the mad great-aunt in question being one of hers, so Mother fears she has brought madness into the family of the Earls of Medway. (Dear me, I don't think I mentioned it before; my father is the current Earl.)

I only met Great-Aunt Edna once, when we all went to my maternal grandparents for Christmas. I was only eight years old, but I remember the occasion well. She was a tiny, toothless old lady, with a sweet, kindly face. They kept her locked in a room at the top of the house, but she wasn't dangerous. She wouldn't have harmed a flea. (Perhaps that's a bad example; everyone crushes fleas.)

Why did they imprison her? Because they were ashamed of her. They kept her presence a strict secret. I wouldn't have known she existed if I hadn't gone exploring in my grandparents' house and spied a maid called Hetty surreptitiously bringing her a tray of food. I peered around the open door of her chamber and saw the old lady seated in a rocking chair.

Hetty set the food down and turned to leave. She saw me and clapped her hands to her mouth. "Oh, dearie me, don't tell on me, please, miss."

"Tell on you about what?" I smiled at the old lady, and she smiled back.

"You never saw me here, miss." Hetty jerked her chin in the direction of the old lady. "You never saw her, neither."

"Yes, I did." I was a truthful child. I still prefer the truth—witness my frankness in this tale—but I have learned, alas, that sometimes it is safer to lie.

"Aye, but you mustn't say so." The maid twisted her hands in her apron. "They'll send me away, and she won't get fed nothing but broth and a bit of toast."

I was puzzling over this strange statement, when the old lady beckoned to me, so I approached her and curtsied.

"Who are you, darling?" the old lady asked. "You're such a pretty little thing." Her speech was a little slurred, perhaps because she had so few teeth.

I told her, and after she had ascertained who my parents were, she introduced herself as Great-Great Aunt Edna. "But you needn't say both *greats*, for it's so cumbersome. I'm your mother's great-aunt, you see."

"Shall you come down to dinner?" I asked. I liked her immediately, more than any of my other relatives on that side of the family.

She shook her head and gave a toothless grin. "They keep me locked up because they think I'm mad." She cackled, just like a witch in a fairy tale. "If I wasn't mad before they imprisoned me, I certainly am now."

More agitated than ever, the maid hustled me toward the door. "We've got to leave, miss, or we'll be discovered."

"Come see me again, dear," the old lady said. "But don't tell anyone. Let it be our secret...for secrets are such fun, don't you think?"

Of course, I agreed—a child can't resist a secret from her elders. I'm not so fond of secrets now.

I don't think my family would go to the lengths of putting me in Bedlam—it isn't appropriate for the daughter of an earl, et cetera. They are more likely to lock me in a room at the family estate in Kent and keep me prisoner until I go mad like Great-Aunt Edna and throw myself out the window, thus proving they were right. Sometimes I think Bedlam would be better, as I would die much more quickly there.

I shouldn't let myself think such thoughts, should I? I should concentrate on maintaining my façade of sanity and get on with life. But despite my determination to ignore them, those letters were beginning to upset me.

Both Albert and another letter arrived the next morning. Actually, Albert had returned to London the afternoon before but went straight to Cynthia's, sending the carriage and baggage home and staying with her until just before dawn. Which would have been perfectly fine, except that my pompous, interfering brother, Julius, had come to Town as well.

In an attempt to control both my impatience and my unsettling thoughts, I'd gone to another musicale in the evening, which meant I was greeted with the news of Julius' arrival upon my return. Worse, he intended to spend the night here rather than at my parents' London house, on the grounds that he didn't wish to disturb the skeleton staff there. Sheer nonsense; by staying here, he would have more opportunity to annoy me and most likely Albert as well.

Julius is tallish, with a ruddy countenance and a tendency to scowl. His best feature is his eyes, which are a clear, bright blue. He has a strong sense of his own importance, hardly surprising in an earl, but while my father wears his worth like a comfortable mantle, Julius wields his like a scythe.

A dull scythe in clumsy hands—likely to do more harm than good. Unkind of me, I suppose, but I dislike him very much.

He had settled in the drawing room with brandy and the newspapers, but had a restful evening helped him compose himself to a semblance of civility? Not at all.

"At last," he barked, the moment I entered the room. "I've been waiting for hours."

No greeting replete with brotherly affection, no solicitous inquiry after my health and that of my husband. Judging by the level of the brandy in the decanter, he had been imbibing all evening. "How delightful to see you, too, brother dear," I said.

He scowled. "Rosamund, I wonder at you, gallivanting about at musicales while in the midst of a scandal."

"My dear Julius, if you spent more time in London, you would know one doesn't gallivant at musicales."

Unfortunately, he has no sense of humor, even under the influence of a little too much brandy. "This is no laughing matter. Your reputation—and that of the entire family, I may add—is at stake."

"Oh, piffle," I said. "No one cares in the least."

"You're a fool if you think that, Rosamund, but you never did have any sense. Perhaps your closest friends have been kind to you, but most of London is laughing behind your back."

"I suppose you spent the few hours since you arrived canvassing the whole of London?" I knew perfectly well he'd been at my house the entire time, because Stevenson had told me so. "What a prodigious feat! I must congratulate you."

His eyes narrowed. His cheek twitched. I would have giggled at this blatant attempt to control his temper, but it would have made things worse. He was winding up for a tirade, and if I placated him a little, it might be over with sooner.

"Don't take offense," I said. "I was merely jesting. I realize you're overwrought."

Oops—I shouldn't have said that. Not only did he take it as an insult—that he, the perfect, well-bred, in-control male could ever be ruled by emotion—but it gave him an opening to fuss about me.

"Nonsense," he pronounced. "I am merely concerned. No, it is more than that—I am deeply disturbed by your behavior. You are addled and out of control."

That was hitting far too close for comfort. "Fustian," I shot back.

"You're the one who should be overwrought. You're the subject of several scandalous prints, and yet you disport yourself about London as if all is well."

"Because that's the best way to deal with such insults, Julius—as I'm sure Papa would agree."

He is too proper to disrespect our father, no matter how much he may disagree with him. "You are far too much like him," he said. One would think this a positive attribute, since the madness is on my mother's side of the family—but no, because father is far too easygoing for Julius' taste. "Being so, you would be better off living his kind of life—pottering about in a garden where you can do no harm."

Temperamentally speaking, Julius is the spitting image of our mother. Literally too, except that he's male, and I think it's not so much his features but the pinched expression that makes him and mother so much alike. "I insist that you accompany me to Kent first thing in the morning," he said.

"The answer is no. If I want to potter, I can do so in the garden here." I'm not much interested in gardening, but we do grow herbs for the kitchen. It was whilst clipping rosemary early one morning that I first noticed the little girl, Jenny, lurking on the other side of the wall. "The country bores me to tears."

I shan't bore *you* with the ensuing monologue. I accustomed myself to Julius' scolds long ago by thinking of something else. It was a more difficult thing to do this time since I *was* a little overset—not by the prints, the gossips, et cetera, but by the anonymous letters. And, I admit it, by Julius' own words. I become cold and shaky inside when one of my family members so much as hints that there is something wrong with me, because they are the only ones who *know*. No matter how long I prove that I am mistress of myself and shan't embarrass them by behaving strangely, they still watch me as if I might at any moment start howling like an inmate of Bedlam.

Suffice it to say that I took a little brandy to dull my senses but not enough to lose my self-control, and waited until he drank enough to run out of orders and reprimands, at which time we both retired to bed.

As I mentioned earlier, the next anonymous letter arrived in the morning. Stevenson brought in the post while we were all at breakfast. Fortunately, Albert and Julius were too occupied with carping at one another to pay any attention to me and my correspondence.

My entire family loathes Albert for carrying on with Cynthia, which is frightfully unfair. I've explained to them that he keeps a mistress with my blessing, but it makes no difference to them. I don't understand it at all—I know for a fact that Julius has a mistress in Town, but nobody fusses at him about it. For all I know, he paid her a visit immediately before descending upon my house to rant about my supposedly scandalous behavior.

Usually the antipathy between my husband and brother is a bit upsetting, but today it was to my advantage.

Julius glared at my husband. "Rosamund *must* return to Kent with me."

"Nonsense," Albert said. "She is a grown woman and can make up her own mind what to do."

"Have you *seen* the most recent of these appalling caricatures?" Julius cried.

"I have not only seen it, I have purchased and burned all available copies."

"Already?" I asked, astonished.

"The instant I returned to town, I ordered my man of business to take care of it," Albert said. "I trust you burned the one Cynthia brought you?"

"That—that strumpet brought a copy *here*?" Julius thumped his fist on the table, rattling the coffee cups.

Albert shot to his feet, fists clenched. Julius stood as well, scowling.

Conveniently, their behavior meant I didn't have to lie; they wouldn't have heard me anyway. I'd pondered burning the print, but in the end kept it as insurance in case Albert found the other copy in my possession, the one Lady Danby had left behind. And why did I need insurance? I had asked myself that question, but I didn't have an answer. I just wasn't quite ready to destroy it, so why not have a safeguard in case the other was wrested from me?

"Cynthia is not a strumpet!" I banged my fist on the table, meaning it as a mockery of my brother's dramatic gesture, but ouch! Men do the strangest things. "Sit down, you two. She is my dear friend, Julius, and I won't have you insulting her."

"Thank you, Rosie," Albert said, still glaring, but he sat as requested. "I should call you out for that, Derwent." (So sorry—I should have introduced my brother properly. Julius is Viscount Derwent, my father's heir. As I mentioned earlier, my father is the Earl of Medway. My mother (obviously) is the Countess, and I have another brother and three sisters, whose names you will learn should they chance to come into this tale.)

"But you won't, because you don't have the guts." Julius sniffed, but subsided into his chair as well. I doubt he has the guts either, but I bit my tongue. "Besides, it would make you look like even more of a fool than you already are," he went on. "By rights, you should call out that Corvus fellow."

"How can I? No one knows who he is," Albert protested.

"Aren't you lucky to have an excuse," Julius sneered.

"In any event, I wouldn't offer a challenge to a low fellow of that sort," Albert said. "I'd have him thrashed instead. He wouldn't find that as stimulating as his lascivious thoughts about my Rosie."

Julius went purple, whether from Albert's laying claim to me when he spent most of his nights with Cynthia, or because he'd mentioned a gross vulgarity in my presence.

Albert took advantage of Julius's momentary speechlessness to say calmly, "I need Rosie here with me in London."

Thank you, Albert.

Julius recovered his voice. "Where she can gad about making scandals? A man in your position should have more sense."

"I'm not making the scandals," I protested. "Corvus is."

"And you're making them worse," he said. "There is something seriously wrong with you, and if you don't go on a repairing lease in the country, I shudder to think where you may end up."

I felt the blood drain from my face. There are times when I really, truly wish I could murder someone, usually Julius or my mother, but I've had horrid thoughts about other people, too. Does that mean I'm mad?

"Nonsense," Albert said. "She is the hostess of my political dinners, and is therefore indispensable to me." Not that we had any dinners planned at the moment, but he might suddenly feel the need to butter someone up.

"Thank you, dearest Albert," I said, and my voice didn't quiver at all, of which I was justly proud. "Julius, I wish you a safe journey home." So infuriated was I that I almost left the room without my correspondence—but at the last second I remembered, scooped it up, and stalked out.

A MAN OF STATURE DESERVES TO HAVE CHILDREN, today's letter said.

What a big nothing that was—and it showed the letter writer's ignorance about me. Was that what all the fuss was about, our lack of progeny? Albert had told me from the start that he didn't want children; that was what made our marriage so practical on both sides. He dislikes children and considers my nieces and nephews loud, smelly brats. (Which is true, but I rather like them all the same. Which reminded me, he wouldn't be too pleased to hear about the far smellier brat I'd had in the breakfast parlor the day before.) I understood the writer's blaming me, as the lack of children is always laid, unfairly or not, at the woman's door. But what was the point of sending me anonymous letters about such an uninteresting subject? If I truly were barren, there was nothing I could do about it.

Ah. Perhaps the letters were sent by some gossip with a mind like Julius's (and my mother's), who assumed I hadn't become with child because Albert rarely bedded me, since he was always at Cynthia's. But in that case, why not send anonymous letters to Albert rather than to me? What, I asked myself, did my correspondent expect me to do in response? Throw a tantrum and demand that Albert bed me more often? Come up with a devious plan to get rid of Cynthia? The whole matter was absurd, and I refused to think about it any longer. I burned the letter.

Yes, I know you find that hard to believe, but I did! It was far too stupid to keep. I had already burned one, so why not another? I didn't burn the rest, though. I would get around to that later.

However, I did record it in code. I freely admit that. I cannot quite explain why; it seemed necessary, somehow.

I left my boudoir and went downstairs, meaning to talk to Mrs. C about the evening meal—a formality she insists upon, although she has usually made up her mind about what Cook will serve us and becomes extremely cranky if I have other ideas.

The front door was open, and Maurice was stowing Julius' valises into his waiting coach. Soft voices in the drawing room brought me to a halt. The door stood slightly ajar.

"I must insist," Julius muttered, "that you keep an eye on her. Her headstrong behavior is part and parcel of the problem, and it's your duty as a husband to curb it."

Albert sighed. "You're fretting about nothing. Rosie may have a mind of her own, but she has never shown herself to be anything but perfectly sane."

The blood congealed in my veins. My heart pounded furiously to get it moving again.

"You didn't know her when she was eighteen or so. We considered having her locked up."

I sucked in deep, terrified breaths.

"So you told me years ago," Albert said, adding caustically, "right after you'd married her off to me. But she has never given me cause for concern, or to regret our marriage."

More aghast by the second, I sank onto a convenient chair by the wall. Thank God Maurice was outside chatting with Julius' coachman, but he glanced at me questioningly and made as if to reenter the house. I gathered my wits and waved him away, pretending to adjust my slipper. No one, absolutely no one, must overhear this conversation.

Julius had told Albert about me, not now, but ages ago. Four years ago, to be precise.

How *could* he have done so? He'd sworn a solemn oath not to. So had everyone else in the family. My difficulties (*not* madness) were our deep, dark (*not* shameful) secret, to be discussed with no one.

"Because she has never been touched by scandal before," Julius said. "She is easily overset, even hysterical, and the sort of gossip these prints have given rise to would affect even the most stoic of individuals."

I am not easily overset. I ask you, and please answer me frankly—have I reacted hysterically to anything that has happened so far?

I thought not.

Julius lowered his voice even more. Fortunately, I have excellent hearing. "I have reason to believe there is already talk about her instability," he said.

Albert huffed. "What reason?" he demanded, and when Julius didn't reply, he said, "You've been drinking too much again, Derwent."

An unkind thrust, but accurate. Julius is so tense that he drinks to calm himself—not that I've seen any indication that it works.

"While I don't necessarily agree with Rosie's approach, she has handled the entire affair with considerable aplomb," Albert said. "You're making a great deal of fuss about nothing."

Thank you again, Albert.

Julius harrumphed. "Mark my words, she will embarrass both our families if she is left to her own devices. If you see the slightest increase in instability, I demand that you send her to the country."

Albert sighed again. "If I judge it necessary, I shall do so. Now, stop insulting my wife and go away before I do something I may regret."

Julius stomped out of the drawing room and almost walked right past without even noticing me. He caught my eye and gasped.

I stood. "You broke your word, Julius, and for that I shall never forgive you."

He paled but recovered himself swiftly. "Don't be a fool, Rosie. I only want what is best for you, and if you had any sense you would realize it."

He left, and I ran upstairs again, needing a moment alone to compose myself. Now I *was* overset—I admit it readily—not by the stupid prints or the gossip, but by my brother's perfidy. I don't like Julius, but I'd always thought him an honorable Englishman. I would never have believed him capable of disregarding a solemn oath.

And dear Albert had defended me so staunchly! Tears of gratitude burned behind my eyes. I dashed them away and scarcely managed a few deep breaths before Albert tapped on the door.

I had to get myself under control, or Albert might start believing Julius' horrid warnings. Thank heavens he asked permission to enter, for that gave me a few more seconds in which to compose myself. Adhering to the rules of polite behavior—on both sides—made our arranged marriage a comfortable one. In this case it proved face-saving.

Still, I didn't want him to see my face just yet, so I seated myself at the desk and bade him enter.

"Thank you for standing up for me," I said without turning around.

"I'm sorry you had to hear that conversation," he said, softly closing the door. "When he came into the drawing room to bid me farewell, he neglected to shut the door behind him."

"I'm glad I heard it," I said, placidly (I hoped) refilling my inkwell. "Now I know how truly horrid my brother can be, and as far as I am concerned, he is no longer welcome here."

"Fine with me," Albert said. "He will be Earl of Medway one day, but he doesn't even take a proper interest in the running of this country. One can only hope the Regent will elevate some worthy men to the peerage."

I don't much like that word worthy, because it far too often means stodgy. Not only that, it reminded me of those horrid anonymous letters. What a pity my correspondent hadn't said un-*stodgy*, for I would have taken that as a compliment.

"How *could* he carry tales about me? Such nonsense, too." I wished I knew exactly what Julius had told him after our wedding—but I dared not ask.

No, I *had* to ask, or else I wouldn't be able to stop thinking and worrying. I turned and asked lightly, "What did he tell you about my supposed instability?"

Albert shrugged. "Nothing much, only that you were prone to excessive emotion and irrational behavior, but so what? That's no different from most young girls, if my sister was anything to judge by." (His sister does not come into this story, so I shan't introduce her for now.)

"If everyone behaved according to his standards," I muttered, "we would be like automatons."

Albert nodded perfunctorily, his thoughts clearly elsewhere. Back on politics, I hoped. I was still quite shaken, and keeping up this conversation was a strain. I wanted to be left alone. I turned away again, screwed the cap on the ink bottle, put it in the drawer, then took it out and checked to make sure it was tight.

Checking it once isn't mad. One doesn't wish to spill ink over the desk or onto one's new gown the next time one opens it.

"But I must tell you, Rosie-love…I couldn't say it within his hearing, but to some extent he is correct."

That set my heart pounding again. Damnation, I'd only checked the cap once! "I beg your pardon?" My voice squeaked horribly. Surely Julius hadn't gone into detail about my impulsive checking.

"As I said at the outset of this Corvus business, you might do better to withdraw from the world for a while."

I frowned, but without much conviction, so relieved was I. Thank God, thank *God* he hadn't agreed that there was something wrong with me. I let out a breath.

"You might consider going to our house in Surrey—it's not far, and none of your family are there."

I got my voice under control again. "No."

He gave his medium-length version of a long-suffering sigh. "Very well then, why not stay in London but remain at home? I merely thought Surrey would provide less temptation to mingle in society."

"Because there *is* no society there." I turned away again. "No, Albert, I will not leave London. I mean to brave it out."

"I have no doubt of your courage, my dear," he said. "But I don't enjoy being made to look a fool, or a bad husband, or a cuckold, or anything of the sort."

Poor Albert indeed. "A cuckold because a low, vile-minded individual finds me attractive?" I huffed. "I don't see how my leaving town will change that."

He put out his lower lip, one of his least endearing expressions. It's too much like a pout and not at all appropriate for a grown man. "I hoped that if you were no longer in London, Corvus would turn his attention elsewhere."

If I had a long-suffering sigh, now was the time to employ it. "The best course is to ignore the gossip, but if it will make you feel better, you may accompany me from time to time, just to show that we are on the best of terms." A concession on my part, seeing as he had already suggested this days ago, at which time I had pooh-poohed the suggestion.

He brightened. "Very well, when I can fit it into my schedule, I shall do so." Which meant most likely he wouldn't, but he would feel that he was doing something, which was all that mattered.

He hovered for a minute or two—most uncharacteristic, and making me more uneasy by the second—and at last asked, "By the way, have you received any more of those anonymous letters?"

Was that all? "Two," I said. How sweet of him to ask, so I told him so. "You see? My brother is an idiot. How could anyone so concerned for my welfare be considered a bad husband?"

His smile was cursory. "The letters?"

"One saying I should be ashamed of myself, and another this morning, implying that I have failed you because we have no children." I paused. "Which goes to show that despite his boast, the letter writer doesn't know everything about me." I paused again. "Before you ask, yes, I burned them."

"Good girl."

I don't much like that patronizing tone of voice, but I could hardly object.

Then he gave the long version of his long-suffering sigh. "I suppose we must expect your mother next."

Fool that I was, I thought we'd abandoned that subject. "I'm sorry, Albert, but I will *not* go to Surrey to avoid my mother. Besides, you don't want to have to face her alone. You're much better off with me here to fend her off."

He grimaced. "But she'll make your life a misery."

"No, she won't, because I shan't let her. At least she won't try to stay in our house." I pondered that. I wouldn't put anything past Mother. "Perhaps we could render the spare bedchamber uninhabitable, just to be on the safe side. Wallpapering or some such."

"As you wish, my dear," Albert said, his smile forced. "I promised I wouldn't interfere with you, and I'll keep that promise."

"Thank you," I said. Dear man, I'm very hard on him. "I'm sorry it distresses you so much, but it will be over soon, I'm sure. What more can Corvus find to say about me?"

***

I know what you're thinking—that Corvus immediately came up with something even more outrageous. But no, he didn't! He did indeed include me his next print, which appeared the following day. In it, I was on the floor on my derriere, looking stunned as if I'd just fallen (but very pretty—I fear Cynthia was right that Corvus lusted after me). However, this time he chose to persecute Lady Danby, who clutched her skirts above dimpled knees as she puffed after a fleeing footman, saying, 'Drat the man, why couldn't he have jostled *me*?' The print was titled *A Narrow Escape*.

"How dare that fiend insult me!" Lady Danby had arrived early, before the usual hour for morning callers, and spread the print on the table in my drawing room.

"I'm so sorry." I sucked in my cheeks so as not to laugh, for it was quite a funny print. "But Corvus insults whomever he chooses." In the drawing, my gown had ridden up, showing part of my calves—shapely and also accurate, I must say, but since Corvus has never seen them, they were the result of his vulgar imaginings, as were my breasts in the print with Cynthia. Good God, I wondered. Had he also imagined the rest of me unclothed?

What horrors!

Lady Danby's wail wrenched me back to reality, thank heavens. "What have I done to deserve this?"

"I have no idea," I said diplomatically, when I could quite easily have listed the reasons: she'd mentioned a *tendre* for a servant, she had bellowed to a footman to return, and when he hadn't, she had pursued him through the crowd. One could easily see where Corvus had come by the idea for his print. The question was, how had he known about that little scene in the first place?

One possibility sprang to mind. "What happened to the footman, by the way? Did Lady Baffleton dismiss him?" An angry footman who'd lost his position might well have broadcast his grievance.

"I couldn't find him," Lady Danby said. "I went straight to Lady Baffleton and complained, but she said she had no such footman. He was of medium height, while all hers are tall—and, incidentally, fair-haired to go with the blue and gold of their livery. What a foolish conceit! And she only has them wear wigs on special occasions, which I say is going too far. A properly-outfitted footman must wear a wig at all times."

I thought back. "He wasn't wearing the Baffleton livery, and come to think of it, a few strands of dark hair protruded from beneath his wig." Corvus had even included that minor detail. I pointed it out to Lady Danby. "Perhaps he was a temporary servant, hired for the evening from an agency, and left in a hurry when he realized you were, er, pursuing him." I bit my lip hard so as not to giggle.

"Believe me, I shall find out," she said. "I'll go to Lady Baffleton directly, and if that is indeed the case, he shall never work in London again."

"For heaven's sake, why not?" I wished I hadn't said anything. "The man shouldn't lose his employment because of a little clumsiness."

"Rather than fleeing, he should have remained and taken his medicine like a man, but that's not the point. He must have told Corvus about it, and for that he deserves far worse."

To be birched? I wanted to say, as laughter welled up again, but ruthlessly I suppressed it. "I doubt if he knows Corvus's identity. More likely he told the story over a pint of ale in a tavern, and from there it spread to Corvus's ears."

But what if he did indeed know who Corvus was? A substantial bribe, and *voilà!* No waiting God knew how long for Jenny. I know, I know, it had only been two days, but as I said earlier, I'm not a patient woman. I'd faithfully kept my bargain, walking in the square whenever possible. I'd even kept an eye on our little back garden, but I'd seen neither hide nor hair of Jenny.

"I shall come with you," I said. I brought her up to my bedchamber while Mary Jane helped me into a walking dress. Otherwise she might have left without me, champing at the bit as she was. Soon we were marching down Henrietta Street. Lady Danby is fifty if she is a day, but I was hard put to keep up with her and the footman who accompanies her everywhere. Not because I was in poor condition—I walk almost every day, whether in a nearby square or to shop—but because whilst she was fuming, I was thinking hard about my role in the upcoming scene.

"Lady Danby, you might consider calming down," I said. "If you storm into Lady Baffleton's house demanding information, she'll take offense."

"If she had temporary help at the ball and neglected to tell me, *I* shall take offense!" retorted Lady Danby.

In which case we would get precisely nowhere, but in any event, I didn't want Lady Baffleton to think I was at one with Lady Danby in wishing to punish the footman. If people were to laugh behind my back, I intended to choose what they laughed about. I'd already feigned amusement and indifference. I would have to maintain that stance in spite of Lady D.

Not only that, I wasn't so sure I wanted her to unmask Corvus. That was *my* project, and damned if I would let her take it over.

I was so deep in thought that I fell behind Lady D—and bumped into Gilroy McBrae.

"Whoa," he said, steadying me with a hand. He doffed his hat. "Good day, Lady Rosamund. Where are you off to in such a rush?"

An impertinent question, but he was that sort of man. "Good day, Mr. McBrae," I said frostily, to cover up the fact that I was disconcerted. Why, I don't know—something about him put me a bit off balance, not for the first time.

He grinned. "Sorry to wrench you out of your brown study, but surely you shouldn't walk unaccompanied."

"I'm not unaccompanied," I said crossly, motioning ahead with my chin. "I'm with Lady Danby. I'd better catch up. So lovely to see you." I attempted to walk away, but he kept pace with me.

"What a pity," he said, "for I was on my way to call on you."

"On me?" I managed to mask my surprise—or perhaps dismay—with hauteur. "Whatever for?"

"In spite of being an uncivilized barbarian, I am familiar with *some* of the customs of the polite world."

If he was trying to embarrass me, he wouldn't succeed. I raised my brows.

"Such as the morning call," he said.

I rolled my eyes, which although vulgar felt perfectly acceptable with this man. "It's a stupid custom." That should have deterred McBrae, but instead he offered me his arm. I looked him up and down. He was dressed rather better than the last time I'd seen him. It would have been insufferably rude of me to refuse to walk with him. I sighed, resigning myself to his company, and placed my hand on his sleeve. We followed in Lady Danby's wake.

"Stupid in what way?" he asked, as if he thought morning calls delightful, and what could I possibly find to object to? His smirk told me otherwise—or maybe he was just pleased at successfully foisting himself onto me. Or perhaps he thought our encounter at the stationer's meant we were now fast friends. Considering the insult I'd dealt his precious country and its untidy cattle, I doubted that.

Oh, what did it matter? "It's bad enough having to be polite to whomever chances to call," I said—and if he took that as in insult, so be it. "But what I truly loathe is the obligation to return the dratted things. Not to gentlemen, of course, but any ladies who leave me their cards today will expect me to call on them tomorrow. Can you conceive of anything more tedious?"

He chuckled. "And absurd. You might have any number of more important things to do tomorrow."

"Precisely! If I don't call, they will feel slighted, so whenever I leave my house during the so-called morning hours, I find myself facing a dilemma—be polite and bored the following day, or rude and therefore slighted in return. Generally, I choose to stay home and put up with whomever arrives."

"But not today?"

"No, because Lady Danby is on a mission." She turned the corner ahead of us, and I withdrew my hand from his arm. "So lovely to see you," I repeated insincerely, "but I must catch her up before she reaches Lady Baffleton's."

He tucked my hand in his arm again and picked up the pace. "I'll come with you."

What possessed the man to cling to me like a barnacle? Perhaps he wanted an introduction to Lady B and could get one no other way. It wouldn't improve my credit to be the one to present him, even though he was better turned out today.

Not that I cared what Lady B thought of me. "Are you acquainted with Lady Baffleton?"

"I was at Harrow with her husband," he said. That explained his accent and acquaintance with members of the *ton*. "What, pray tell, is Lady Danby's mission?"

Another impertinent question, but it was my fault for phrasing her intention in such a way. I shrugged internally; it didn't matter if I told him, as he would find out soon enough. Far more important, I had yet to decide how to explain my own presence.

"She is incensed by the latest print by that Corvus fellow," I said.

"And so she should be."

"You've already seen it," I said glumly.

"By now, it's in every print shop window in town."

"I suppose so," I said. "What a bore. I told Lady Danby to ignore it, but she is determined to unmask Corvus and make him pay."

"Ah, now your haste makes sense. You are joining Lady Danby in her mission."

Exactly what I was afraid of! "Not at all! I'd rather she *didn't* unmask him." Now, why had I blurted that out? It was true, but I couldn't explain why.

"No? As I recall, you're in the latest print as well."

"I don't care about that."

"Then why does it matter whether you catch up?" We halted while a boy swept the crossing. I dug in my reticule for a penny, but McBrae forestalled me. I suppose my assumption that he didn't have money to spare was another insult, but I didn't have time to worry about that. I had to come up with an answer to his question.

He tossed the boy a coin, we moved forward again, and at last I knew what to say. "If Corvus is unmasked, my husband might feel obliged to call him out. Albert is a poor shot, so Corvus might easily be better." I sighed. "And if Corvus proves to be of the servant class, Albert might hire someone to thrash him, which would be horrid." Drat, I was blushing.

He chuckled. "That's not the sort of thrashing Corvus seems to hope for."

"He can hope until doomsday," I retorted.

He smirked. "I wonder what sparked his latest effort. Is Lady Danby known for pursuing lusty footmen?"

"No, of course not." Needless to say this reminded us both of the first print. I frowned, hoping it would chase away the heat in my cheeks, and told him about the incident at Lady Baffleton's ball. "Corvus has exaggerated what happened. The footman jostled me, but I didn't fall over. Lady Danby demanded that he return and apologize, but she didn't go charging after him.

She merely complained to Lady Baffleton, who said she had no such servant in her employ—all her footmen being tall, whilst the man in question was of medium height. Also, I happened to notice a few strands of dark hair peeking from beneath his wig, while all Lady Baffleton's footmen are fair-haired to go with their blue and gold livery." I barely refrained from rolling my eyes at this folly. Regardless of McBrae's opinion and his assumptions regarding me, I didn't intend to make a habit of stooping to his level. "It was truly much ado about nothing, and I wish I hadn't mentioned the dark hair to Lady Danby. I told her not to make a fuss, but once she makes up her mind, there's no stopping her. She'll upset Lady Baffleton for no reason at all."

"You didn't mind being jostled by a servant?"

I had no intention of explaining why the man had jostled me. "Everyone is entitled to occasional clumsiness," I said, as I decided which portion of the truth to impart. "That's why I accompanied her. She thinks the footman in question may have been hired from an agency just for the ball. If this is indeed the case, and she finds out who he was, I wish to make sure the agency doesn't dismiss him, or if they do, I shall make it up to him somehow, perhaps by furnishing a recommendation."

"Why should you? It wasn't your fault he jostled you."

Actually, it *was* my fault to some extent, but again, I couldn't admit it. "Perhaps I moved suddenly, and he wasn't quick enough to get out of the way," I improvised. Conversing with McBrae could be quite exhausting—one had to think the entire time! "Regardless, he doesn't deserve to find himself out of work for such a stupid reason."

"Definitely not, but I fail to see the connection between the elusive footman and the latest print."

"Lady Danby thinks he must have told Corvus about the incident. But what is the chance that a stray footman is acquainted with him?"

McBrae shifted a shoulder. "It's not impossible."

"But highly unlikely. I expect he told his friends at some tavern or other and the story eventually reached Corvus. Either that, or another servant at the ball spread the story, the same way the servants on my street gossiped about poor Harold falling down the stairs." There! In spite of having to do way too much thinking in too short a space of time, I had remembered to call Harold by his given name.

Which meant, I realized with dismay, that I *did* care what McBrae thought of me.

Chapter Six

She inspires me. I don't know what to do.
—From the diary of Corvus

Why in heaven's name should it matter to me what he thought? It was such a ludicrous notion that I had to sort it out in my mind, but by then I'd had enough of thinking. At last we arrived at Lady Baffleton's door.

Whilst the footman plied the knocker, Lady Danby looked McBrae up and down. "You've been to a tailor, I see." She sniffed. "Better than before."

"You're too kind, my lady," McBrae said, bowing over her hand. She was a literal-minded woman, but it was hard to miss the sarcasm beneath his bland response.

But no, her thoughts were elsewhere. She jabbed an accusatory finger in the direction of McBrae's wavy black locks. "Was the footman's hair that color? Raven's wing, I call it."

"I beg your pardon?" McBrae asked as if he was all at sea, for which I silently thanked him. I'd been frightfully indiscreet discussing the matter with him. Not that he wouldn't hear all about it any minute, but it was hers to bring up in company, not mine.

"It was only a few strands," I said. "Not enough for me to say how dark."

"I've never liked that color," she said. "There's something sinister about it. Foreign. Distinctly un-English."

"As a Scotsman," McBrae replied, "I cannot but take pride in my un-English hair."

Luckily, the butler appeared to show us to the drawing room, at which point I had a brilliant notion. I smiled at the man and said, "I was most impressed by the service at Lady Baffleton's ball. Tell me, were you obliged to hire extra footmen?"

"Yes indeed, my lady," he said.

"From which agency did you hire them?"

"Waller's," he told me, while Lady Danby glared indignantly. I thanked him, and he ushered us into the drawing room.

"Clever of you," McBrae murmured, a smile in his voice.

A thrill of pride washed over me. Aghast at the degree to which I appreciated his approval, I shrugged as if it was nothing—which it might well prove to be, as Lady Danby was perfectly capable of making a fuss anyway. She refrained, however, and a boring twenty minutes later we took our leave. Fortunately, Lord Baffleton rode up just as we reached the door, and while he and McBrae embarked on a discussion of horseflesh, Lady Danby and I made our escape. I did not wish to spend any more time in the company of that man until I recovered my sanity.

Come, come, you know what I mean. This bizarre response to McBrae had nothing to do with my other problem, the one I'm sick and tired of discussing. Still, it disturbed me that I cared about the approval of a man I hardly knew and for whom I had little respect.

"Dratted girl, you spiked my guns," Lady Danby said as we set off toward the nearest hackney stand. "I was looking forward to giving that chit a good talking-to."

"I know, but think how unpleasant for poor Lady Baffleton." She is the same age as I and wouldn't appreciate being scolded in front of her other guests. "She probably didn't even know whether the butler had hired extra help." I smiled deprecatingly. "Will you forgive me? I just wanted to get over heavy ground as lightly as possible."

"I realize that. Where did that Scottish fellow spring from?"

"He was on his way to call on me," I said, "and I literally bumped into him."

"To call upon you? How presumptuous of him. He may be acquainted with a few peers, but he is still a nobody."

Precisely—and I don't care about the opinions of nobodies. I don't even care about the opinions of my social equals much of the time. How vexing all this was.

As the hack pulled up in front of the employment agency, Lady Danby said, "This time, you will not butt in and take over the conversation."

"Yes, my lady," I answered meekly. I hadn't the slightest intention of taking over; in fact, I hoped she would make such a mull of it that the owner, Mr. Waller, would divulge just enough information before clamming up.

Once her wealth and status were established—a good footman takes care of that—Lady Danby explained to the polite (but not obsequious) Waller that she wished to hire extra help for a party and that his agency came highly recommended. So far, unexpectedly tactful. She proceeded to discuss rates, dates, and so on, without committing to anything. "Very well," she said at the end, "I shall have my butler contact you to make the final arrangements."

"Excellent, my lady," said Waller. "I look forward to hearing from him."

She turned as if to go, then swerved and put up a finger. "But!" she said. "Not that black-haired fellow with the dirty wig."

My mouth dropped open. As I recalled, his wig had been unusually clean.

"I beg your pardon?" asked Waller.

"There was a footman at Lady Baffleton's the other night. Some of your people helped at her ball, is that not so?"

"Indeed, my lady, but—"

"One of the footmen was extremely rude to Lady Rosamund." She indicated me with a jut of her chin.

Drat the woman, I had nothing against the footman. I tried to indicate this to Waller by a slight shake of the head. He remained properly impassive.

"Medium height, with very dark hair, so dark as to be called raven's-wing, and I'm sure he was one of yours, since he didn't wear the Baffleton livery," Lady Danby said. Despite knowing only that the absconding footman's hair was dark, she had decided it must be the particular shade she disliked. She is not a stupid woman; how can she be so unaware of her prejudices?

"None of my footman have black hair, my lady," Waller said.

"You have already dismissed him!" Lady Danby trumpeted. "I'm glad to hear that."

"No, my lady, I meant that I have no black-haired footmen at the moment. Not only that, all the servants I sent to Lady Baffleton's ball were tall, to match the height of her own footmen, and she had sufficient livery that I had no need to use our own." He glanced at the wall, where two sets of livery were displayed—one trimmed in red and the other in silver and blue.

I'd only had a glance at the fleeing footman, but I was almost certain he wore neither of these, but rather something more subdued.

Perhaps Waller was lying. I wouldn't blame him for doing so.

Lady Danby narrowed her eyes at him. "You're certain of that."

"Indeed I am, my lady," he said. "I assure you, I have no such employee, and if someone of that description should happen to apply for work here, I shall not send him to work at your party."

"But you would hire him? He should never be permitted to work in London again."

I exchanged glances with Mr. Waller. I even rolled my eyes, but he didn't bat an eyelash in return. I couldn't keep my mouth shut any longer. "Lady Danby, that's not fair. He was a bit clumsy, that's all."

She scowled at me. "He was far worse, Rosie, and you know it." She turned her scowl on Waller. "Well?"

"I would first ascertain whether he served at the Baffleton ball, my lady," he said obligingly.

"I should hope so, my good man." Lady Danby stalked to the door. Waller bowed to me and sketched the slightest wink. Thank heavens, for if the footman sought work there, I thought he should be given a fair chance.

Except that...maybe he wasn't a footman at all. I scurried out the door after Lady Danby, possessed of another brilliant notion. Since the dark-haired man wasn't one of Lady Baffleton's...nor one of Waller's...who was he?

What if he was Corvus himself?

***

Needless to say, I did not confide my astonishing deduction to Lady D, and evidently she didn't come to the same conclusion. We took a hackney home, and she complained the whole way about wasting time and getting nowhere.

Not at all! This was my first real clue to Corvus's identity, and it made complete sense. At a very large party, such as Lady B's ball, it would be quite easy to slip inside as a temporary footman, eavesdrop on any number of conversations, and take note of embarrassing occurrences. It explained how he knew a great deal about the *ton* without being one of us. And I already knew he was dark-haired, judging by the birching print.

Admittedly, he could have drawn himself dark when he was actually fair to throw people off the scent. But why bother? No one seemed to be trying hard to unmask him, or they would surely have done so by now. He probably thought himself completely secure. Ha!

Lady Danby dropped me at home, and I went upstairs feeling rather more cheerful than for the past few days. The clue didn't bring me much closer to actually finding Corvus, but it meant I had a far better chance of recognizing him when I did. I would keep my eyes open for stray dark-haired footmen at any balls I happened to attend.

***

THERE IS SOMETHING SERIOUSLY WRONG WITH YOU.

The anonymous letters had begun to affect my enjoyment of breakfast. My fault, to some extent—I shouldn't have ripped the dratted letter open before eating my coddled eggs—but being alone in the breakfast parlor, I wasn't thinking about concealment at the time.

Panic swarmed inside me, but almost immediately, realization replaced it. Julius had used those very words just yesterday.

I say realization, but at first I couldn't believe my mind, for two substantial reasons. Number one: much as I dislike my brother, I simply couldn't imagine him sending anonymous letters. Julius doesn't mince words. Unlike Albert, who, as a politician, is often devious in attaining his ends, Julius invariably says what is on his mind. (This is one reason he and Albert don't get on. Their political views are not so very far apart, but their methods differ greatly.) Julius had already told me—and Albert—what he thought of me.

However, he was one of the few people who knew my secret. If he wanted me banished to the country, he might see a series of insidious threats as a means to a desired end. He might well think that although I would remain stubborn, Albert would take fright and order me to vegetate in Surrey.

Reason number two: Julius doesn't live in London. He might have posted this morning's letter yesterday afternoon, but he couldn't have sent the others.

But…someone else might have done so on his behalf. It didn't take long to guess who.

I folded the letter, hid it under my other correspondence, and forced myself to finish my eggs and toast. If I didn't consume my usual hearty breakfast, it might be noticed. I didn't want to give the servants reason to wonder if something had caused me to lose my appetite.

Yes, I know that sounds excessive, but I had begun to feel persecuted. I felt that I must avoid the slightest unnecessary deviation from the norm—especially since there might prove to be many of them in the near future.

Such as visiting Julius's mistress this morning. Her name is Esme Concord. I had never met her, but thanks to Cynthia (in whom Albert confides a great deal of unsavory information), I knew who she was and where she lived. I couldn't go there unaccompanied, but it must remain a secret. I would have to take Mary Jane.

"I wish to dress simply today," I told her. "Fashionably, but not in the sort of ensemble that shows off your expertise in dressing me."

"But…but why, my lady?" she whined.

By rights, I should have told her off. Good servants do not question the commands of their masters and mistresses. However, Mary Jane has been with me since I was sixteen. I trust her more than any other servant, and in this situation I needed the utmost discretion.

"Not those old clothes you wore the other day, I should hope," she muttered. She'd tried to throw them out after finding them on the floor where I had discarded them, but I insisted on keeping them.

"Not this time," I said. "This morning, I merely wish to avoid attracting attention."

"May I ask where you mean to go, my lady?"

"No, because you'll disapprove. You'll find out soon enough, since you're coming with me."

She pursed her lips but did as she was told, even providing a veil when I asked for one. I tucked it inside my bonnet, for it would look extremely odd were I to wear a veil here, where I am well known, but once we were in Kensington, it would conceal my identity. We left the house on foot as if we intended nothing more than shopping in Oxford Street. Instead, the instant we had turned the corner, we headed for the closest hackney stand.

And whom should we encounter there but Gilroy McBrae! The man always seemed to be underfoot.

"Well met, Lady Rosamund." He bowed. "Where are you off to this fine morning?"

"That's none of your business," I retorted. I should have known better. It's a stupid response, the sort that arouses people's curiosity, but as I've said earlier, something about McBrae sets me off balance. (Which has nothing to do with being *unbalanced*—let me make myself perfectly clear.)

"Returning morning calls?" he asked. "No, that can't be it. It's far too early for that sort of boredom. Shopping it must be, then."

"You are nosy and impertinent, Mr. McBrae."

He grinned. "Aye, that's the truth."

I glared. "I didn't mean it as a compliment."

"No, but I always take it as one. Nosiness and impertinence are among my most useful attributes."

"Then pray employ them elsewhere. Good morning." I put my nose in the air and stalked over to the hack Mary Jane had chosen. "Kensington High Street," I told the driver, and climbed in.

If I'd been with Cynthia, I would have railed about McBrae during the entire ride to Kensington, but I never condescend to that sort of familiarity with Mary Jane. Instead I stewed internally. I try to be truthful with myself, and I had to admit that when it came down to it, I wouldn't have minded in the least strolling down Oxford Street with McBrae. No matter how impertinent, he was vastly more interesting to talk to than most of my acquaintance. Not only that, just because he deserved a set down didn't mean I should have given him one. I'd been rude not so much because of his nosiness but because I had to keep my final destination secret, even from the hackney driver. That was why I gave such a vague address. I had him let us down within a short walking distance of the house in which Julius keeps Esme Concord.

Excessive again? I don't think so. I do understand Albert's concerns, if not my brother's. I can't afford to be caught in such scandalous behavior as visiting my brother's mistress. I know, I know, I visit my husband's mistress all the time, but Cynthia is almost as well-born as I and an independent widow, whilst Esme is a nobody—a merchant's daughter turned fallen woman.

I glanced about me before descending from the hack. There was absolutely no reason to do so. No one in this area of town was acquainted with me, and yet I couldn't quite get rid of the feeling of being watched.

By whom? I asked myself. Delivery boys ran this way and that. A few ladies glanced in shop windows, and two men in outmoded coats conversed outside a tavern. Another hackney drove past us and pulled up. A man in shirtsleeves and a red cap jumped out, paid the driver, and strode into the tavern. No one looked my way.

I shook off my uneasiness, put down my veil, and climbed out of the hack, waiting in the brisk breeze whilst Mary Jane paid him. "Just where are we going, my lady?" she asked.

She would have to know soon enough. "To visit Miss Esme Concord."

Her eyes widened. How is it that everyone knows all the gossip but me? It is pure luck that my best friend is a very worldly woman.

"Yes, she's Lord Derwent's mistress, and yes, it's improper of me to visit, but don't waste your breath scolding me. Just keep your mouth shut about it." *Oh, dear.* I had offended her; I should have phrased it better. She would just have to swallow the insult, but it is unwise to offend one's inferiors, particularly one's trusted servants. They can make one's life quite uncomfortable if they choose—frightfully unfair, but so it is.

She sniffed. "Certainly, my lady."

Fortunately, Miss Concord was at home to visitors—or perhaps she was too surprised to refuse me access. I consigned Mary Jane to a chair in the vestibule and allowed the housemaid who had answered the door to escort me to a small parlor, comfortably furnished but not in the latest style.

My hostess, a pretty, well-formed dark-haired woman about the same age as I, stared at me from across the room and said absolutely nothing. Perhaps she couldn't—she was deathly pale and her hands were shaking. I don't know what I had expected—someone with a brassier personality, I suppose. The prostitutes one glimpses at Covent Garden tend to be loud and vulgar.

Perhaps she trembled from guilt. "You have nothing to fear from me, Miss Concord," I said. "I merely wish to ask you a question and get a truthful answer. I shan't blame it on you, I swear."

"B-blame what?" she stammered and then, recovering her poise a little, "Will you take a seat, my lady? May I offer you some refreshment?"

"Thank you, but no. I can't stay more than a minute or two." I sat, framing my words. If it weren't for that encounter with McBrae, I would have spent the hackney ride planning what to say instead of stewing about his effrontery. "I don't blame you for obeying Lord Derwent."

"Obeying him…in what way?" She appeared genuinely confused. Perhaps she was a good actress. She must be, to remain ever polite and agreeable to my brother. "I beg your pardon, my lady, but I don't understand what you're asking. I always obey him."

"I suppose you have no choice." How ghastly that must be.

She was silent, her shoulder twitching in the slightest shrug, as if anything she said might put her in the wrong. She had recovered her complexion, which proved to have a lovely golden tone.

I sighed. Best to get this over with. "I merely wish to know if Lord Derwent ordered you to post some letters for him."

After a pause: "N-no, my lady." Her perplexed frown didn't quite convince me, but perhaps that was due to my suspicion rather than her guilt.

"This would be within the past week or so," I said.

"Lord Derwent wasn't in London during that time." She reddened. "Except..."

"Except for one night." I paused, watching her narrowly, detecting nothing but mortification. Why would a mistress be ashamed? I mean, what is the point? If shame were a concern, why become a fallen woman in the first place?

Carnal desires, you say, and once again, I don't understand. The consequences of an unmarried woman's indulging her carnal inclinations are appalling. Why would anyone exchange ruin for a little pleasure? It makes no sense.

"I am aware of that." I hoped I didn't sound disapproving. Just because I didn't understand, it didn't mean I should add to her embarrassment. "I refer to letters that he sent you to post for him in London, in a specific sequence, perhaps."

"N-no, my lady. He never told me to post anything for him."

Was she lying or not? I simply couldn't tell. I tried once more. "At Lombard Street post office, perhaps?"

"Lombard Street?" she burst out. "Why ever would I post anything there? It must be three miles away! I would simply put a letter in the postman's bag."

That rendered me speechless. What an idiot I was! If only I'd thought before acting, I could have avoided an embarrassing and risky situation. "Very well," I said at last. "I apologize for disturbing you, Miss Concord. I would appreciate your discretion on this subject."

She curtsied. "Of course, my lady."

"If there should be any repercussions...... That is, if my brother should find out that I was here..."

"I swear, I shall say nothing!" Esme said. Was she frightened of me or of my brother? He would probably have told her not to admit me.

"Is my brother unkind to you?" I asked.

Her eyes widened. "Never, my lady. He is..." She paused, her voice brimful of emotion. "I shall be eternally grateful to him. He is the best man I have ever met."

Heavens! She must have met very few men, if that's how she feels about Julius.

"You'll have to say something if he finds out. Tell him I surprised you. That I only wished to meet you." I grimaced. "And that I was all kindness and condescension—that sort of nonsense tends to placate him."

"Very well, my lady." Did I sense a gleam of humor in her eyes? If so, it vanished immediately.

"Thank you," I said. "I am happy to have met you."

It was the truth, but I wasn't the least bit surprised when she didn't reply in kind.

***

I arrived home discouraged. It was now toward the end of the third day since I'd hired Jenny, and I'd begun to fear she had run off with my nuts and shillings, never to return. But I couldn't let discouragement affect me any more than those stupid letters, so after a bracing cup of tea, I set out for the nearby square. It's the one place I go on my own—it's so close to home that I need no escort.

I walked four times around the square. Children played in the garden, overseen by their respective nursemaids. One little boy shrieked repeatedly while throwing a stick for a tiny, yapping dog. All very domestic and uninteresting, and meanwhile, no sign of Jenny. Grumpily, I stalked toward home. I didn't regret the three shillings, but I didn't like the feeling of being cheated. Even more, I would have to find someone new to watch the print shop, and meanwhile—

"Psst!"

I swiveled. A small face peeked through a crack between two boards of a shed at the end of a mews. "Jenny?"

"Shhh! Keep walking and I'll catch you up."

I glared, sorely tempted to admonish her, for how dare she order me about? Any other lady of my acquaintance would have taken umbrage. But something told me not to, and I strolled slowly on, idly twirling my parasol.

She came up next to me just before I reached Henrietta Street.

"Heavens, what happened to you?" She was dirtier than ever and had a ghastly purple and black bruise near one eye.

"Got into a fight," she said with the slightest of shrugs. She glanced behind her. "I don't think no one saw me, but I'd best not hide in there again."

"Then why didn't you meet me in the square, as I requested? It's a lovely garden with children playing."

"They don't let the likes of me past the gates," she said.

I hadn't thought of that. Only residents of the square hold keys to the garden, and the nursemaids wouldn't let their charges near a little guttersnipe. For all they knew, she carried some dread disease—but it was extremely inconvenient for me. "Then why didn't you wait on the pavement outside the fence?"

"They don't like me there, neither. They had a footman run me off."

"What a nuisance," I said, but she looked even more disreputable than before, so I could hardly blame them. Her dress was torn, and now I spied a scrape on her arm. "You've hurt your arm. Was that in the fight as well?"

She nodded.

"You must avoid fighting," I said in what I hoped was a firm, no-nonsense voice. "Girls don't fight. It's what boys do."

"It was a boy I fought, weren't it? And I kicked him good, but Fat Alice said there was plenty room for us both, long as I brings her a handkerchief a day. Otherwise, that boy will fight me again."

None of this made any sense to me. "Who, may I ask, is Fat Alice?"

"The woman what has the barrow next to the stationer's shop."

"You want to sell handkerchiefs now instead of nuts?"

She shook her head. "Like I said, I got to give Fat Alice handkerchiefs, or the boy will fight me again."

I didn't understand the logic, but it hardly mattered. "Very well, but do you have any information for me?"

"I knows which fella brings the prints from Corvus, but I ain't had a chance to follow him yet."

"Tell me about him," I said, thinking that perhaps I could do the following.

"What does he look like?"

"Just a fella."

"A boy? A grown man? How tall? Fat or thin? What color hair?"

"A grown man, I'd say." She screwed up her face in concentration. "Middling height, maybe shorter. Not fat nor thin. He had on a cap. I didn't see no hair, but I didn't see him clear, 'cause it was almost dark."

That made me most uneasy. "You were out after dark?"

She rolled her eyes. "If I comes here in daylight, they drives me away. I always comes home after dark."

And home was a shed in the neighbor's garden. How I wished I could give her better shelter, but I knew Albert would never permit me to hire her to work in the kitchen. He will only hire servants who come with reputable references. Well, once I had paid her the five pounds, she would be able to afford food and decent lodging for quite some time.

That settled my mind enough to continue. "How do you know he's the one who brings the Corvus prints?"

"'Cause I heard him talking to Mr. Charles."

"But he didn't see you?"

"Naw. I sneaks into the yard to piss behind the cistern, see, and then he comes and knocks on the back door, so I stays still and waits."

Good Lord Almighty. The more I learned of this child's life, the more appalled I became. But where else could she go to relieve herself?

"He knocks on the door, and Mr. Charles himself comes out. They jaws for a bit, and then Mr. Charles says, real soft like, 'Nothing from Corvus?' and the other fella says, 'Maybe tomorrow.'"

Perfect, I thought.

"So I peeks round the cistern to take a gander at him, but like I says, it was too dark to see much. Then he and Mr. Charles goes out together, and I sneaks after them, but Mr. Charles stands at the gate chewing the fat with the barrow woman while the other fella leaves."

"Did you see which direction he took?"

"East," she said immediately, "but he coulda turned north or south after that. But I'll be ready to follow him tomorrow."

"Excellent work, Jenny," I said.

She grinned, a wide-mouthed, ecstatic smile, and my heart twisted. "Come with me. I'll get your money and some more nuts."

"And handkerchiefs."

"That's right," I said, and we turned the corner—to be faced with an appalling sight. A familiar travelling carriage had pulled up before our house. An equally familiar footman opened the carriage door, while Maurice unstrapped the baggage from the boot.

I stopped short. "*Merde.*" Excessively crude, I know, but it doesn't sound quite as bad in French as in English—at least to my English ears. I have reserved it for moments of shock and upset and fury.

My mother had come to Town.

Chapter Seven

*S*he arouses my conscience, which is bad enough. If only that were not all she arouses in me.
  —From the diary of Corvus

"Beg pardon, my lady?"

Jenny's confused voice broke through my shock. "It's my mother. God damn her to hell, what is she doing here?"

Jenny gaped at me and whispered, "That's bad language, my lady."

I tempered my fury. A child of the streets admonishing me for cursing!—but she couldn't be expected to understand. "I hate my mother," I said, watching the footman let down the carriage steps.

Jenny looked even more appalled. "Better than not having one," she murmured.

My heart twisted again. "In your case, yes. In mine, no. Come with me."

I stormed up the pavement and arrived at my doorstep just as Mother descended from the carriage.

"Why is Maurice unstrapping your baggage here?" I demanded.

"Rosie, dearest! There you are. Why in heaven's name are you out unaccompanied?"

"I was just walking around the square." I don't know why, but I always, always feel obliged to explain myself to my mother. "I repeat, why is Maurice bringing your baggage indoors? You can't stay here." Why hadn't I called someone in to strip the wallpaper in the spare bedchamber? After thinking of it, I'd completely forgotten.

She blinked and looked about. "Who is Maurice?"

"My footman. James, then. Mother, you can't stay here." I tried to think of an excuse, but failed utterly.

"But I must, darling," she said, smoothing her skirts. She turned to her maid, who was climbing out of the coach with a dressing case in one hand and a bandbox in the other. Her voice changed to the one she uses for servants. "Hurry up, girl. Bring my dressing case upstairs and put it under lock and key."

"You have a perfectly good house only two streets away," I said.

She sighed. "Indeed, and I should be much more comfortable there, but you need me, and the welfare of my dearest Rosie matters more than anything."

She should have been on the stage. She convinces everyone that she has my best interests at heart, when all she really wants is her own way. Her eyes lit upon Jenny, and the sweet, syrupy voice became strident. "What is that filthy child doing?" She flapped her hand. "Shoo! Go back where you belong."

I grabbed Jenny's grubby little hand. "She belongs right where she is," I retorted. "Jenny is my protégée. I'm helping her earn an honest living."

My mother's eyes went round with distress—I don't doubt that her distress was a real emotion—and for a moment her façade dropped. "Good God, you truly have gone mad."

I didn't answer. I couldn't. I fled indoors, taking Jenny with me to my bedchamber, where I slammed the door and took several deep, gulping breaths.

"Are you ill, my lady?" The child's tentative voice brought me to my senses. Something about my mother makes me lose control—the last thing I can afford to do.

"No, I'm fine. It's just that she makes me—very angry." I collected myself and found three of my older handkerchiefs. "Will these do?"

Her eyes widened. "Oh, aye, my lady, they're perfect."

"Here are three shillings for three more days," I said, "but do your best to come to me immediately if you have more information." I paused to think. "I don't know how I shall manage to meet you. My mother will watch my every move…"

"Why, my lady? You don't look mad to me."

How I wished she hadn't heard my mother, but strangely, her reassurance made me blink away tears. "I'm not, but my mother—my whole family—are terrified of scandal, and there's been a lot of it lately, all related to me." I don't know why I tried to explain to her. I suppose I needed someone to talk to, and McBrae wasn't there.

What an unexpected thought that was—and not at all comforting. I scarcely knew the man and didn't particularly like him, and yet I saw him as a confidant.

Now that…that truly *was* mad.

"Let me see how much I gave you again," I said.

"It were three shillings, my lady."

"Yes," I said, knowing perfectly well what I'd given her, but I had to *see*. "Let me count it again. And—and perhaps I have a shinier coin or two." Well, I had to have *some* excuse, didn't I? Reluctantly, she took the three coins from her pocket and showed me. I glanced in my reticule, added a sixpence, the coins disappeared into her pocket, and immediately I longed to count them again, just to *see*, even though I already was completely sure what I had given her.

"Thank you, my lady." Her mildly perplexed expression pricked me.

I took a deep breath. Did it really matter whether I checked the coins again? No. If I'd given her too much, I didn't care, and she would have told me if I hadn't given her enough. I had saved myself this time—the extra sixpence had distracted her—but if she didn't think me mad yet, she might come to do so if I didn't watch myself.

Back, then, to the real problem: my mother was here, determined to get me under her control again, and I couldn't allow it. I didn't expect any help from Albert. He doesn't like my mother either, but he wouldn't risk offending her by ordering her to leave. He would simply spend more time away from home—just when I would actually welcome him underfoot, as a shield if nothing else.

If I behaved myself (according to my mother's tedious notions), she would eventually go home to the country, but I couldn't let her ruin my chances of finding Corvus. Besides that, I didn't like the idea of Jenny scurrying through the streets at night, or fighting with boys, or relieving herself behind a cistern. Five pounds would last her a good long time. She would have proper lodging and food, and if I continued to help her, she might find work. I had to get my search for Corvus over with, whether or not my blasted mother was in London.

I had never stood up to my mother before, but I had no choice but to do so now.

I brought Jenny to the kitchen, where I purloined more nuts and several muffins in spite of Mrs. C's disapproval; she was far too preoccupied with my mother's sudden arrival to do more than glare at Jenny and get on with ordering the cook and scullery maid about. I sent Jenny on her way and steeled myself to be polite but firm with my mother.

I hesitate to write about my mother. It is very, very hard to do, because I can't help but fear your judgment of me. I've told you what I think of her, but I have to ask myself—could I be wrong? Does she really care about my welfare, or simply about what people think?

When she is elsewhere, I have no problem knowing my own mind, maintaining my composure, et cetera. I am one hundred percent certain that she is as selfish and heartless as she seems. But if that is the case, why, oh why do I feel an urge to please her when she is nearby? Why can't I simply—to put it in vulgar terms—tell her to go to hell and stay there?

Because I'm a lady, you say. Because I was taught to be polite, despite any feelings to the contrary. Fine, but it's not that simple. It's not just a matter of not being rude to her. Some part of me wants her to think well of me—of the real me, though, not some imaginary Rosamund molded in her image.

In any event, I tried, because that is what I always do. I ordered tea and cakes, got out my knitting, and sat with her in the drawing room—all very polite and proper.

"I've been invited to a small party at Lady Logan's tonight," I told her. "Cards, and maybe some dancing, but nothing formal. Would you like to come along? I'm sure she'd be delighted to see you."

"After a grueling drive from Kent? I'm far too exhausted to go out."

"Very well, I'll give Lady Logan your best."

"My dear child," she said gently, "good manners dictate that you stay home and entertain me."

My insides began to squirm, but I couldn't simply acquiesce. "They also dictate that I attend a party when I have said I will do so."

"Send a note to Lady Logan. I'm sure she will understand."

Guilt wracked me. "Mother, I don't want to stay here with you. We'll just end up arguing."

"Not if you don't insist on contradicting me, dearest," she said.

I stood. If I stayed there, I might start shouting at her. As a child, I would have wept, but now I would rather die than weep in front of my mother. "I'm sorry to have to contradict you, but I'm going to the party whether you like it or not."

She sighed. Then she sighed again. "Sit down, Rosie," she said with a third sigh, a longsuffering one that is far worse than any of Albert's. "I see one of your tantrums coming on, and I couldn't bear that. They distress me so very much. They make me fear..." She let the words drift to nothing, suggesting you know what. I longed to strangle her.

Instead, I picked up my knitting. "In fact, I'd best go speak to Mary Jane about which jewelry to wear tonight. My best diamond eardrops are being cleaned, such a bore, but perhaps another pair will do." My voice didn't shake at all, and I left the room with entirely adequate composure under the circumstances.

Needless to say, she choose to come with me to Lady Logan's, since she couldn't do much to control me otherwise. She took forever getting ready, and I almost left without her (promising to send the carriage back for her), but she came downstairs just in time to make the short ride unpleasant.

"I'm so very weary," she complained, getting into the carriage as slowly as a stiff old lady, which she isn't. "So heartless of you to insist that I come along."

I didn't bother retorting that I had done no such thing. What was the use?

"Where is dear Albert? If he had accompanied you, I needn't have done so."

"I have no idea where he is, nor do I care. We don't interfere in one another's lives." If only she would take the hint.

"You poor darling," Mother said, "abandoned for a loose woman. How can you expect to have children if your husband is disporting himself elsewhere? You're looking rather pale. I must say, a little rouge might help to make you more appealing. Although perhaps it's for the best; much as I dislike Albert, you're perhaps not the ideal candidate for motherhood."

Et cetera.

Lady Logan professed great pleasure at seeing my mother. She probably meant it; Mother is the perfect aristocrat, aloof and well-mannered, cordial to her peers, an excellent guest. You see, I do recognize that she has some good qualities.

Much as I didn't want her there, it was better than staying at home. At Lady Logan's, she wouldn't glue herself to my side, as that would look odd. I could play cards or dance or converse in relative comfort. Perhaps she would even realize that the scandal wasn't so very bad, that I was perfectly sane, and that she could return to Kent immediately.

Foolish of me, I know.

Almost immediately, we found ourselves confronted by Mother's arch-enemy, Mrs. Brill. She reminds me of a reptile—cold, grey eyes and a tendency to show the tip of her tongue. They greeted each other with false professions of delight.

"How selfless of you to come to Town, my dear Lady Medway," Mrs. Brill said. "Exhausting, I'm sure, at your age." She paused to let this jab reach home, but not long enough for Mother to form a rebuttal. "Poor Rosamund needs you just now." She turned her lizard eyes on me. "You're not looking at all well, child."

"I'm perfectly fine, thank you," I said in a sprightly voice.

She chucked me under the chin. She does this every time she meets me in company with my mother. Otherwise, she ignores me.

Which makes it abundantly clear that she does it to annoy Mother, so I repressed a shudder, as I do every time, and offered her a sickly smile.

"So very brave," she said. "Don't let the gossip disturb you."

"I don't," I said.

"Of course you don't," Mother said crisply. "It's all nonsense."

"Precisely," said Mrs. Brill, "so don't you *dare* believe a *word* of it, no matter *what* you hear."

"Thank you *so* much for the kind advice, Mrs. Brill," I simpered. "It means so *much* to me."

Actually, come to think of it, she doesn't *always* ignore me. This dig from me was in response to her disapproval of one of the stories I read aloud at the Home for Indigent Female Orphans. She is also a patron, and also reads to those poor, hapless little girls—but whereas she prefers harrowing tales of the horrors that befall disobedient children, I read them adventure stories I have penned myself, based on exciting legends such as the Knights of the Round Table or Robin Hood. The matron must have complained about me, for Mrs. Brill came to the orphanage specifically to remonstrate with me for reading stories that did not have a suitable moral. "Robin Hood was an outlaw. A thief! Hardly a good example for children to follow."

I didn't entirely blame her for disapproving of stealing from the rich to feed the poor. I am quite well off and would prefer to remain so. However, I am not uncharitable, and greediness in the face of extreme deprivation, even starvation, is downright stupid. "But there is a moral," I told her. "Don't be a bad King, or your subjects will take the law into their own hands." Which is exactly what happened at Runnymede, so I had history to back me up.

That infuriated her even more, and now her eyes narrowed dangerously.

Mother yanked on my arm. "Look, there's Lady Danby. Come, dearest, I mustn't neglect her." She dragged me away, hissing. "I have enough problems with that woman without your sarcastic remarks."

"I was trying to be helpful," I protested. "Sticking up for our side."

"I don't need help from an idiot," she snarled.

Stung, I bit my lip hard.

"Do you have no idea of the harm she can do spreading gossip about you?"

"Everybody's already gossiping about me," I said, but then we approached Lady Danby.

She and Mother are old friends, so after a short while, I was able to slip away.

"That's your mother?"

I turned to find—you guessed it—McBrae smiling at me. I don't know why I was surprised to see him; I knew he was a friend of Lord Logan's.

"Well met, Lady Rosamund," he said. "If you would cease torturing your sash, I might be able to take your hand."

Drat it, I'd been twisting and turning the blue sash that Mary Jane had draped so elegantly about my gown. Now it was a crumpled mess. I tried to smooth it, but to no avail.

I gave up. "Take my hand? Why?"

He curled his firm, strong fingers around my limp, sweaty ones and raised my hand to his lips—a charming, old-fashioned gesture. "That's why."

I felt my color rise. Heavens, was the man flirting with me? "Yes, that's my mother," I said flatly.

"She's a pretty woman. You favor her greatly."

"Don't say that," I blurted. "I don't want to be anything like her."

What is *wrong* with me? For some reason, I always became indiscreet and stupid in his presence, but this was worse than usual. I do know better than to disrespect my mother in public.

He didn't respond to my foolish remark, merely saying, "Will you dance with me? There's a quadrille forming."

"I was thinking of playing whist," I muttered, embarrassed and wanting to get away.

"Later. Dance with me now."

"Oh, very well." I know I sounded surly, which made no sense, since in a way I was relieved. I like dancing, and one isn't obliged to make conversation, so it would give me time to recover my composure. He proved to be an elegant dancer, and by the time the quadrille ended, I was feeling much better than I had all day.

"Whist now?" he asked. "Or may I get you some refreshment first?" Without waiting for an answer, he led me to a table. Soon we were partaking of wine and cakes and discussing harmless subjects like seals (had I succeeded in finding a design I liked?) and vanishing footmen (no, thank heavens, Lady D hadn't identified the poor man).

"Darling Rosie, do introduce me."

I should have known my enjoyment was too good to last. "Mother, this is Mr. Gilroy McBrae from Scotland." Quickly, I added, "A friend of Lord Logan's. And Lord Baffleton's." I feared she would snub him otherwise. "Mr. McBrae, this is my mother, the Countess of Medway."

McBrae, who had very properly risen, bowed and said, "Charmed to meet you, Lady Medway."

"Likewise, I'm sure," she said in an indifferent voice. "Come play whist, Rosie dear."

"I'd rather not. I don't enjoy whist." I don't know what had possessed me to mention it earlier to McBrae. The stupidest things pop out of my mouth, don't they?

"Nonsense, darling. Come now. This is primarily a card party. People will think it very queer if you don't play at all."

"No fear of that, Lady Medway," said McBrae. "Lady Rosamund just promised to play piquet with me."

"Well then, how lovely," she said in her gentlest voice. She drifted away, calling to some others to make up a four for whist. I knew full well I was in for a scold later.

We only played one game of piquet, which should have been fun, for McBrae and I were very well matched. But my dread of what was to come destroyed my pleasure.

"Thank you," I told him when he suggested another, "but I feel a headache coming on."

"I don't blame you," he said. "Take it from me, Lady Rosamund, you're nothing like her." With that he left, and I joined a group of ladies drinking tea, but by the time we said our goodbyes I really did have a headache.

***

It proved to be far worse than a scold. She harangued me the whole way home for spending too much time with a man unrelated to me, and a nobody to boot. People might think I had a *tendre* for him, and next thing we knew, Corvus would produce a print about that. My head throbbed to the point of nausea by the time we reached my house. By dint of a supreme effort, I held onto my composure. I took a few drops of laudanum—a weakness in which I rarely indulge—and fell into a deep, yet uneasy sleep.

Albert had returned before dawn, as usual. I found him doing his best to placate my mother at breakfast. "My dear Lady Medway, Rosie is perfectly fine. You may return to Kent assured that all will be well."

"And count on you to take care of her?" Mother demanded. "You're the worst possible influence. She refused to play whist with me, which was extremely disrespectful, and before a Scotsman of all people."

"Which Scotsman?" Albert asked.

"A Mr. McBrae," I said. "Sir Edwin introduced us. He's perfectly respectable—educated at Harrow, a school friend of Lord Baffleton's. I had already promised to play piquet with him, so it would have been impolite not to."

"Quite right," Albert said. "We have enough problems with the Scots without going about insulting them."

"This has nothing to do with politics, and the man's a nobody," Mother said. "Rosie's wayward behavior is entirely your fault."

Albert and I exchanged speaking glances. We both knew better than to argue with my mother.

"Look at her," Mother said. "She's pale and wan. I fear for her well-being. The country is a much healthier place to be."

"You *are* looking a little peaked, Rosie." Albert put up a hand, anticipating my protest. "But I know how much you dislike the country, so as always, it's up to you."

Shortly after that, he left. "What a stupid man you married," Mother said.

"No, he's actually quite clever," I protested. Otherwise, he wouldn't have achieved so much in politics. He has hopes of being on the honors list someday. But I didn't say as much to my mother; why waste my breath?

"I always said the match was beneath you—not that I would have risked giving you to a nobleman," Mother said. "We can't afford instability in our ruling families."

I'd heard this before, years ago. If she was so worried about instability, she should be relieved I'd had no children.

She shouldn't have married my father, if she cared so much about the ruling families. She shouldn't have had children herself, if she feared the spread of madness.

I have often been tempted to say exactly that, but so far I have always refrained. I don't want to upset and infuriate her. When Mother is truly upset, everyone suffers.

The post arrived, and I flipped through it.

"Pass me the invitations, darling," Mother said. "I'll decide which to accept."

My heartbeat quickened: another argument. "You needn't stay here, Mother."

"Albert can't see the nose before his face," she said. "You're not well. You disobey me. You feed dirty, vermin-infested ragamuffin children. Yes, I have spoken to Mrs. Cropp about it, and I am appalled."

"There's nothing wrong with feeding the hungry," I retorted.

"Through appropriate charities, my love," she chastised me. "Even in proper company, you choose to associate with your inferiors. You actually giggled at that man last night—how indescribably vulgar."

She may have been right that I'd giggled; I didn't remember, but McBrae was an amusing man.

"And then you got a headache for no reason at all, which only goes to prove that you're not in the best of health. You need solitude and good nursing."

I gritted my teeth. "I'm fine, Mother. You're imagining things." I ripped open another letter.

I LEFT OUT PART OF YESTERDAY'S MESSAGE. THERE'S SOMETHING SERIOUSLY WRONG WITH YOU, AND SOON ALL LONDON WILL KNOW.

Terror assailed me. With a supreme effort, I refolded the letter and tucked it in my pile of correspondence. Only by pressing my hands on the table did I keep them from shaking.

She was smiling at me, her head cocked like some sharp-beaked bird.

"Darling Rosie, we know you're not in your right mind. You put up with an adulterous husband. You laugh at scandalous prints. If you continue to gad about, feeding urchins, giggling at nothing, dancing with inferior sorts, and so on, soon all London will know."

I stood, staring at her, nausea rising in my gorge. Had my *mother* written those letters? No, surely not. *Surely* not.

"London may go to hell," I said.

She paled and clapped a hand to her chest. It wasn't an act; I truly had shocked her. Indeed, I had shocked myself. "Oh, my dear child, what has become of you? These palpitations will kill me. It's worse than I thought. You *need* your mother to care for you, and therefore I must stay."

So much for standing up to her. I had to get out of there before I was sick all over the breakfast table. I couldn't afford to be sick, not here, not anywhere, because that would give her more ammunition.

Finally, almost too late, a notion came to me—not one of my more brilliant ideas, but I blame that on the nausea. "I shall not run away from London at the first sign of scandal. Nor shall I flee because some horrid caricaturist chooses to mock me. Such cowardly behavior is unworthy of a daughter of one of England's noble houses."

Mother blinked at me. I believe I had for once surprised her. Not for long, though. "It's not cowardice, Rosie. It's common sense, of which you evidently possess none."

I ignored her. "I shall consider going to the country when the season is over." Hopefully she would be long gone by then, and if I left Town, it would *not* be to go to Kent. I stood and gathered my correspondence. "Stay if you must—I'm sure you mean well—but this is my house, and these are my invitations. I shall let you know which ones I have accepted. You may choose to accompany me if you wish."

Wrapping myself in what I hoped passed for dignity, I stalked toward the door.

"Stop right now!" my mother cried. I obeyed—out of habit, drat it—and she leapt up and slammed the door shut before I could get away. "Sit down and *listen* to me."

So I did. I blew out a long breath, trying to overcome the nausea. I mustn't let my imagination run wild just because of some stupid letters. I composed myself to listen to another harangue.

Unexpectedly, she spoke in a low, urgent voice. "I didn't want to tell you this for fear of upsetting your delicate balance even more, but I must." She paused. "Your brother Julius fears he may have let our little secret slip whilst in his cups."

Aghast, I blurted, "How *could* he?" Well, the answer to that was obvious. "He was too drunk to remember what he said?"

"So he tells me, foolish boy. I am all out of patience with him."

Was that what Julius meant when he told Albert he had reason to believe there was talk about my instability? How craven of him not to admit why—but it wasn't as worrisome as it might be. "Then most likely whoever he was with doesn't remember either."

"My dear child, what if they do? And what if the suggestion spreads and ends up in the hands of Mrs. Brill?"

That didn't worry me much either. Mrs. Brill and my mother were once equals on the Marriage Mart, but they became rivals for my father. Mother won, so now she has precedence over Mrs. Brill. "People take anything she says about you or your family with a grain of salt," I said. "They know she hates you."

"Tsk," Mother said. "It will get into other hands as well. Surely you now understand why Julius and I want you to stay out of sight for a while."

"That's a pity," I retorted, "for I shan't." This time, I made it successfully out of the room.

***

By the time I reached my bedchamber, I realized my error. I know better than to give in to my temper with my mother. The freedom of my life in London had made me careless.

I also knew my mother hadn't written the letters. What earthly reason would she have for doing so? She was terrified of scandal. The last thing she wanted was for the *ton* to whisper about madness in the house of Medway.

For those letters seemed...calculated...to make me go mad.

This thought gave me such a blow that I fell into a chair. It made no sense, and yet it did. Horrifyingly so.

I took a deep breath. And another. After a while, the nausea subsided, but not the... I refuse to call it fear, for a member of the house of Medway cannot succumb to such an unworthy emotion. (Perhaps you'd thought it mere posturing, but I was quite serious earlier, when I'd said much the same to Mother. I do have some familial pride, and I refused to let the nasty letter-writer get the better of me.)

Suddenly, identifying my horrid correspondent had become a matter of urgency—far more urgent than unmasking Corvus. Not that I intended to give up on that front, but for the moment, I must turn my attention once again to the letters. To do that, I must stay in London, and I must also find ways to avoid my mother at least part of the time. (I would wish to do that anyway, but this time I had a far more compelling reason than that she drives me mad.)

What a poor choice of words! How can people speak so lightly of madness? They wouldn't if they knew what their careless words truly signify.

How *could* I imagine that my mother or brother would seek to drive me mad? Their goal is to avoid scandal, whilst madness in the family would cause just the opposite. And although I don't usually agree with them, they aren't evil. It was as absurd as suspecting Albert or my dearest Cynthia.

Oh, how I missed Cynthia. To the devil with her scruples; I intended to go see her.

First things first. I would have to apologize to Mother; that went without saying. And I would have to give in to her to some extent—or at the very least, make her believe I had done so. She wanted me to withdraw from society for a while. How might I do so without repairing to the country?

Aha! There must be a storehouse of brilliant notions in the ether, poised to descend on those who truly need them.

I glanced through the little pile of correspondence, chose the two invitations least likely to appeal to her, and quickly wrote to accept them. I would hand her the rest, with my apology. Let her accept or refuse as she chose; it would be up to her to decide whether I was fit to accompany her. When she didn't want me along, I would find other, more productive ways to occupy my time.

Several invitations a day, to accept or refuse, should keep her satisfied. In fact, I might even hand her all of my mail, to show how much I trusted her to take care of me.

Oh, drat! What if she saw the letters sealed in black?

Now, you might think it made sense to show them to her. To arouse, you say, her maternal instincts (which, I am obliged to admit, she does possess in her domineering way). But no, because if she saw them, she would be even more desperate to hurry me out of London, because 1) such horrid letters might upset the delicate balance of my sanity, and 2) (more importantly), it would confirm her fear that someone out there *knew* about me. *Out of sight, out of mind is our only hope*, she would say. Albert might well agree and let her whisk me away to Kent.

I hurried downstairs—no, first I hid the latest letter, after copying it out in code. I am ashamed to admit that my hands shook a little as I copied it, and that I took it out of its hiding place and replaced it again several times before finally getting a hold of myself and going downstairs. A daughter of the House of Medway should not be so easily rattled, but so it was.

I accosted Stevenson as he exited the passage to the service area. I handed him the two acceptances I'd written with orders to have them delivered. "Stevenson," I whispered. "Where is my mother?"

He jutted his chin toward the drawing room.

"Very well. She insists on staying here, but I can't have her appropriating my correspondence. If she tries to do so, tell her the master said my letters come to me and no one else."

"The master already ordered me to do precisely that." Stevenson allowed himself a small, conspiratorial smile.

How thoughtful of Albert! He knows how much it annoys me when Mother tries to run my life. Unfortunately, I would have to let her do so to some extent.

I carried on to the drawing room, where Mother was engaged in some stitchery. I put on a contrite face and curtsied to her. "Dearest Mother, do please forgive me for that unladylike outburst."

She didn't raise her head (what a waste of a perfectly good curtsey), but merely kept on stabbing the needle in and out of the fabric, no doubt envisioning doing it to me.

Or perhaps not. Mother doesn't have much imagination.

"My only excuse is that I'm accustomed to managing my own household and my own invitations. However, I know you mean well, Mother. I'm *frightfully* sorry."

Still the silent stabbing. I suppressed a sigh and went on with my lines.

"I believe you're right, that I should perhaps—not precisely withdraw, but be much less in sight. If I go to fewer parties, Corvus is likely to forget me and find someone else to caricature." That is, if he didn't hear about my supposed madness. I shuddered at the thought, but I wasn't about to put *that* notion into Mother's head.

The stabbing became slower, less violent. I knew what she was thinking—that now she was halfway to her goal of removing me from society. Which I didn't like much, but it was the only way to stave her off.

"I have accepted a few invitations—one to accompany Miss Tubbs to an exhibit of Roman pottery at the British Museum, and another to a poetry reading. I hardly think Corvus will find me at either of those." I tittered.

How sickening. In real life, I never titter, but needs must. "Here are my remaining invitations." I proffered the little pile, and when she didn't reach for them (no surprise), I laid them on the table before her. "Feel free to answer them as you choose. I shall of course accompany you or remain home, as you think best."

Without glancing at the invitations, she said, "We shall dine at home tonight. A light menu, suitable for an invalid. I shall inform Mrs. Cropp." Irritating pause. "Unless you don't trust me to do that either?"

The temptation to roll my eyes almost mastered me. It is as if I have a pot of vulgarities within me which boils up in mother's presence. "I should be most grateful if you would do so," I said. Mrs. Cropp would far rather deal with Mother, of whom she is in awe, and in any event would likely override my orders in favor of hers. And although an invalid menu always leaves me ravenous, I would find ways to supplement it with refreshments elsewhere, or by sneaking down to the kitchen at night.

Feeling as if I had got easily over rather heavy ground, I left the room. I had given way in one respect—one step towards placating her. Whether or not she forgave me was another question entirely, but she would certainly deal with the invitations. She wouldn't be able to resist.

Relieved, I donned my half-boots and pelisse and went out for a walk. Hopefully, exercise and fresh air would 1) put a bloom into my cheeks, and 2) assist me in deciding on the next step in identifying my horrid correspondent.

Number two, above, could be approached from one of two angles, by asking: a) who was writing the letters, and b) why. I decided to concentrate on why. Apart from my family, there were a number of people who might know my secret—acquaintances of my blabbing brother, for example, and through them, any number of gossips. It was also possible that one of my sisters had confided in a bosom friend. Or even some elderly person might know about Great-Aunt Edna. But whoever knew must also have reason to harm me. Why else torment me in such a way?

So far, Mrs. Brill was at the top of my list—well, so far it was a list of one. I couldn't quite imagine her penning nasty letters, but it would be foolish to dismiss her.

Particularly since I had recently read a story to the orphans about Queen Elizabeth's friendship with the famous female pirate from Ireland, Grace O'Malley. Stupid of me, you say, for it was bound to provoke both the matron and Mrs. Brill, but I saw it as an excellent example two strong women. Those little orphans need to hear tales of strength and fortitude, for their lives will surely be hard.

It is no great fun imagining who might wish one ill. I suppose that is why my steps turned automatically toward Cynthia's house. Yes, she'd said we must pretend to be at odds with one another, but I didn't feel like doing what I was told. Rather, I wanted to feel safe and comfortable, and she is one of the few people whom I trust absolutely.

Cynthia lives in a charming little house, which is hers for life or until she remarries, at which point it reverts to the present Lord Benson. If I could live alone, it's just the sort of adequate but unpretentious house I would choose. I rapped upon the door, enjoying my unescorted state. Usually one takes a carriage to a morning call, so this felt delightfully free.

A harried maidservant opened the door. "I'm sorry, but Lady Benson isn't home to callers today." I was about to take umbrage—I am not just any visitor—when I realized what time it was—still morning, and morning callers don't come until after noon.

"This isn't a morning call," I said. "Lady Benson will receive me."

"Mrs. Delabole told me not to admit anyone," the maid said. "Milady is ill."

"Good heavens." I pushed my way past her into the house. "What's wrong?" My answer came in the form of the sound of retching.

I hurried up the stairs to the first floor, to come upon the distressing sight of Cynthia reclining on the drawing room sofa, vomiting into a basin held by her personal maid. Mrs. Delabole watched grimly. None of them noticed me.

After a moment, Cynthia passed a handkerchief across her lips. "Take it away, Agnes. I shall be fine for a while now."

"Perhaps some barley water, milady?"

"Later, please. Take the basin away." Cynthia spied me in the doorway. "Rosie!"

"Lady Rosamund!" Mrs. Delabole straightened, her frail fingers tightening on her cane. "What are you doing here? I told the girl not to admit callers." Her prim, wizened face twisted into a scowl.

"Surely that doesn't include me," I said sweetly. "Dearest Cynthia, how frightfully boring to be unwell."

"It's nothing. Agnes, bring tea and cakes." The maid left, and Cynthia added, "Don't frown, Mrs. Delabole. Lady Rosamund is always welcome here."

"It will cause talk," Mrs. Delabole said, "as if there isn't enough already."

"A short visit won't hurt," Cynthia said irritably.

The old lady's scowl deepened. "Sir Roderick ordered me to deny Lady Rosamund access to you."

"He did *what?*" Cynthia sat up, clenching her fists. Such a display of emotion was unprecedented on her part—not that I blamed her. "Sir Roderick has no right to decide who may visit me."

"He only wants what is best for you," Mrs. Delabole said.

Cynthia huffed. "Yes, yes, I know he means well." She subsided against the back of the sofa. "He just doesn't *understand.*"

"He understands that it's all that woman's fault." The old lady jabbed her cane in my direction. For an instant, I feared she might strike me, but luckily she can't walk without it. "You should be ashamed of yourself, Lady Rosamund." With brisk, angry taps of the cane on the floor, she left the room.

Whatever had upset her so? Usually, despite her disapproval, she treats me with ordinary civility.

Honestly, I don't know why Cynthia puts up with her. I have often suggested that she get rid of the old bat, but Cynthia refuses, because for some reason she doesn't want to be unkind to Sir Roderick. Which makes no sense at all—she already *has* been unkind by remaining as Albert's mistress. Surely cutting off all contact would make more sense than keeping him dangling after her.

"Perhaps a tisane would be better for you than tea," I suggested.

"My stomach is a little upset, that's all," Cynthia said crossly.

"More than a little, I think. Why aren't you upstairs in bed?"

"Truly, it's nothing." She swallowed again. Her usually rosy cheeks were pale. "I can't keep anything down, but it will pass."

"But why sit in the drawing room feeling poorly if you're not receiving callers? It makes no sense."

"It's *nothing,*" she repeated. "I can't *stand* lying in bed feeling sorry for myself. I shall be well directly."

Heavens, I'd never seen her so crotchety. This illness had seriously upset her customary equilibrium.

"Yes, of course, dearest." I eyed her. She must be laced up particularly tight, for those voluptuous breasts were almost bursting from her bodice. Exactly the opposite of what she should do when unwell...

Good God Almighty! Just because I'm inexperienced in certain aspects of life, it doesn't mean I don't recognize the signs. I have three married sisters, after all. I glanced behind and shut the drawing room door.

"Are you increasing?" I asked baldly.

Cynthia glared at me, but didn't deny it.

I shouldn't have been surprised—I do know how babies are made—but Cynthia had been Albert's mistress for years, and the wife of Lord Benson before that. (The current Lord Benson was the son of his father's first wife; Cynthia had been his second.) I'd assumed she was barren.

Well, this certainly explained why everything was my fault even more than usual. Mrs. Delabole must be suffering fits of horror. No wonder her façade of civility had slipped. Even Sir Roderick might be forgiven for trying to keep Cynthia's condition secret—although he shouldn't even have known about it. Mrs. Delabole had tattled to him, no doubt.

I sat next to her on the sofa. "This is quite a complication. Does Albert know?"

"Yes, of course." She let out an exasperated sigh. "He asked me not to tell you. He said it would upset you."

Honestly, men can be dense as bricks. "I hope you didn't believe that nonsense. I am *concerned* for you, of course, but not upset." That got me thinking. "You *were* going to tell me, weren't you?" I was not pleased at being the last to find out, so to speak.

"Yes, darling, but I've scarcely had time to become accustomed to the idea myself, and what with calming Albert down..."

"He never wanted children," I said. "He calls them dirty little beasts."

"He need have nothing to do with this one," she said. "He keeps telling me not to worry, that he will handle it, but I can take care of myself perfectly well. It's obvious what I must do—leave London and find someplace to have the baby where no one knows me."

It is one thing to have a scandalous liaison, but to have a child out of wedlock is another matter. Which makes no sense, in my opinion, as all too often one leads to the other. The only alternative to having the baby elsewhere would be to marry immediately—but what respectable man would want Albert's mistress and child?

"I can't go to France because of the war," she said. "I'm wondering about Ireland."

"Ireland? But it's so far, and horridly barbaric," I cried.

"America, then," she said.

"Just as bad, and even farther away."

"That's what Albert says, too, along with a lot of useless talk about suitable arrangements."

"How tiresome of him," I said. "I'll give him a good scold."

"No, no, please don't! He'll be so vexed with me. He already is."

"For falling pregnant? That's his fault as much as yours."

"No, not because of that. He's agitated because of how it will appear to society, but he doesn't want me to leave."

"For he will miss you," I said, and realization and sadness swept over me. "I shall miss you, too."

"I shall miss you as well, Rosie, but perhaps it's for the best," she said briskly. "As I said before, we must pretend to be estranged from one another to avoid further talk. My departure will aid in that goal."

I didn't give a hedgehog's bum about the gossip caused by Corvus' prints, but this pregnancy was another matter entirely. A dreadful notion struck me. "You mustn't foster it out. You're going to keep the baby. Aren't you?"

"Of course, darling!" She patted my hand. "I wouldn't dream of giving it up."

That was a relief. "You must vigorously oppose Albert if he suggests such a horrid measure. When you return, we will say it is the child of a relative who died."

"A transparent excuse which will cause talk of another sort," she said flatly. "It's one topic of gossip or the other, take your choice."

It was then that a brilliant and delightful notion swept over me.

"That is exactly what we'll do—take our choice!" I cried. "What if we two were to go on a long journey together? If people believe we are more than friends, they will not be surprised if we leave Town."

Her brows drew together. "I don't see how that will help."

"It will, because they will think you are fleeing to escape gossip. They won't even suspect you're hiding a pregnancy. We'll go north and live retired for a couple of years, and Albert can come visit us."

She shook her head. Her lips quirked up the tiniest bit. "I doubt if he will agree."

"He *must* agree, for your sake." The more I thought about it, the more I liked the idea. "The season will be over in another month or so, and it won't seem unusual if we leave London for the summer, and then stay away longer than planned." Two birds with one stone: if I was traveling with Cynthia, I couldn't be dragged back to Kent by my mother. "You can convince Albert of anything if you put your mind to it."

"To do without me for a few years? I don't think so."

"Very well, I shall have to do so," I said stoutly. Her customary expression of mild amusement was back—but although I was glad to see her restored to her usual self, it rather annoyed me this time. Albert was stubborn, and she was the one with influence on him—so why wouldn't she at least try?

"Don't bother him about it just yet," she said. "I'd rather see what he's planning first."

"But, Cynthia—"

"I mean it, Rosie," she said. "This is my problem, not yours. Let me handle it my way."

I kissed her goodbye, trying not to feel to out of charity with her. I would have to muster my patience as best I could. In the meantime, I had work to do here in London. During the walk home, I enjoyed myself devising various plans.

Unfortunately, what I encountered there put pleasurable journeys right out of my head.

Chapter Eight

ould she be amenable to a spot of adultery? More to the point, would I? I don't usually look to other men's wives. I'd rather keep it that way, and yet this one is neglected...
—*From the diary of Corvus*

A weeping maidservant emerged from the house next door to mine, pursued by both Lady Beddoes' housekeeper and personal maid (who styles herself a dresser, to which Mary Jane takes exception, insisting that a dresser must have a sense of style, which neither Lady Beddoes nor her maid possesses). I recognized the young woman as Lucy, the maid of all work, with whom I occasionally exchanged a word over the garden wall. She wore an old bonnet and a tattered cloak, and carried a string bag which, by the look of it, contained a few articles of clothing.

"Begone, you lying trollop!" the housekeeper cried.

"Be thankful my mistress allowed you to keep your clothing," the personal maid said primly. "You deserve to be cast naked into the street."

Lucy faced them, chin up. "I'm an honest maid. She's my sister, I swear!"

This was greeted by a loud guffaw from a rough-looking fellow unloading coal from a nearby cart. Already, onlookers were gathering. I don't know how it happens, but at the slightest hint of an altercation, a deserted London street suddenly boasts a crowd.

"I have never before heard such a barefaced lie," the housekeeper said.

"The gall of the strumpet!" said a self-righteous female amongst the onlookers, whom I recognized as the desiccated paid companion of one of my elderly neighbors. She'd probably never had an opportunity to behave inappropriately.

Which, I admit, is a horrid thing to say. One cannot help but feel sorry for ladies obliged to serve as paid companions or governesses. Surely their very misfortune should make them more sympathetic to others—but quite the contrary.

On the other hand, Lucy should have known better. I cannot comprehend why women whose livelihood depends on their virtue do not cling to it for dear life. How difficult can that possibly be?

"You'll end up in a brothel, and rightly so." The personal maid's eyes gleamed with malice. "And if the child shows her face here, she will be sent straight to the workhouse."

Child? Oh, good *heavens*. Surely not.

"Please, *please*, no," Lucy cried. "I'll come fetch my Jenny."

"Don't you dare," the housekeeper said. "If you're seen nearby, I'll have you put in charge. How dare you house and feed your ill-begotten daughter in my mistress's shed? You should be hanged for theft."

"Come along of me, sweetheart," said the coal heaver with a lascivious leer. "I'll take care of you."

Titters and guffaws erupted from the crowd. The maid shuddered and hurried away, muffling her sobs in her cloak.

Appalled, wondering what in God's name to do, I glanced at my own house, and spied my mother's face at the window. Immediately, she drew back; vulgar inquisitiveness is unacceptable in a lady.

It was obvious what I had to do: find Jenny, who was evidently the illegitimate child of the dismissed maid, and see that she didn't end up in the workhouse.

My front door opened a little way, and my mother hissed, "Come into the house, Rosie. Don't stand there gaping."

I obeyed, seeing as there was no point in remaining outdoors. "That poor woman," I said. "How callous of them to send her off with nothing but the clothes on her back."

"It's no more than she deserves." Mother shut the door behind me. "She had a baby out of wedlock, and what's worse, she hid her shame and concealed the child in Lady Beddoes' garden."

"What else was she supposed to do?" I demanded. "No one would hire her if they knew about her daughter."

"She should have thought of that before she gave in to her base urges," Mother said.

Exactly what I'd been thinking, so I couldn't disagree. Easy for me, you say, as I have no base urges. But to be ruined by one little mistake seems frightfully unfair. "I suppose she could have given the child to an orphanage," I said.

"She would still be a lying slut," Mother said. "And a thief, stealing food and bedding and God knows what else, too!"

This was illogical. If the maid had given the child up, she wouldn't have had to steal anything. "Lady Beddoes can afford to feed and clothe one little girl," I huffed.

"It was *theft*," Mother said. "They should have sent for the constable, and so I told Mrs. Cropp."

I opened my eyes wide as it dawned on me. "How did they find out about little Jenny?"

Her cheek twitched. She didn't answer, and changed the subject. "Upstairs, child, and ring for your maid to dress you." She tugged on the strings of my bonnet.

"This was your doing, wasn't it? Yours and Mrs. Cropp's."

"My dear Rosie, it had nothing to do with me." She removed my bonnet and dusted it off. "Mrs. Cropp saw the child lurking next door, talking to the maid of all work, and felt it to be her duty to inform Lady Beddoes' housekeeper."

Duty, my foot. She did it to curry favor with my mother, but I didn't say that. "And to get rid of that poor child."

"Rightly so. The situation was not to be borne. She understands that I cannot allow my daughter to concern herself with beggar children."

Did she mean what I thought she meant? Did Mrs. Cropp *know*?

Surely not. Whatever my mother might do, she wouldn't confide in a mere servant. Mrs. Cropp was merely as obsessed with propriety as my mother. That was all. I let out a breath.

"It presents such a very odd appearance," Mother added complacently.

"And therefore you had a hardworking woman thrown penniless into the street, and her child threatened with the workhouse? Because of *me?*"

"It was *necessary*," Mother said.

"And now it's necessary for me to find that child before such a hideous fate befalls her." Conditions in the workhouse are horrid—or so I have heard. Naturally, I have no direct experience with such places.

"Nonsense," she said briskly. "Come upstairs and change into something more suitable for morning callers. Where have you been? Walking about on your own is most improper; you should have taken a footman. You're windblown and disheveled, for heaven's sake."

As if the footman could have protected me from the wind. "You'll have to deal with the morning callers yourself. I'm going out to find Jenny."

I marched to the door and threw it open.

"Come back, child! You must not—Rosie, you cannot *afford* to behave so oddly."

I whirled. "You have given me no choice." I stormed out, slamming the door behind me.

And bumped into—you guessed it—Gilroy McBrae.

He put out a hand to steady me. "Going someplace?"

"Yes," I retorted. "What are you doing here?"

"I came to pay a morning call," he said mildly. "You appear to be overset, Lady Rosamund. Enraged, even, judging by the bloom in your cheeks."

"I am furious," I muttered before I could stop myself. Really, it was none of his business.

"Anything I can do to help?"

"No, but thank you anyway. Feel free to call; my mother is there." I started off down the street.

"Yes, I see her in the window, wearing a scowl." He kept pace with me. "I came to call on you, not your mother."

He had meant to call on me before—the day we met on the way to Lady

Baffleton's, if you recall—but this time, for some reason, it made me blush. I am not without admirers, but my lack of prurient interest means I find it easy and natural to treat them with cool friendliness.

Not so with McBrae. I frowned, trying to understand my reaction. Since it was not a question of physical attraction—not that McBrae was unattractive, mind you—it must be that I valued his friendship.

How very odd. He wasn't my sort. I'm the daughter of an English earl, and although he seemed fairly well-bred, he was far below me socially, and a Scot to boot.

I shook off such ponderings. I had more important concerns for now. "Frightfully kind of you, but I have an urgent matter to take care of."

"I can see that." His sympathetic smile and the kindness in his eyes couldn't but affect me. "I should be happy to escort you."

I couldn't possibly explain it all to him; I didn't need yet another person suspecting I was mad. "Thank you, but—"

He glanced behind, interrupting me. "Unless you prefer the footman hotfooting it after us."

I turned. Our one remaining footman hurried up, puffing. He held out my bonnet, which I'd forgotten in my haste. Oh *dear*; a lady without a hat does indeed appear extremely odd, if not precisely mad. I thanked him and tugged it on over my wayward hair.

"Milady sent me to accompany you, Lady Rosamund," he said.

So he could report my every move? McBrae was by far the lesser of two evils. "Thank you, Maurice, but Mr. McBrae will escort me." I was proud of myself; I'd remembered not to call the footman James, an accomplishment considering my state of mind.

"I'll take good care of Lady Rosamund and bring her safely home," McBrae said. "You tell that to the countess."

Maurice looked to me for confirmation. I nodded, and he retreated, looking relieved.

Thus I was stuck with my Scottish escort, but by then it had occurred to me that I needn't tell him *everything*. "Thank you," I said.

"My pleasure. Poor fellow, it's not easy for a servant caught between conflicting orders."

"Is that why he seemed relieved? I assumed he just didn't want to accompany me, as I'm likely to be out much of the day." He'd probably heard the altercation and wondered where I meant to search for Jenny, and how long it would take. He would much rather laze about in the kitchen drinking ale and polishing the silver.

"Perhaps that too, but mostly because your mother wanted him to spy on you."

That shook me; my heart began to pound. Did McBrae suspect my instability? Why else would anyone spy on me?

My unease must have shown, for he added, "Isn't that so? She's that sort of woman, determined to control everyone. You left the house in a temper, so naturally she is worried you will do something that reflects badly on her."

I let out a long breath of relief. "You judge her with uncanny accuracy," I grumped. Yes, it was rude of him to describe my mother to me in such terms, but it was wondrous—not an exaggeration, I swear—to have someone on my side, so to speak. "No one dares defy her."

"Except you." He grinned charmingly, coaxing a small smile out of me.

"I do try not to, but I've already lost my temper with her twice since she arrived."

"Tsk," he said, laughing. We reached the street corner. "Where are we going?"

"To the Strand," I said. "Not far from Mr. Charles's shop."

"Then we'll need a hack." He would have steered me towards the hackney stand, but I resisted. It is one thing to walk with a man or ride with him in an open carriage, and another entirely to take a closed carriage. Not that I had the slightest apprehension of improper behavior on his part, but people always assume the worst. What if Corvus happened to find out? I shuddered to think what he might make of it.

"I prefer to walk off my annoyance," I said.

"Very well," he said. We set off east along Oxford Street. "Now, tell me what has upset you."

"If you'd arrived just five minutes earlier, you would know. The maid of all work next door was dismissed in a truly horrid way." I blushed again, hesitating to bring up such a delicate subject when conversing with a man, but there was nothing for it. "She was secretly sheltering her little illegitimate daughter, Jenny—the girl must be seven or eight years old, I judge—in the shed in the back garden. When the housekeeper found out, she dismissed the maid with nothing but the clothes on her back."

He frowned, and his expression grew dark—but somehow I knew he wasn't angry at me for bringing up such an improper matter. He had, I recalled now, defended servants once or twice in my presence.

"That poor woman," I said, emboldened. "She was a hardworking maid—much more so than the housekeeper, who is forever chatting over tea with my own housekeeper, Mrs. Cropp." Now I felt my face darken. "It was she who reported seeing Jenny in the back garden, encouraged by my mother. They both believe that such women deserve their fate. That they would be better off dead."

"And you don't?"

"It does seem rather a harsh punishment," I said. "One little mistake shouldn't ruin an entire life. It's particularly unfair, when one realizes that for people such as—" I broke off with a gasp. What had come over me? I'd almost blabbed the secret of my dearest friend.

"People such as…?"

"It would be impolite to name names, but people with money can have a child fostered out and go on with their lives. They can even keep the entire occurrence a secret and suffer no repercussions at all."

Hopefully, that would dispel any suspicion that I was referring to Cynthia, whose liaison was public knowledge. Besides, she was believed to be barren.

"Shouldn't some allowance be made for passion?" I blundered on. "As you said on our first meeting, everyone experiences it, and for some, it's well-nigh impossible to resist."

"True," he said, with a hint of…a smirk. Suddenly, I wasn't quite so comfortable with him. I supposed that, as a man, he must have passionate urges, but I certainly didn't want to know about them. I preferred to assume they didn't exist.

Which may be stupid, but the alternative is thinking of everyone as simmering pots of desire, ready to boil over, which is far, far worse. What a ghastly notion; surely you agree.

"But women whose employment, whose very survival, depends on their virtue, should control themselves," I said. "I simply can't understand why they don't."

"What about the men who couple with them?" he asked. "Shouldn't they control themselves, too?"

A blush roared up my cheeks. "I have heard," I replied stiffly, "that men cannot do so."

"Nonsense," he said. "They choose not to."

That surprised me. "Most men would disagree with you."

"The child's father was equally at fault, if not more so, for not standing by the maid," McBrae said. "Even if he was a married man, it was his duty to support his mistress and child."

"If he was married, he shouldn't have bedded that poor girl at all." I blushed again; what a stupid, *stupid* thing to say, considering my husband's behavior.

McBrae didn't respond, which immediately got my back up. He was probably doing his best to muffle a guffaw.

Out of sheer annoyance, mostly with myself, I dug myself in deeper. "He should have chosen a woman of experience." Now I sounded completely immoral! "And don't you dare say that that sort of woman would have many lovers, so a man would feel no obligation to support a child possibly not his own."

"I wasn't going to say that."

"No?" I retorted. "What were you going to say?"

"That I assume we are going in search of the woman in order to offer assistance."

"No," I said regretfully. "I should like to help her, but I have no notion where she went. I can only hope that disgusting coal heaver didn't get ahold of her." There'd been no sign of him on the street as I walked away with McBrae. "He made her a crude offer, and people laughed." My throat swelled at the memory. "I should have prevented her from leaving. I should have offered to help right then and there. Heaven knows I don't care what Lady Beddoes thinks of me, but I was transfixed with horror, and then she was gone."

"Your mother would have raised a fuss if you'd tried to help," he said.

"Yes, but she couldn't have stopped me from giving the woman some money," I said. "She would have scolded me about my odd behavior and said that I can't afford to appear…" I bit my tongue. Once again I was babbling, as if he were a safe confidant.

No one was a safe confidant.

"Appear…?"

"Oh…" I fumbled for words. "Different from her beliefs about proper, ladylike behavior."

"Why should you care what she believes?"

I shrugged, hoping to set the topic aside.

"Would your husband object to your charitable impulse?"

"He lets me make my own decisions." Albert might think my behavior peculiar, but if I provided examples of ladies who are patrons of societies for rescuing fallen women, he would nod agreeably and change the subject. As you surely have realized by now, he prefers not to make a fuss.

"We're going to look for the little girl, Jenny," I said. "As far as I know, she is selling nuts on the Strand, not far from Mr. Charles' print shop. I must find her before she returns to the shed next door, for they will be watching for her—Lady Beddoes' maid and housekeeper, and doubtless my housekeeper, too. They mean to send her to the workhouse."

McBrae muttered an oath. "That's not much better than starvation, or a number of other fates she might meet."

"She is to some extent my responsibility. I gave her some walnuts and filberts to sell, encouraging her to support herself."

"Ah," he said, "I begin to understand. You feel this situation is your fault."

I glared at him. "You've been wondering all along why a lady such as I would trouble herself over the fate of a fallen woman and her child. Haven't you?"

"The question had crossed my mind."

For some reason, that hurt. Do I really appear so callous and unconcerned?

"Sympathy doesn't often lead to action," he added.

"Well then, yes, definitely it's my fault!" I said. "My housekeeper caught her in our henhouse some days ago and wanted to put her in the hands of a constable. Instead, I fed her and gave her the nuts, which upset Mrs. Cropp." Infuriated her, more likely. She prefers an obedient mistress. "I wish I could dismiss her, but she's my husband's servant, not mine."

"Surely, as the lady of the house…"

"Yes, but she's been with the Phipps family for years, so I can't possibly get rid of her. I'm sure she kept an eye open for Jenny, saw her skulking next door with the maid of all work, and told the housekeeper there, after which it all came out. Jenny wasn't there when they dismissed the woman, so she will return all unawares. But if I hadn't hi—befriended Jenny, none of this would have happened."

"You don't know that," he said. "Sooner or later, someone would have noticed."

"Maybe not. Maybe the two of them would have been safe until the maid got her year's pay, at the very least. As it is, they are both destitute. I must find Jenny and see what I can do to help both her and her mother."

"Understood. Come, let's take a hackney. We'll get there more quickly."

In my concern for my reputation, I hadn't seen the urgency of the situation. This time, when he steered me toward a hackney stand, I didn't resist.

"If she's not there, I can ask the people at Mr. Charles' shop to keep an eye open for her," he said.

"How very kind," I said, meaning it.

The streets were busy, so it was slow going in the hack, but faster and far less tiring than on foot. I kept to my side of the seat, as near the window as possible. Even so, he took up most of the rest of the seat and therefore was uncomfortably close to me. Not that his person was offensive in any way; my sense of smell informed me that he bathed regularly and changed his clothing often. If anything, I found his subtle personal aroma rather pleasant.

But the situation smacked of impropriety, and besides that, I didn't want a witness to my conversation with Jenny. What if she brought up our bargain? It was none of McBrae's business.

"Why do you suppose she chose a spot so far from home?"

Startled, I froze. He had a knack for asking the most awkward questions. My mind fluttered about chaotically, seeking excuses. "Because the clerks in the area like nuts?" I ventured weakly.

"People everywhere like nuts." He rolled his eyes. "Surely you can think of a better explanation."

What in heaven's name did he mean by that? Did he *suspect*?

Suspect *what*, for heaven's sake? He had no cause to suspect anything; he knew nothing of my twin goals. I was descending into paranoia, which from my sporadic reading I knew was a form of madness. Perish the thought!

I have done my best to educate myself about the various forms of lunacy—not an easy task, as I dare not let anyone know, since it was to prove to myself that I am *not* mad, not to reinforce the fears of my family.

I shook off my foolish thoughts and put my intellect to work at getting me out of this mess. "I could probably think of dozens," I said pettishly, "but why would I? Her reason hardly matters; her predicament does."

He chuckled. "I stand admonished." He had a charming grin, boyish and engaging.

By now I had calmed somewhat. "She did say something about a woman named Alice who has a barrow," I recalled. "And asked me for some handkerchiefs. I can't say I understood why, but it had to do with a boy who gave her a black eye."

He tsked. "The boy didn't want her hawking her nuts in what he saw as his territory, but Fat Alice lets her have a spot nearby in exchange for a handkerchief a day."

"Protecting her! How kind. But what can the woman want with all those handkerchiefs? Surely she doesn't blow her nose that often."

"She doesn't *use* them, she sells them. Fences most of them, actually."

"Fences?"

"She receives stolen handkerchiefs from little pickpockets thereabouts, removes any identifying stitchery, and sells them to a shop."

"Oh, dear," I lamented. "I didn't mean to expose Jenny to criminals."

He snorted. "What else would a street urchin do with her days but meet criminals of various sorts? She must have her wits about her, if she has managed to avoid being forced into prostitution."

I gaped at him, shocked beyond measure. "She's a *child*!"

He shrugged. "Aye, and some men prefer children."

Horrified, I clapped my hands to my mouth. "Surely not...not *you*, Mr. McBrae!"

His eyes blazed. I quailed, shrinking against the window.

"Damn it to hell, Lady Rosamund. No, not I!" He pressed his lips together as if holding back more curses.

I got ahold of myself enough to sit up straight again. "I apologize, but in that case, how do you know of such vileness?"

"Unlike you, I haven't been sheltered from every adverse wind."

That was too much. "Nor have I," I retorted, meeting his now skeptical gaze. "Mine were different adverse winds, that's all."

"I daresay." His tone indicated he didn't believe me, and I certainly did not intend to enlighten him. Besides, my stomach was protesting vigorously, although whether due to the disgusting subject of our conversation or the rocking of the coach, I couldn't say. I wrapped my arms around myself.

"Your innocence is appalling, Lady Rosamund, although only to be expected." He glowered. "You're not going to be sick, are you? Because if so, we'd best get out. The coachman won't appreciate having to clean it up."

I swallowed and sat back, grimly determined not to waste even a minute getting to our destination. "No, I'll be fine. Oh, I *must* find Jenny and get her off the streets."

"Don't worry, we shall," he said.

Soon after, McBrae tapped on the roof and the hackney came to a halt.

"Why did we stop?" I demanded, peering out the window. "Mr. Charles's shop is farther down the street—near the next corner, I believe." If there's one thing that annoys me, it's a man who assumes he has a right to order my affairs.

Or a woman, I corrected myself, thinking of my mother. Surely, by now, you can see why I married Albert.

I scowled at McBrae, who had let down the window to open the door.

"Because," he said, "caution is warranted, and you, Lady Rosamund, are in anything but a cautious mood. If we find Jenny, don't discuss her mother's predicament in front of Fat Alice or anyone else who's lingering about."

"Why not?"

McBrae let out an exasperated sigh, as if he were a schoolmaster with a particularly dim pupil. "For the very reasons I mentioned above. If she has any sense, she invokes her mother regularly, to show that someone is looking out for her. It would be stupid to make her appear more vulnerable than she already is. She may mention a father, too, even if she hasn't one."

That I understood. I invoke my father as a last resort. He doesn't precisely look out for me—he can't, since he lives far away in the North, but nor does he pay any heed to my mother's nonsense. Sometimes, I am actually grateful that men have dominion over their wives.

Mostly not, needless to say, but fortunately, I had found myself the one man who didn't exercise his.

McBrae helped me down, and I gazed down the street. "I don't see her."

"The barrow's around the corner. It's a good spot for hawkers." He asked the jarvey to wait and tucked my arm in his, but halted me just as we reached the corner.

Sure enough, there sat an enormous woman on a stool. She wore a grimy straw bonnet with an even grimier crimson ribbon, a faded green round gown (a decade out of fashion) with a stained fichu, and an appalling violet shawl around her broad shoulders. In front of her, a length of dingy canvas was spread over the top of a barrow, and on it were displayed a number of scarves, gloves, and handkerchiefs.

Her barrow stood between the stationery shop and a little alley to the side, which led to the building at the rear which held the printing press. In the mouth of the alley stood Jenny and a barefoot boy in a tattered coat and ragged breeches, glaring at one another.

"You can't keep the spot if you ain't here," the boy said. Or something

133

to that effect. I shall not attempt to convey his almost incomprehensible accent.

"I had to run an errand," Jenny said.

"Too bloody bad," the boy said. "Off with you."

"Fat Alice and me's got an agreement." Jenny turned to her protector.

"Aye, girl, but only if you're here," Fat Alice said. "An empty spot loses me money."

"That makes no sense," Jenny said, hands on her skinny hips, "since you get the same payment from me whether or not I'm here."

"Aye, but you're a pretty little thing, so people stop and take a look. Helps me out."

"Oh," Jenny said. "Then this ugly boy and I can take turns. He can have it whenever I'm not here."

"Tsk," Mr. McBrae murmured next to me. "She should know better than to take a dig at him. It's not his fault he's ugly, poor little bastard."

"Take turns?" cried the boy. "Not a flipping chance. Then I'll lose this spot *and* me other one."

The barrow woman ignored him. "We might change the terms of our agreement, dearie. Two hankies a day, and the spot's yours even when you're not here."

"Oi! No fair!" The boy clenched his fists.

Jenny dodged out of his way. She frowned at the woman. "I dunno as I can get two a day."

"You can if you tries," Fat Alice said slyly.

A shudder of horror passed over me. "She wants her to steal them!"

"Aye, what else?" McBrae said.

"She couldn't pick a pocket if her life depended on it," the boy scoffed.

"Rightly so," I cried, descending upon them in fury.

"Hades, woman, have you no sense?" McBrae muttered behind me.

I planted myself before the barrow. "How dare you encourage her to steal!"

A purple flush swarmed up the woman's cheeks. She surged to her feet, a huge, furious creature. I almost cringed. Of course I didn't, being the daughter of an earl, but it was a close run thing.

"Oi! Did I say a word about stealing?" she demanded of the street at large. This evinced a snort from a nosy passerby.

"Lady Rosamund!" Jenny ran over and grabbed my hand with her grimy one. I resisted the temptation to shake myself free of her clutch—which my mother would do, if any ragamuffin child took such a liberty—and not just because my glove was already soiled. Jenny must be frightened or upset and therefore sought my protection, so it behooved me to provide it.

"Well?" Fat Alice bellowed. "Did I?"

"You implied it," I said, on my mettle, "and that boy confirmed it."

"Tsk," McBrae said again, trying to take my arm. "My lady, these people are beneath your notice."

Lord, how frightfully stuffy and unlike him! I gaped, astonished and, I admit it, dismayed.

He took my arm. "Let us take your business with Jenny to a more private location."

I shook him off and jabbed a finger at the woman. "I supplied Jenny with nuts and handkerchiefs so she could *make* a living, not steal one!"

Meanwhile, the boy ran canny eyes over me. I clutched my reticule tighter.

"Hop it, Tom." McBrae flipped him a sixpence.

The lad caught it with a grin and dodged his way through the growing crowd of spectators. My mother—if she were ever caught in such a situation, which is of course impossible—would have ignored them as if they didn't exist, whilst enjoying the deferential attention, but I don't like being watched. I assume that by now you understand why.

"One would think," I said irritably, "that the inhabitants of our fair city have nothing better to do than gawk."

A few chuckles greeted this. How annoying, as it was meant as a reprimand, not a sally.

"Shall we go elsewhere?" McBrae asked, wisely not attempting to steer me away.

"Oh, very well," I muttered. "Come, Jenny."

"Who's he?" She frowned at McBrae. "I seen him here afore now."

"No doubt you have. Mr. McBrae is acquainted with Mr. Charles, who owns the shop. Come with me."

She did, still clutching my hand as McBrae ushered us up the alleyway to the tiny cobbled yard at the rear of Mr. Charles's premises. "You can let go now," I said, trying to extricate myself.

She had a powerful grip for a child. "You told me to keep it a secret." She indicated McBrae with a lift of her chin. "Is he in on it?"

"No, not at all, but the thing is, Jenny, that—"

She tugged me to the side and dropped her voice to a whisper. "I got what you wanted." Seeing that McBrae had stayed well back, she released me.

A tiny folded paper fluttered to the cobbles. She'd been attempting to pass it to me in a secretive manner, and I hadn't even noticed it through my glove! So much for Jenny needing my protection.

She snatched it up and passed it to me with a blinding smile. I opened it, to see the penciled number 19 and the letter A. "What does it mean?" I asked softly. I took a sideways look at McBrae, but he had seated himself on a stone bench by the wall and was picking a pebble out of the sole of his boot. Uninterested in our conversation, thank heavens.

"That's where the errand boy gets them," she whispered. "The drawings! I followed him up there this morning. He went all over town, he did, fetching this and dropping off that, but last of all he stopped there. He gave the fella at the door a bottle of ink, and took a folded paper from him, and put it in his marketing basket under everything else, all sly-like. He went into a tavern on the way back here, the lazy sod, while I near perished of thirst outside. Then he came out with another fella carrying a jug of ale and a cheese. I near busted a gut following them, but it was easier, cause they was jawing and not looking about themselves. I saw him go in that there door." Her swift, sideways glance indicated the door of the room which held the printing press.

"That's wonderful news, but what is 19A?"

She rolled her eyes. "The number of the house."

There must be a thousand 19As in London. "On what street?" I put up a hand to cover my mouth; I had squeaked the word.

"It's not as posh as yours." She grubbed in her pocket and took out another scrap of paper. "I think I got it right."

I glanced at the second scrap: *Bradford St.* "Excellent."

She put out a hand. "Me five quid, please and thank you."

I hadn't thought of that. "I don't have that much on me, but I'll give you what I can now, and the rest later." I went over to the bench, sat down next to McBrae, and opened my reticule.

Jenny planted herself in front of me. "How much later?"

"Tomorrow, I imagine—" I stopped, pondering. This wasn't going to be as simple as I'd anticipated, now that she dare not approach my house for fear of being snatched up by the beadle. "Jenny, I have some bad news for you. Your mother was given the sack."

Her eyes went wide, her mouth agape. "Me *mother*?"

"Yes, your mother. She lost her position at Lady Beddoes' house. I don't know where she's gone, but—"

She heaved an exasperated sigh. "Me *sister*," she said. "She's me sister, not me *mum*."

I huffed. "You needn't keep up the pretense with me, Jenny. Truly, it doesn't matter to me that she's your mother."

Jenny narrowed her eyes and clenched her fists. "She ain't me *mum*."

I cast my gaze heavenward. When a servant is found out in a lie, why must he or she invariably attempt to insist on it? "For heaven's sake, what difference does it make? I certainly don't care whether or not you were born in wedlock."

"Tsk." McBrae put a restraining hand on my arm.

I turned to him, bewildered. "What are you tutting about? I'm far more open-minded than the rest of my family. It really doesn't matter to me; I wouldn't dismiss a maid for such a reason."

"I daresay," he said dryly, "but that's not the point."

Jenny's gaze was hot and angry now. "Me mum's *dead*."

Dismay washed over me. That poor child, grieving for her mother, and I'd said something that made it seem as if she were alive. "Oh, I'm so sorry. You must miss her very much." Despite my own exasperating mother, I do recognize that some daughters get on well with theirs.

"That's not the point either," McBrae said.

"Then for heaven's sake, what *is* the p—"

Jenny thrust her dirty little face close to mine and said, "I wants me five quid, and I wants it *now*."

Naturally, I shrank back. Despite what Fat Alice said, Jenny didn't seem pretty to me. As for her unmitigated gall! Sometimes I think my mother is correct. Give the lower classes an inch and they'll take a dozen leagues. "How dare you address me in such a way?"

"I thought you was different," she shrieked, "but you're just like the other nobs!" Judging by the contorted expression on her face, she was moved by some powerful emotion. I couldn't for the life of me think what it might be.

I took a deep breath. A lady of good breeding—unlike a low-bred brat—does not let her emotions affect her behavior. I opened my reticule again. "My dear child, as I said earlier, I shall give you what I can now and the rest later. However, since you—"

"Don't!" snapped McBrae.

Astonished, I raised my head. McBrae had gripped the child by the arm and pulled her away from me. A glob of spittle hung from her lip.

"She was about to spit in your face," he said. To Jenny, he growled something incomprehensible, sounding very much like a chimney sweep, or perhaps a dustman. A *London* dustman, mind you, not a Scottish one. I may not understand more than half the words, but I do recognize the accent.

Even when I'm in shock. Good God, she would have *spat* at me! When I meant nothing but kindness, too.

"Lemme go!" she cried, squirming in his grasp. She uttered a shockingly foul curse.

"Don't be a fool. If you run off now, you'll be without protection and in the hands of a pimp before nightfall." He swept the struggling girl under his arm and jerked his chin at me. "Come along, Lady Rosamund. We must find Jenny's sister." He led the way down the alley.

Jenny cursed again, thumping his thigh to no avail. "I wants me five quid."

"You shall get it, but only when it's safe to give it to you," McBrae said. "If you don't allow me to protect you until I can hand you over to your sister, you'll likely never see her again."

Jenny burst into tears and subsided. He set her down gently—better than she deserved—and took her by the hand. I followed them into the street, wrapping myself in haughty dignity. I do know how to follow my mother's example when circumstances require it.

At last we got through the gauntlet of onlookers and reached the hackney. He opened the door, lifted the child in, and offered me his hand. I climbed in and seated myself opposite her—facing the rear, mind you, which was totally inappropriate considering my station in life, but I was quite, quite furious with the child. I considered offering her a handkerchief, but decided against it. Judging by the hatred in her gaze, she would most likely have slapped my hand or thrown it in my face.

McBrae sat beside her, took out his own handkerchief, unfolded it, and passed it to Jenny. Needless to say, she accepted it. She blew her nose, wiped her eyes, and passed it back to him. He took it without the slightest sign of distaste, as if he was used to dealing with filthy children in squalid circumstances.

Who the devil was he? I wondered, as the hackney began to move. Not that I questioned his name or provenance, since Sir Edwin and at least two respected peers vouched for him. But why was he so familiar with the lower orders—so much so that he could switch from the accents of a gentleman to those of a dustman with ease?

I found myself watching him and Jenny with a combination of bewilderment and envy. Up until now, I'd thought Jenny rather liked me, and that she trusted me to pay her.

Now it transpired that she both despised and mistrusted me, but why?

"Now then, Jenny," McBrae said. "Where do you suppose your sister has gone?"

"To Grannie Agnes," she muttered.

"Your grandmother?" I asked.

She shot me a look of loathing. "Boarding house," she told McBrae. "In St. Giles." She named a street.

McBrae lifted the hatch and gave the jarvey the direction. Much as I agreed with—indeed was thankful for his assumption of authority over Jenny, however highhanded—I did not in the least wish to visit St. Giles, a location of considerable squalor.

"Unless you would prefer that we drop you at home first, my lady?" McBrae asked.

"Not at all," I retorted. "I intend to speak to Jenny's…sister." I still wasn't entirely convinced. For all I knew, the maidservant had pretended to Jenny from the start that they were sisters, not mother and daughter. Not that it mattered, you see, but the lower classes lie out of habit. They can't help themselves.

Jenny narrowed her eyes at me. "Why? What about?"

You see? She feared I would expose her falsehood. Or berate the maidservant for requiring her to lie. Or something of the sort; one never knows for sure.

Happily conscious of my magnanimity, I said, "To tell her that I shall supply a reference so she can find another position."

If I expected a softening in her manner (notice that I do not admit to doing so), I was doomed to disappointment. She sniffed and turned her head away.

McBrae crossed his legs and sat back, entirely at his ease. His gaze, resting briefly on me before it shifted to the window, was cool and ironic.

How dare he judge me? Damned if I follow my mother's lead, and damned if I didn't.

It was a long, slow, silent drive through the crowded streets, and (this I will admit), I was feeling sorry for myself.

Gradually, the streets grew narrower, seamier. McBrae straightened. "How much can you pay Jenny today?"

I heaved an annoyed sigh. "I have tried to ascertain that twice already, and have met with nothing but disrespect." Lips pressed together to emphasize my displeasure, I opened my reticule once again and counted a little under two guineas into his hand—not hers. Thereby making a point, I hoped, though I wasn't quite sure what that point was. Perhaps that one does not deign to deal directly with a brat who tries to spit in one's face? Regardless, I avoided his gaze.

"That ain't all you got," Jenny said. "I hear them coins a-clinking in there."

"I have to pay the jarvey, too," I snapped back. "Consider yourself lucky, you ungrateful child. I intend to pay the rest and help your sister, despite your unwarranted rudeness. I don't even have proof that you did the job correctly."

"I did," she cried. "I *did*. I got it right!"

"Fortunately for you, I believe you," I said with quiet dignity.

Well, that's what I thought it was, until I caught McBrae's ironic eye once again. Jenny gave me another of those looks of loathing but wisely held her tongue. McBrae dropped the coins into the little sack in which Jenny carried her nuts.

My nuts, not that I cared. I'm not usually petty, truly I'm not, but I was upset.

The hackney came to a halt. I peered doubtfully out the window at a narrow, ramshackle building. Four stories of grimy windows seemed to glower down upon the cobbled street. A woman with untidy blond hair and a great deal of bosom leaned out of one; ragged clothing hung in another, flapping in the breeze. A shriveled crone rocked in a chair by the door.

McBrae opened the coach door, jumped out, and let down the steps. He swung Jenny out and set her on the pavement.

I put my nose in the air and descended. Someone made a vulgar comment about my appearance; I refused to look about me to see who it might be.

"For God's sake," McBrae muttered, "don't make yourself any more conspicuous than you already are."

"I beg your pardon?" What an odoriferous slum! I raised my handkerchief to my nose.

McBrae threw up his hands. He tossed the jarvey a crown and asked him once more to wait for us. We followed Jenny, who was speaking to the crone, but before we reached the door of the tenement, the maidservant surged out, pulling Jenny into her arms.

"Thank the good Lord!" Tears ran down her cheeks. "Oh, thank God, thank God. I was afeard the beadle would snatch you up."

Jenny indicated McBrae. "Thank that there gent." Not one word of appreciation to me—not even one glance, mind you, despite the fact that McBrae wouldn't have known about Jenny's plight if not for me!

I swallowed my displeasure, and was much mollified when the maidservant, in the midst of thanking McBrae, recognized me and dropped a startled curtsey. "My lady!"

At least *someone* recognized where respect was due. I nodded in gracious acknowledgement. "I'm sorry you lost your position, Lucy. I came to let you know that I will gladly supply you with a letter of reference."

"Thank you, my lady!" She wiped her eyes. "I'm ever so grateful."

Quite rightly. "It is my pleasure to do so. Lady Beddoes dismissed you unfairly, and I am happy to do anything in my power to rectify the situation." I took a breath. "I hired Jenny to perform a small service for me. I paid her part of what I owe her. I should like to arrange to meet you later to pay the rest."

"Why, thank you kindly, my lady," she said. "Any small sum, even a sixpence or two, will come in handy now."

I was about to disabuse her of the assumption that I owed such a trivial amount, when McBrae cut in. "Might we go indoors to discuss the references? I shall be happy to provide one as well." He herded us toward the door. Reluctantly, I overcame my distaste at entering such a dwelling, for I didn't wish to make a fuss in the street.

We climbed four dingy flights of stairs to a tiny, airless garret. The floor, its planks pitted and worn, was bare but for a rickety cot with a faded blanket, a chipped jug in a stained basin, a cracked chamber pot, and the pitiful pile of Lucy's belongings. Not even a table or chair!

Jenny opened her little sack and poured it onto the cot. Lucy clapped her hands to her mouth, disbelieving.

"I earned it." Jenny preened. "For us."

"How? Are you sure, love?" Lucy gaped from me to McBrae and back as if she couldn't believe such fortune. For only a few pounds, too!

I preened a little also, but was too well-bred to show it. "She did indeed earn it. I am at a loss as to how to pay the remainder. I haven't it on me now, and I daren't come here again; my husband would not permit it." Not that I would let that stop me, but he wouldn't like it, and it would give my mother more ammunition. "And there is the business of the reference, too. Since you mustn't risk being seen near Lady Beddoes' house…"

"I'll take care of it," McBrae said.

Amid profuse expressions of gratitude, we left. I was perfectly happy to let McBrae deal with Lucy and Jenny from now on. In fact, I was relieved to be done with that appalling child and free to get on with the next step in my attempt to identify Corvus.

But no matter how thankful I might be at McBrae's willingness to help out, I wasn't about to demean myself by asking him for an explanation of Jenny's extraordinary behavior. What, I asked myself, did her crude, childish motives matter to me? Much as I try to be kind and understanding when dealing with my inferiors, one must draw the line somewhere.

So I feigned interest in my surroundings. Fortunately, a few streets away the streets widened. The houses appeared respectable, and the denizens were decently dressed. It's not that far from St. Giles to Mayfair. Soon I would be home.

"You made an unwarranted assumption," McBrae said.

I made a point of looking down my nose at him. "I *beg* your pardon?"

"You accused her of lying. You insulted her. You hurt her pride."

Faced with this barrage of accusations—from an upstart Scot, mind you—I took refuge in languid hauteur. (Along with the usual well-bred manners, every daughter of England's aristocracy learns the various grades of hauteur.) "One at a time, I beg of you," I drawled. "What unwarranted assumption?"

"That she is an illegitimate child."

I huffed. "It's a completely logical assumption. I'm still not convinced that she's Lucy's sister, but what does it matter?"

Instead of answering, he posed a question of his own. "Why aren't you convinced?"

"Because the woman is a servant, and servants invariably lie to cover their mistakes."

"Tsk." He shook his head.

"Whatever you may choose to believe, it's true." Charitably, I added, "One

LADY ROSAMUND AND THE POISON PEN

can scarcely blame them. A great many employers expect them to pay for broken dishes from their meager wages. Most unfair, as accidents will happen from time to time. Nevertheless..." I gave an elegant shrug. (Another of the accomplishments of a true lady.) "Lucy may have told Jenny that she's her sister—I grant you that much." Nobly done of me—and quite a tidy summation, too.

"And what if a servant isn't lying?"

Damn the man. "Then he or she is telling the truth. But since one can never know for sure, one has no choice but to assume the worst."

"Tsk," he said again.

"Would you kindly stop making that irritating noise? Who do you think you are, to treat me in such an odious manner?" Imagine—I'd actually begun to like the man! "As a matter of fact, I have my doubts about *you*, Mr. McBrae. No gentleman worthy of the name condescends to speak with the accent of a laborer. He should not even know how to do so."

I cringed inwardly even as I said this, for it wasn't precisely true. My brothers used to imitate the villagers in Kent. On the other hand, I justified to myself, they were boys at the time, not full-grown, supposedly mature men.

"It's more appropriate to assume the best," he said. "What if she *was* lying? In what way does that harm you?"

I felt myself reddening. "Well, I—I cannot tolerate being taken in."

"Whereas falsely accusing an innocent person is acceptable?"

Now it was a full flush. "No, of course not, but—"

"But nothing. How do you feel when someone insults you? When your pride is hurt?"

"But she's a servant!" I defended myself. "What use has a servant for pride?"

"The same as any other human being!" he roared. "By God, to think I—"

"To think you what?"

"Nothing," he snapped. "You sheltered, pampered sorts can't be expected to understand."

"Sheltered?" I cried. Yes, to the extent that some of my family members considered shutting me away from the world. "Pampered?" Forced into an

144

intolerable mold, more like. "You know nothing about *my sort*."

"And am happy not to," he retorted.

Thank *God*, the coach pulled up before my house. Unfortunately, McBrae was between me and the door, so I had to wait for him to get out. I know better than to make a scene on the street, so I accepted his proffered hand and stepped down.

To find myself confronted by my husband.

Not standing on the doorstep, mind you, scowling like some dustman whose wife has spent his hard-earned wages on a new hat. Albert strode out the door, all affability. My mother's eyes glowered from the dim interior. She was biding her time.

"There you are, Rosie!" Albert said. "You're a little late. Have you forgotten that we're dining early to go to the opera?"

This was the first I'd heard of it. "Dear me, I had indeed. So sorry." I dug in my reticule to pay the jarvey, but Albert waved me off, tossed the man some coins, and sent him on his way.

He turned to McBrae. "Thank you for accompanying my wife," he said, offering his hand to shake as if they were already acquainted—which, as far as I knew, they weren't. "Do come in for a nip of brandy." It was borne upon me, belatedly, that Albert was doing his best to prevent gossip.

"Thank you, Mr. Phipps, but I have an engagement elsewhere. Your servant, Lady Rosamund." McBrae turned to go.

"Wait a moment," I said. "I must give you the money I owe Jenny." I felt myself blanching—for perhaps he had changed his mind about acting as my agent.

"Ah, yes," he said coldly. "Very well, I can spare a few more minutes."

Much as I longed to throw his few minutes in his face, I accepted this offer—for Lucy and Jenny's sake, you understand.

"Excellent," Albert said. "It's marvelous French brandy, not easy to acquire nowadays. Unless you prefer your countrymen's contribution to the cultured palate?"

"We keep the best whisky in Scotland," McBrae said, "so I'll stick to brandy."

I would have giggled at this dig at the English, if I hadn't been so angry.

Albert laughed good-naturedly and ushered him into the house. "They probably keep the best of the brandy in France, for the use of the Emperor. We'll make do with what we have. " He clapped McBrae on the back and shepherded him to the drawing room. "I'm most obliged to you for taking care of Rosie today."

The instant the butler shut the door, my mother opened her mouth to start scolding. I shoved my way past her. "Later, Mother." I ran up to my boudoir and locked the door. Hurriedly, I fingered through the drawer of my *secrétaire*, where luckily I had a few guineas. That, with the assorted coins in my reticule, should suffice. I didn't know the precise amount still owed, but I daren't ask McBrae if he recalled how much I'd given Jenny, while Albert or my mother were listening. The questions and comments would start and might never end.

I rummaged in my bedchamber for a tiny velvet bag in the shape of a frog—Lucy would be able to sell it for a few shillings—and counted out what I thought right, adding a little more for good measure. McBrae would have no reason to judge me inconsiderate or vindictive or anything of the sort. He would see what a generous, kind-hearted person I am.

Not that I cared what he thought of me.

No, perhaps I did care, although for the life of me I couldn't understand why.

I took a pen and paper to write the reference I'd promised—and decided against it. If I passed a sealed letter to McBrae, Mother would demand to know what it was. I couldn't refuse to say with my husband there in the room, and if I told the truth, she would do her best to counteract it. I couldn't put it in the post, for then Lucy would have to pay for it.

I might have to bring it to Lucy in person. I shuddered at the prospect, but steeled myself. The daughter of an earl does not give in to fear.

Mother was hovering at the foot of the stairs. "You stupid girl. How much more fodder will you give to Corvus? Do you wish to ruin us completely?"

I marched past her into the drawing room. "If Corvus criticizes you or Lady Beddoes for your cruelty to a helpless woman and her sister, it will only be what you deserve."

"Well!" cried Mother. "I have never been so insulted in my life!"

"Rosie dear," Albert said, "I think your dear mother fears, rather, that Corvus will mock *you*."

A smile hovered on McBrae's mouth. He seemed almost friendly again, perhaps due to the mellowing effect of the brandy. "Why would he? Lady Rosamund's mission today was a charitable one."

Mother gave him a look of withering scorn. "The daughter of an earl has a responsibility to her country. What sort of example does she set by aiding an immoral servant and her bastard child? The worst! Not to mention fleeing her home hatless and disheveled, and accepting the escort of a man she scarcely knows. She is a figure for mockery of the worst sort."

"A little ill-judged, perhaps, but I don't suppose it's quite that bad," Albert said. "Ladies are supposed to be charitable."

"At a distance, and to the deserving," Mother said.

I could, I suppose, have argued that Lucy *was* deserving, but it would have accomplished nothing.

"Rosamund has no discrimination, as her actions today show," Mother said.

See what I mean? "Corvus may do as he pleases," I said loftily. "I certainly don't care."

"Because you're addled in the head," Mother snapped.

Terror assailed me. I took a deep breath to stave it off. I mustn't let them see!

"Do please excuse my daughter, Mr. McBrae," Mother said hurriedly, no doubt realizing the unwisdom of that last remark. "She is young and behaves foolishly at times. I hope I can count on you not to spread gossip about her...escapade today." Judging by the stiffness of her manner, making such a request to a nobody dealt quite a blow to her pride.

"I have already reassured Mr. Phipps on that score," McBrae said. "I shouldn't worry about Corvus, Lady Medway. Most likely, he doesn't even know about it."

I wasn't so sure about that—Corvus was uncannily omniscient—but it was kind of McBrae to try to reassure my mother. It calmed me a little, too, and with scarcely a tremble I passed him the frog-shaped purse. "Pray tell Lucy the purse is hers to keep or sell as she chooses."

"I shall do so, Lady Rosamund." He tossed back the rest of his brandy. "Delightful to meet you, Mr. Phipps. Always a pleasure, Lady Medway." A bow, and he was gone.

"Seems a decent enough fellow, for a Scot," Albert said, once the door was shut behind him. He passed me a much-needed brandy. "Friend of Lord Baffleton, I believe?"

"And of Lord Logan," I said. "And Sir Edwin Walters, too. It was most considerate of him to accompany me today. His behavior is chivalrous and gentlemanlike." Most of the time, at least.

"He is as much of an idiot as Rosie, if he believes that trollop was deserving," said Mother. "And you're an idiot too, Albert, for not curtailing her folly."

I reminded myself that I had no need to worry. Mother always demands that Albert control me, and he nods agreeably and goes on exactly as before—and yet, every time Mother challenges him, I fear he will give in. I held my breath...

"I daresay you're right, Lady Medway, but one cannot fault Rosie for having a kind heart."

I let out a sigh of relief. "Thank you, Albert." Isn't my husband a dear, wonderful man?

But now it would be harder than ever to convince my mother to return to Kent.

Chapter Nine

H ow damned inconvenient. An ideal subject for caricature, but my hands are tied...at least for now.
—From the diary of Corvus

For the next fortnight, I forced myself to agree meekly with everything my mother said, planned, and did. It was dreadfully taxing but—I confess it—I was fearful. Quite frankly, I felt endangered. True, she couldn't do anything drastic to me without Albert's consent, but she simply would not let up. She ranted morning, noon, and night, prophesying disaster.

Couple that with the last letter I had received from my anonymous correspondent, threatening to tell the world all about me, how could I help but be afraid?

Not only that, she tried to keep me to that blasted invalid diet, which always makes me cross. Tea and sops for breakfast if I'm lucky (otherwise, gruel!), a bit of fruit in the middle of the day, washed down with beef tea, and a small portion of boiled fowl and a soggy vegetable in the evening. Mary Jane did her best to smuggle me more sustaining food, and I crept down to the pantry at night if I woke hungry—although I had to be careful not to take too much, or Mrs. C would suspect and tell Mother, or blame the other servants. I shouldn't be forced to such shifts in my own house; I'm sure you agree!

No wonder the maid at my grandparents' house smuggled food to poor Great-Aunt Edna. Thank God for servants!

If all this wasn't bad enough, it was my turn to read an improving tale at the Home for Indigent Female Orphans, but my muse had entirely deserted me. I'd been thinking of retelling Romeo and Juliet, in which the star-crossed lovers escaped and lived happily ever after, the moral being that one should defy one's parents in the name of true love. It wasn't such a bad notion, but I didn't want to encourage the orphans to disobey their headmistress, for she would probably inflict some dreadful punishment upon them. But try as I would, I couldn't come up with anything better, so I wrote cancelling my visit.

I hated the thought that my unpleasant correspondent was getting the better of me—particularly if said correspondent should chance to be Mrs. Brill.

Ah, well—in any event, I was so exhausted from lack of sufficient nourishment that I hadn't the energy to compose anything but acceptances as directed by Mother. Maintaining the appearance of obedience was the only hope of getting rid of her. The hardest part was carrying things in my reticule that I wouldn't be tempted to check over and over, such as extra handkerchiefs. This probably makes no sense to you, but I was dealing with two problems at once: 1) suppressing my tendency to check things, always worse when my mother is watching me, and 2) making my reticule appear full enough that I could sneak food into it at a party without her noticing. I could easily tuck a handkerchief into my corset and bring it home that way.

For a while nothing too dreadful happened. I managed to write the letter of reference and carried it with me whenever Mother allowed me out into company, hoping to give it to McBrae. One would think, judging by past experience, that I would meet him frequently, but on the contrary, he was nowhere to be seen.

Perhaps he was avoiding me. I shouldn't be at all surprised. Very lowering, seeing as he had sought me out in the past, but doubtless it was all for the best. He wasn't the sort of person with whom the daughter of an earl should associate.

After several days, Mother allowed me to attend an evening party at the house of one of her old cronies. Cards of course, polite conversation, a bit of music, but no dancing. She permitted me a single macaroon and a glass of ratafia—which I dislike, but even that insipid beverage tastes good when one is ravenous—and left me with a group of younger ladies around the pianoforte while she went off to play whist. Which gave me the opportunity to sneak over to the refreshment table and get what I really wanted—plum cake!

"So that's what a reticule is for."

I jumped, muffling a squeak, and almost dropped the slice of cake, which I had just wrapped in a handkerchief. McBrae caught it and slipped it into my open reticule.

"Dear God, you startled me!" I tugged the drawstrings shut. "My mother didn't see, did she?" I glanced about, but apart from us, the refreshment table was deserted.

"No, I made sure she was in the card room before approaching you," he said.

Which made it sound like a clandestine assignation, which it certainly wasn't. I felt the blood rising to my cheeks.

His smug smile didn't help. "Do you commonly purloin cake at an evening party, Lady Rosamund?"

"Only when I've been living on invalid rations," I muttered, loading two more slices of cake onto a plate. "I beg your pardon, but I'd better eat this quickly, before she realizes I'm not sitting with the other ladies." I took a big bite. Ah, delicious!

"Invalid rations. Are you unwell?" His brows drew together. "Your color isn't as good as usual."

Not the sort of remark one wants to hear from a gentleman—not that I cared what he thought of my appearance. "Nor would yours be, if you'd had nothing but gruel and boiled chicken for days on end." I stuffed the rest of the slice of cake into my mouth before it occurred to me that he might want an explanation, which I couldn't possibly give.

Fortunately, someone had taught McBrae the good manners to wait until my mouth was empty before asking a question, so I forestalled him by changing the subject. "Have you given the money and your letter of reference to Lucy?"

With a touch of reproof, he said that indeed he had.

Drat, I'd offended him. Recalling his opinion of me—which I had now made worse—I scrambled to explain. "I'm too late, then. I was going to beg you to give her mine as well. I cannot get away nowadays without an unwelcome escort—the sort who will tattle to Mother." I paused, feeling the need to explain myself even further. "She might make it difficult for Lucy to find work, if she knew."

"I should be happy to do so," he said with a bow.

Relieved, I removed the letter from my reticule—fortunately, no crumbs had escaped the handkerchief—and passed it to him. He tucked it in his pocket and said, "Don't forget to clean all traces of cake from your face." With that, he strode away.

Such an admonition would have been mortifying under ordinary circumstances, but it's impossible to eat daintily in a huge rush. He meant well, which was kind of him, seeing as he well-nigh despised me. I wolfed down the second slice, wiped my mouth, brushed the crumbs off my hands, and turned—to find myself face to face with Mrs. Brill.

She smiled evilly, and her tongue flicked out. "Passing love notes, Lady Rosamund?"

I was taken aback—but not for long. I tittered. "I? Dear me, Mrs. Brill, what a vulgar imagination you have."

Her eyelids drooped and rose again in the usual reptilian manner—the only sign that she had registered the insult. "It's the obvious conclusion. You're neglected, that Scotsman is attractive, *et voilà*. Your poor mother will be mortified when she finds out."

I rolled my eyes, vulgarity being entirely forgivable in this instance. Good God, this woman could have married my father! Much as I dislike Mother, imagine being the daughter of Mrs. Brill instead! Would I have had those lizard-like eyes? That flicking tongue? (She has only one child, a son, with eyes rather like hers. I've never seen his tongue and hope it remains that way.)

I laughed—a mistake, but I so was relieved that I'd been born to the right mother that I couldn't stop myself. Also, I wasn't hungry any longer, and therefore more my usual self. "Surely you can find something more worthy of your spite than that," I said.

Malice flashed in those eyes. "Oh, yes," she hissed. "I'm sure I can. There is plenty of fascinating gossip about you, Lady Rosamund." Cackling, she sailed away.

Dear God, did she mean *madness*?

No, I told myself. She wouldn't have hesitated to say so.

Or maybe not, if she wished to torment me... To pen evil missives and draw my torture out until I truly went mad.

With a gargantuan effort, I shook away these useless speculations, and yet they lingered, jerking me awake at night.

Corvus' next effort ignored me, my mother, Lady Beddoes, hapless servants, et cetera, instead mocking one of Albert's political rivals, which pleased him very much. "Perhaps Corvus isn't such a bad fellow after all," he said.

I wasn't so sure about that, but I crossed my fingers. Did this mean we were safe from yet another scandal?

"Just you wait," Mother said.

So wait we did...and wait...and wait. Perhaps, I surmised, Corvus had done with me for now. Strange to say, I was a little disappointed. I don't know what I'd hoped for...perhaps that he would indeed stand up for the wronged maidservant and shame my mother and Lady Beddoes. Much as they deserved it, though, my mother would have been livid with fury and made life even more miserable for Albert and me.

If he'd mocked me instead, she would have felt justified in her prediction. Either way, no good would have come of it. It was best by far that he knew nothing of that particular scene.

I set aside my hope of unmasking him, at least for the moment. I couldn't possibly escape to investigate the address Jenny had given me. Sooner or later, I thought with a sigh.

I hadn't received any more horrid letters, either. Maybe my correspondent had tired of me, too. I surely hoped so. Now if only Mother would go home...

But then another of the unsettling missives came, sealed, this time, in red.

Which you may see as less fraught, since it's a common color for sealing wax, but I recognized the same forceful lettering and dreaded opening it. I tucked the disturbing missive and another, more welcome one under my saucer and dutifully passed the rest to my mother.

She glowered at me and said, as she did *every single day*, "I hope you are not concealing invitations from me." It's astonishing that I kept my temper. Or maybe not; terror gives one incredible self-control.

"Of course not, Mother. It's just a letter from my godmother and an account from my perfumer."

"Very well." She began her usual business of sorting through the mail, exclaiming at the impertinence of this person or the tediousness of that, while I made agreeable sounds at the right moments and tried not to wolf down my breakfast—a modified invalid diet, for now she permitted me a boiled egg and a bit of honey with my toast.

At last, I excused myself and hurried up to my bedchamber.

WHY THE RED SEAL? my correspondent enquired nastily. *SO LADY MEDWAY DOESN'T GET TOO CURIOUS. THIS IS BETWEEN YOU AND ME. THE REMEDY IS IN YOUR HANDS, AND YOURS ALONE. IMAGINE WHAT CORVUS WILL DO WITH THE TRUTH ABOUT YOU!*

THINK ON THIS, AND THINK WELL. YOU NEED NOT LIVE TO SEE IT.

I sank onto a chair, dizzy with shock.

As you may recall, I'd thought the last letter was intended to drive me mad.

On the contrary. My correspondent already believed I was mad.

Was he suggesting that I should kill myself?

After several shattering minutes, during which I wondered if I truly would go mad, I got a hold of myself.

To some extent, at least. Mary Jane came in to tidy my bedchamber, and pride took hold—a pride that any human being, from the king down to his humblest subjects, would understand. (I'd had plenty of time to contemplate McBrae's words to me on that unpleasant ride home. Apart from his unfair conclusions about me, he was most likely correct. All unknowingly, I harbored prejudices about the lower classes, some of which were faulty—and some of which, I assumed, were entirely correct. I still wasn't certain which were which, but I intended to find out. When I had the time.)

I opened the letter from my godmother and pretended to peruse it. Meanwhile, I glanced at the postmark on the odious missive: Lombard Street, as always. I was utterly without a clue to my correspondent. I was completely at his mercy.

I cast my mind about, desperately trying to imagine who he might be. Or she—for I was in constant dread that Mrs. Brill did indeed know about my affliction, and intended to reveal it to the world. She hated my mother enough to destroy her through me.

But I couldn't think of a way to find out, short of having a boy watch her house and follow the footman with the outgoing mail. This was clearly impossible as long as my mother was in Town.

I turned my mind to other enemies. My brother Julius gets into the occasional dispute, but I couldn't imagine his opponent settling it by sending unpleasant letters to me. They would more likely indulge in fisticuffs (if drunk) or a duel (if sober). Or both. Regardless, I couldn't even imagine a way to inquire into Julius' affairs.

Albert has enemies, too, but they're not in the same set as Mother and I. The likelihood that one of them would know about my secret was very low.

But whoever my correspondent was, he or she could reveal my supposed madness to the world, and Corvus would mock me and my entire family, and…oh, God help me, Albert would feel obliged, for the sake of his political ambitions, to pack me off to genteel captivity in the country.

Bitter tisanes and invalid diets, locked doors and pitying looks. I would be lucky to be permitted a stroll in the gardens, with keepers watching my every move.

I couldn't bear it! But nor did I intend to kill myself. I would fight this to the last possible ditch…

At this moment, poised between fury and despair, a positively diabolical notion occurred to me. I had no idea why this unknown person wanted to destroy me, but the best way to counter a scandal is to distract society with a far worse one.

I would identify Corvus, and then unmask him. Not immediately, but at the first indication that London was whispering about my affliction. Even if Corvus managed to caricature me, society would revile him. They would say he had made up the gossip because I had laughed at his earlier efforts to mock me, and life would go on as before. My horrid correspondent would be foiled...

But at what, I wondered? Why did he want me to kill myself? Had I perhaps misunderstood his intent?

I had no answer for that, but having a plan was all that mattered for now. The time had come for action. In order to prepare myself, I must find out who lived at the address Jenny had given me.

"Is something amiss, my lady?"

I started. I'd been staring at the same crossed and re-crossed page of my godmother's letter for I don't know how long. "My mind was wandering." No more. I had to escape, if only for an hour or two. I pinched the bridge of my nose. "It must be this dreadful headache, and trying to read this handwriting only made it worse. Ring for a tisane, please. Better yet, make it for me; you always do it better than Cook." I tottered to my feet. "I shall try to sleep it off. I should hate to miss the assembly at Almack's tonight."

I must have appeared sufficiently wan, for she believed me. When she tried to take the letter—heaven forbid, for the bottom sheet was the one from my persecutor—and help me to bed, I waved her away. "Just hurry and bring the tisane."

She curtsied and left. I scurried to the shelf, pulled out the book on knot gardens, and put the threatening missive inside. I would set it down in code as well later, when I had the chance.

But I couldn't just set the book in its place again. I had to check that all the letters were still there. (I forgot to mention earlier that I moved them back to the book from behind the headboard of my bed.) You are entirely justified in asking, for God's sake, why? (About either move, or about checking them now.) No logical reason, except that in my ghastly position of having no idea who had written them, I found myself suspecting everyone. My family, my friends, my servants—for if it wasn't an obvious enemy, it might be someone who knew me well.

So it was partly this growing paranoia on my part that prompted me to check all the letters once again.

But it was my lifelong affliction that forced me to check them twice more after that. Only my apprehension that Mary Jane would soon return made me stuff them into place and return the book to the shelf.

Just in time, for I had scarcely rolled myself under the coverlet when she returned with the tisane. "Her ladyship's right behind me. She says it's the egg you ate for breakfast."

I groaned. Not back to the invalid diet! I was sick to death of sneaking down to the pantry at night. I'd managed to make up for it at a few balls, but the refreshments at Almack's were atrocious. "What are my mother's plans for today?"

"Morning calls on her friends."

"I'd almost rather have a headache. Pull the window curtains, Mary Jane. The light hurts my eyes." Fortunately, it was a sunny morning—not the usual for London—so this complaint made sense. Mother came in then, and instead of tucking me in—during which activity she might have noticed that I was abed fully clothed, and demanded to know why—she instead closed the bed curtains as well and left, adjuring Mary Jane to take good care of me while she was gone.

"As if I wouldn't," Mary Jane muttered, throwing one of the curtains open again. "How are you to reach the tisane with it shut, I ask you?"

"Thank you," I said. "I'll drink it after it cools a bit. That, and some peace and quiet, are all I want. I'll ring if I need you."

She left, and I sipped a little of the tisane. I am leery of such preparations, especially when my mother is about, for she has been known to dose me with laudanum. Mary Jane knows I avoid the stuff, but…

Hell and the devil confound it! (Pray excuse my unladylike language.) I was beginning to suspect my dear, kind maid. I sipped a little more of the foul concoction, then tipped the rest out the window, after ascertaining that no one was below. Did I get rid of it because, deep down, I couldn't help my suspicions? After all, Mary Jane is as sane as they come. Most likely she believes me to be unbalanced at the very least, however unlikely she is to say so. And although I would never accuse her of taking my mother's part against me, she might yet be influenced by Mother's fears.

I set such thoughts aside, lay back in bed, and waited, ears a-prick, for my mother to leave. I tried to while away the time by reading my godmother's letter, but I couldn't concentrate. It is difficult to decipher a crossed and re-crossed letter at the best of times. I was in a frenzy of worry; I had decided upon a course of action and was desperate to carry it out.

Finally my mother descended the stairs, fussing at her maid as she did so. I heard the front door close behind her and the carriage draw away. Now, at last, was my chance. Mother might learn that I had left, but by then my mission would be complete.

I donned my half boots, a plain straw bonnet, and an old, unfashionable pelisse—the kind I would wear in the country, never in London. Despite what McBrae thought, I did understand the concept of appearing inconspicuous. Actually, I prefer it, but when one is in the forefront of fashion, one must dress to be seen.

I made sure I had enough for hackney fare and a box of pastries, which I intended to devour before Mother found out about them—

What if Mother took it upon herself to poke about in my bedchamber? She was nosy by nature. What if she came upon my cache of letters? I was seized by an urge to check the anonymous letters again—an irresistible need to do so. Ridiculous, you say. Foolish beyond words, given my need for secrecy, the limited time at my disposal, and the fact that she had just gone out. And yet, I couldn't help myself. I took the book down, removed the letters, unfolded them, folded them once more, unfolded them again—

Enough! Terror was making me a lunatic in truth. Hands trembling in my haste, as well as dismay at my folly, I shoved them into their hiding place once again, returned the book to the shelf, and crept down the stairs. Fortunately, no servant appeared. I slipped out the front door without let or hindrance, hastened to the nearest hackney stand, and was on my way.

Bradford Street proved to be a good distance, almost to the City and not far from Lombard Street....Where my correspondent posted his letters!

The answer sent me reeling—or would have done, if I hadn't been safely seated in the coach. Were the letter-writer and Corvus one and the same?

Did *Corvus* want me dead? Or merely insane with terror, so he could mock me even more? Or destroy my family, just as Mother feared?

But—but how could he be aware of my affliction? I knew no one whatsoever in this part of London! Thousands of people lived near Lombard Street. Not only that, all London mail passed through the Lombard Street office, as far as I was aware. It must be a coincidence.

And yet, it made perfect sense. Perhaps he bore my family a grudge. My father is a kindly soul without an enemy in the world, but not so my husband, my mother, and my brother Julius. Somehow he knew of my affliction, and the death of the footman had given him the idea. Accuse me in jest via a caricature, send letters designed to unsettle me, mock me in more caricatures, and emphasize my odd behavior... I had played into his hands by ignoring the advice of my nearest and dearest, saying and doing precisely what I pleased. Poor Albert, who tried in vain to advise me! I didn't feel sorry for my mother or brother, but sadly, I had to admit that perhaps they were right to want me to withdraw from society for a while.

I had the jarvey set me down at the corner of Bradford St. If possible, I wished to ascertain who lived at 19A without actually knocking on the door.

Glancing around me, I saw what Jenny meant about posh but not as posh as where I dwelt. Shabby-genteel, my mother would call it. Most likely some lesser merchants lived here. It would be no surprise if Corvus smelled of the shop.

I strolled along the pavement. Number 19 seemed a perfectly ordinary house, divided into three dwellings, designated A, B and C. A sandy-haired servant weeded a window box on the ground floor; there was no sign of movement on the first; a maid shook a duster out of a second-floor window; and on the top floor, lace curtains fluttered in the breeze. It all seemed perfectly ordinary, calm, and safe. I should hesitate to seek admittance to an unknown household under any circumstances, but in this case, I feared that someone who dwelt there wished me harm. I could hardly knock on the door and announce myself to him.

I could have slapped myself for such a lack of preparation. If I hadn't been angry and fearful, and yes, I must admit, stupidly unbalanced, I wouldn't have wasted time by taking my letters out of their hiding place and putting them back again. And again. I would have planned what to do when I arrived at Bradford Street. What a ninny I was!

I must invent a persona of sorts—a reason to ask questions in the area, or even better, an excuse for knocking on the doors of strangers. Too late, I had a brilliant idea. All I needed was several improving tracts and a collecting box, and I could pester any number of households.

But I had no tracts and no box, so I continued along the pavement, pondering a role which required no props. The result was less than perfect, but it would do: a lady who'd come to visit an ailing friend in Bradford Street—except that the address would prove to be wrong, because (insert name of villain) dwelt there.

So far, so good. At the far end of the street was a pastry-cook's shop. My stomach rumbled eagerly—and shopkeepers know a great deal about the neighborhood in which they do business. Two birds with one stone!

Pleased with myself, I pushed open the door. The heavenly aroma of fresh baking wafted over me. A few customers were there before me, but being dressed simply and lacking my usual footman, no one rushed to serve me first. I trod hard on my impatience—ordinary people must have to do this constantly—and contemplated the array of breads, cakes, and other delights. Salivating—how unladylike of me!—I lingered over everything from fresh sausage rolls to rock cakes to macaroons. How many, I wondered, could I eat in the hackney before I reached home?

My turn soon came. The shopkeeper took a swift glance at me—sizing me up, to which I shall *never* become accustomed—and smiled. "How may I help you ma'am? I saw how you was eyeing them macaroons."

"Yes, they do look scrumptious," I said. "As do the rock cakes, and the petit fours, and—oh, dear, I don't know quite what to choose. I'm here to visit a friend, you see, and I don't know her tastes." Clever of me, don't you think? He would, of course, ask who my friend was, and I would say—

A lad hurried into the shop. "Order from Mr. McBrae in 19A, sir," he called out. "Six sausage rolls hot from the oven, and a pound cake, *if* you please."

"Mc—McBrae?" I blurted.

"Yes, ma'am." The shopkeeper began to bustle about, filling the order. "He buys from us almost daily. Are you acquainted with him?"

"N-no, I don't believe so. But—but the lad said 19A, and that's the direction my friend gave me." I paused, searching frantically for a name. "Miss, er, Collins."

"Miss Amelia Collins?" Swiftly, he wrapped sausage rolls and a pound cake. "That would be number 29, I believe."

Drat, there *would* be a woman of that surname close by. "No, her Christian name is Amarantha." A ridiculous name, but that's what popped into my disordered mind.

McBrae lived at 19A?

The baker passed the packages to the boy, who took them and dashed out again. He shook his head. "Can't say as I know of her, ma'am."

"Dear me. Per—perhaps the street name is wrong," I said. *McBrae?*

Impossible. Oh, worse than impossible—devastating.

Come now, I told myself. My McBrae wasn't the only Scotsman in London, and likely not the only one of that name. That explained it.

On the other hand, Jenny had followed the errand boy here. But...but perhaps she had been mistaken in the lad's errand. He could have come to McBrae's to fetch something unconnected with caricatures. A folded paper, she'd said.

Oh, why fool myself? McBrae was well acquainted with Mr. Charles, the printer. He went about in society, and therefore saw and heard a great deal. A nobody, as Mother put it, whom one would scarcely notice, much less think to suspect.

"Now, what have you decided on, ma'am?"

The baker's voice intruded upon my thoughts, and I pulled myself together. The daughter of an earl, even if a madwoman, does not give way to her emotions in public. Not only that, I had to decide what to do next, and it seemed best to maintain my persona. "How inconvenient, but typical of

Amarantha Collins. Perhaps she used to live there? How long has this Mr., er, McBrae resided at 19A?"

"A year, maybe more."

It was a little over a year since Corvus' caricatures had first appeared. Every indication pointed to my so-called friend. A Scotsman who easily identified the seal as a highland cow—because he had sealed the letters himself! He even had black hair, just as in that infamous birching caricature.

The shopkeeper shrugged. "I can't say as I recall another Miss Collins, ma'am. How about some macaroons?"

My appetite, needless to say, had deserted me, but I would look a fool if I fled in disarray. "I'll take two sausage rolls and four rock cakes, please."

Somehow, I managed to complete the transaction with composure, and by the time I left the bakery, I had made up my mind.

I had no choice but to confront Mr. Gilroy McBrae.

The more I thought about his perfidy, the angrier I became. I think, if I hadn't been so furious, I would have lacked the courage to knock on his door. I trod firmly to the entrance marked 19A, lifted the knocker and banged it hard. When the door didn't open on the instant, I snapped my parasol shut and rapped it on the door as well.

A head popped out the window to my left—the same sandy-haired servant who'd been weeding the flower box. "Dinna break the door, mon." He realized I was female and looked me up and down with bright, dark eyes. "Wrong house, lassie. This is a gentleman's residence."

Another Scotsman. I assumed my haughtiest pose. "Mr. McBrae's, I presume?"

"Aye, but—"

"We are acquainted. He will see me."

"I canna admit ye," he said, "for it's no' proper. Awa' wi' ye."

I stared him down, for which ability I have my mother to thank. (I loathe being obliged to admit that.) "My good man, don't be a fool. Open the door, or it will be the worse for you."

He snorted at that—typical, disrespectful Scot that he was. "Very well, lass," he said with a crude wink, "what name shall I tell him?"

I am sure my face was flaming by now. Whatever did he imagine, that I was his master's fancy piece? "I do not intend to broadcast my identity for the entire street to hear." I rapped my parasol on the door again. "Let me in!"

He considered me for several seconds. I was sorely tempted to rap him on the head with my parasol. However, that would not help me gain entrance, so I mustered what little patience I possessed. At last he let out a long sigh. "It's on your head, not mine." He disappeared and soon opened the door, ushering me ungraciously inside. "All right, you're in now. What's the name?"

I didn't have much choice. In any event, he would most likely overhear the ensuing scene. "Shut the door, please." Grudgingly, he did so. "Tell him Lady Rosamund Phipps is here."

His brows rose and his mouth dropped open. He goggled as if I were a freak at the fair.

"For heaven's sake, fellow, stop staring and fetch your master!"

This further imitation of my mother got him moving. "I'll see what he has to say. Wait right here." Ahead was a staircase; on the left, a door stood ajar. Pointedly, he shut the door before taking the stairs two at a time.

How dare he leave me to kick my heels like a tradesman? I opened the door he had recently shut and found a simply-appointed parlor with a chintz-covered sofa and two chairs. A servant of discrimination would have shown me in here.

I set my bakery box on a small table and paced up and down before the sofa, dreading the upcoming confrontation. Already my courage was flagging—and then I noticed the drawing board near the window, slanted for ease of use and to catch the light from outdoors. On it were papers, an inkwell, an open bottle of ink, a penknife, and a cup containing a number of pens.

And above it, pinned to the wall, was a huge pen-and-ink sketch....

It was the scene I had feared would come next from Corvus' pen. My mother and Lady Beddoes were exaggerated to look like withered, malicious crones, but recognizable all the same. Lady Beddoes, flanked by two sneering maids in mobcaps, pointed a long, gnarled finger at the fleeing Lucy. A burly footman in the Medway livery (how unfair, as none of my family's footmen would be required to do any such thing, even by my mother in a rage) whipped the torn and tattered maid down the street before a cheering crowd.

Meanwhile, Mother gripped my arm with talons like those of a hawk, as I, a disheveled lunatic, tried desperately to save a child from being dragged away by a grinning beadle.

There was no need of a signature; no need of any more proof.

"Lady Rosamund."

I turned. McBrae stood in the doorway; he didn't smile; he didn't bow. For the first time since we'd met, he appeared uneasy. "You have found me out."

The servant's voice came from behind, trembling with indignation. He appeared, shaking an admonitory finger at me. "I didna put ye in that room." He scowled at his master. "I didna want to let her in at a'."

"Calm yourself, Hamish," McBrae said. "This was inevitable." He came into the room, shutting the door on the outraged servant.

"How dare you?" I cried. "How *could* you?"

"You weren't supposed to know," he said simply, as if that was a good enough excuse for tormenting me. "And then you didn't seem to mind, so…" He shrugged.

"Not *mind*?" Much as I tried to maintain my dignity, my fury would not stay contained. "All your kindness and helpfulness was nothing but a sham."

"That's not so," he began.

I would have none of it. "I suppose your next masterpiece was to be me in the back slum, cavorting like a madwoman with a wanton, a filthy little bastard child, and the coal heaver."

"Coal heaver?"

I jabbed at the horrid drawing with my parasol. "What a pity you omitted him from here. He wanted Lucy to come along with him." McBrae looked utterly blank. "What, didn't I tell you? Well, now you know. You'd better add him grabbing the poor girl's bosom, so society can slaver over that, as well."

"Yes, I recall that you mentioned the coal heaver, but my dear Lady

Rosamund, I didn't—"

"You disgust me." I poked him in the belly with the point of my parasol. "Is that why you sent me those vile letters?"

He moved the parasol aside and assumed a baffled expression. "Letters?" He put up his hands to fend me off. "I sent you no letters."

"Stop pretending to be innocent," I raged, batting his hands away. "You're a liar and a fraud." Oh, damn; if I didn't control myself, I would burst into tears. I jabbed at him instead. "I don't seem quite mad enough for your purposes, so you sent me those vicious letters to make me go insane in truth?"

"Lady Rosamund, I have no idea what you're talking about," he said gently, as if I were a madwoman indeed. "Put the parasol down, and we'll discuss this calmly and rationally."

"Calmly, my eye!" I shrieked, and raised the parasol to whack him.

He snatched it from my grasp. "Stop it," he ordered. "Stop it *now*."

I grabbed my package from the bakery. "I thought you were my *friend*." I threw it at him, but he caught it easily.

"I *am* your friend." He set the packet on a table by the sofa.

"Don't *lie* to me!" Deprived of weapons, I threw a cushion at him.

He tossed it aside. "For God's sake, woman, talk sense." He moved toward me.

"You're as good as a murderer." I backed away. "Do you know what they do to lunatics? Or did you really want me to kill myself?"

He stopped. "*What?*"

I found the cup of pens and threw it at him. "Either way, it would have made a lovely caricature."

He didn't even try to catch the pens. He simply stared at me.

"Either chained in an asylum, or dead with a dagger between my breasts—take your choice." I grabbed the bottle of ink and aimed.

"Don't!" he cried, lunging toward me, but he was too late. The ink splattered all over him—his chin, his shirt and waistcoat, his breeches, and onto the carpet.

"Caricature that!" I cried. My breath caught on a sob—but somehow, God help me, I managed not to burst into tears. I just stood there, fists clenched, heart pounding, gasping for breath.

He pulled me into his arms, and I subsided weakly against him, ink and all. I can't say why, for it made no sense at all; and yet I did.

"Darling Rosamund, I'm sorry about the caricatures, but I have never written you a letter, vicious or otherwise."

"No?" I was trembling all over.

"No. Definitely not."

I heaved a huge, shuddering sigh. I felt so safe there in his arms.

Which was absurd, considering I'd just accused him of wanting me dead. "Then who *did*?" I quavered, but I didn't try to extricate myself from his embrace.

He tightened his arms about me. "I have no idea, but I mean to find out." He sounded harsh and determined, and it was suddenly borne upon me that he had called me *darling*. And had used my Christian name without my title. I had never given him permission for such a liberty. And he was *hugging* me, gently caressing my spine.

All frightfully improper, so I extricated myself in a hurry, and was confronted with the dreadful mess I had just made. He took a rag from the drawing table and began to blot the ink off his face.

I opened my mouth to apologize, but shut it again immediately. Just because I'd felt safe with him, it didn't mean I was. I bit my lip, wishing I could believe him, but how could I know for sure?

The corner of his mouth quirked up. "Your pretty pelisse is ruined, too."

I glanced down—sure enough, my bosom had ink all over it, where I'd been pressed against his chest.

He moved swiftly to the door and opened it a few inches. "Hamish, bring us tea. Hot and strong, with the sausage rolls and pound cake. But first, some rags and a basin of water." He shut the door again. "You needn't worry about my man. He won't gossip."

I heaved another shuddering sigh. "I have some s-sausage rolls, too." I indicated my package from the baker's. "And r-rock cakes."

"Just the thing we need." He sought in his pocket for a handkerchief and passed it to me. I wiped my eyes and blew my nose, but kept hold of the handkerchief. I was still in a fragile state of mind.

"Now, let's sit down, and you can tell me all about it," he said.

I obeyed, for what else could I do? I know it seems absurd, but I had realized that, deep within me, I believed and trusted him.

Or perhaps I simply wanted so desperately to trust someone that I couldn't help myself. Albert is an extraordinarily good husband, but his is not a strong character. Someday he may buckle under pressure from my relatives. Mary Jane means well, but she is influenced by their view of me. And of course I trust Cynthia, but I could never confide in her about such a vile subject.

Perhaps I was being a fool. I couldn't tell for sure, so I gave up trying. "When do you mean to publish that monstrosity?" I demanded, indicating the drawing up on the wall.

He grimaced. "Mr. Charles distributed the prints this morning." He shook his head ruefully. "They'll be in every stationer's in London by now, and on the outbound coaches as well."

I closed my eyes, imagining my mother's reaction. The great Lady Medway, a wicked crone? She would be livid.

She might even have an apoplectic fit, I thought hopefully. For otherwise, once she got over the insult to herself, she would point to the madwoman, lament the imminent ruin of the Medway family, and insist on my immediate departure for Kent.

"Sorry, but I felt that your mother and Lady Beddoes deserved it," McBrae said. "I assumed you would agree with me."

I didn't know whether to laugh or cry—for it was a truly wonderful caricature, and with that aspect of it I did agree. If only I didn't look so utterly hopeless. I shook my head despairingly.

"You didn't seem to mind the other caricatures—you even mentioned that you liked them. I meant no insult to you, Lady Rosamund, which is why I portrayed you as an avenging angel."

I opened my eyes. "I'm an angel?" I blinked blearily at the drawing. "I thought I was a madwoman."

"Don't you see the halo? And the pretty little wings?"

"Now that you mention it..." I felt my lips tremble into a smile. How kind of him, and how unexpected after his disappointment in me that day. "Thank you."

He contemplated me. "Perhaps I made you look a little too enraged. Why in God's name would I portray you as mad?"

I felt myself pale. Oh, dear, what a fix I was in! If he didn't know about my affliction, the last thing I wanted to do was tell him about it. I floundered about for something to say.

"It's your mother again, isn't it?"

I pounced on his supposition. "She believes I am unbalanced, because I do not adhere to her standards of behavior. When she is visiting, she tries to control where I go, to whom I speak, and even what I eat. That's why I was on invalid rations, and it's why I went to the bakery at the corner of your street. I intend to eat as much as I can cram inside me before going home, because once she learns that I went out on my own, she will insist on an invalid diet again."

"But surely she can't force you to obey her."

"No, but she makes everyone dreadfully uncomfortable. If I give in, she calms down, and if I'm obedient, she's more likely to go back to Kent. And if I get too hungry, I creep down to the pantry at night." My stomach, which had been churning, now rumbled again. I reached for the packet of goodies and untied the string.

"What's the matter with that husband of yours? Why doesn't he take your part?"

"He tries." I took a bite of sausage roll. Yes, it was impolite of me, but I was so *hungry*. I chewed and swallowed. Such bliss! "He takes my part perfectly well against my brother Julius, but no one knows how to manage my mother. He does his best, but then he leaves. His parliamentary duties keep him from home most of the time."

"You mean he has no spine."

Poor Albert; that was so unfair, but I understood McBrae's point of view. If my husband ordered Mother to leave, she would have no choice but to go. It is not as if we would put her into the street. She would merely be driven two streets away to Medway House. I wiped my greasy fingers on the handkerchief and took another bite of heaven. A tap sounded on the door, and McBrae took a basin and rags from the servant, who exclaimed at his master's ruined coat.

"Dinna fash yoursel', Hamish," McBrae replied in broad Scots. "It's naught but a coat, and an auld 'un forbye." Or something of the sort; I was mesmerized by his facility with accents. The upper class drawl, the incomprehensible lower-class Londoner, and now this.

He ordered Hamish to hurry with the tea and shut the door again. How thoughtful of him not to let the man in to witness my disheveled state as well. He got down on hands and knees and scrubbed the ink out of the carpet.

"I'm so sorry," I said, meaning it. "It was frightfully ill-bred of me to make such a scene."

He laughed up at me. "It was well worth it to have you ring a peal over me, Lady Rosamund. You are magnificent."

What a sweet thing to say! It was a much better compliment than many, many I have received.

He did a good job of scrubbing—one could scarcely see where the ink had fallen—and soon Hamish returned with the tea tray. McBrae joined me on the sofa. He poured the tea—how lovely not to be obliged to do so, merely because one is female! But it made me even more aware of my own unmannerly behavior. I tried not to eye the sausage rolls with longing.

"You hired Jenny to find out where Corvus lived." He offered me a whole plate full of sausage rolls and pound cake.

Gratefully, I took one sausage roll. I was not so lost to propriety as to appropriate more than my fair share. "Did she tell you so?" I took another ecstatic bite.

"No, and I didn't ask. Given your secretive behavior, the location she chose to sell her nuts, and the ridiculously high reward you gave her, I wondered if you hoped to unmask me."

I couldn't help but grin. "Wasn't she clever? She followed the errand boy from Mr. Charles' shop all over London until he fetched a drawing from here."

His brows knit. "Mr. Charles' boy doesn't come here for drawings. I do etchings for Mr. Charles—not usually of my own work, but that of others. Perhaps the boy brought me supplies, and I returned an account of the work I had done." He laughed ruefully. "What a farce this is! All Jenny stumbled upon was my acquaintance with Mr. Charles, which you already knew about."

I digested this. "So Mr. Charles *does* know you are Corvus!"

"I expect he has guessed, but we maintain a mutual fiction that I am merely a messenger. I deliver the drawings myself, if I'm bringing an etching, or I have Hamish do it by a far more circuitous route. I'd better not let him know that if he had put you in another room, instead of tempting you by shutting this one, you might never have unmasked me. He'd be mortified."

At that point, I didn't care much for Hamish, but I wouldn't wish mortification on anyone, not even my mother. I sighed. "Did you see Jenny when you brought my letter of reference? Is she well? Does she hate me?"

"She is well, but she didn't mention you until her sister insisted that she ask me to convey her thanks for the payment." His shrug was sympathetic, and I felt myself color. I cannot help being a daughter of the aristocracy, and although this is supposed to confer superiority upon me…sometimes I cannot help but feel that it makes me just the opposite.

I drowned my sorrows in tea and another sausage roll, followed by a slice of pound cake.

"Lucy now has a position with Lady Baffleton, who sympathizes with her plight," he said after a while. "Jenny is to help out in the kitchen."

"You arranged for them to work for Lady Baffleton," I said, astonished. "How very, very kind of you."

He shrugged again. "She was happy to hire them. She became indignant when I told her Lucy's story."

How self-deprecating of him; he had helped far more than any other gentleman of my acquaintance would have done. "Once I was assured that Lucy and Jenny had a haven there, I felt free to publish the print," he said.

How thoughtful, for Lucy's loss of reputation might make the difference between life and death, whereas all my mother and Lady Beddoes had to weather was embarrassment.

Together, we demolished all the sausage rolls and several slices of pound cake. "We'll leave the rock cakes for you to enjoy on the ride home."

I smothered a burp. "I won't have any room left." I popped a final morsel of pound cake into my mouth.

"Then you must stow them in your reticule for a midnight feast." Such an engaging, mischievous grin he had! "Hamish will find something to wrap them in." He put his head out the door and shouted for a cloth and a fresh pot of tea.

I almost opened my mouth to refuse. Although I had unmasked Corvus, I was no further forward in my attempt to find the noxious letter-writer. How dispiriting. I should thank him and leave, and make a new plan of action on the way home.

And yet, how comfortable this was. How much, much more so than I ever felt at home. I'd had a little time to take stock of my surroundings. Adequate, certainly, with nothing of the execrable taste one often finds in the homes of the middling sort—

Yes, in the homes of the wealthy and well-connected as well. Remember the ghastly striped cushion in Sir Edwin's house? And, though I would never do so, I would gladly rid my own home of some of Albert's favorite pieces.

The tea and a checkered cloth for my rock cakes duly arrived, and McBrae poured again. "Now, about this business of the letters."

"It doesn't matter," I said. "It has nothing to do with you."

"It does if someone signed Corvus' name to letters you received," he retorted.

"No," I said, "oh, no, the letters were anonymous... But the circumstances led me to believe..." Another realization struck me—that I would now have to confess to accusing him with very little genuine evidence to back me up. I wished I needn't explain it all to him, but now that I'd thrown ink all over his parlor, I had little choice. "Oh, drat. I've been an idiot again."

"I doubt it," he said. "You identified Corvus."

"By accident," I muttered.

"No, your theory of how the drawings might be passed to Mr. Charles was sound, but Jenny, however clever for her age, took too much for granted."

171

So did I, I thought glumly.

"If you could have investigated it on your own, you would have succeeded." His rueful smile appeared again. "It was fun while it lasted."

I frowned, unsure what he meant. "What was fun?"

"Caricaturing the beau monde." His lip curled ruefully. "Society will not look kindly upon me, once my identity is revealed."

"Surely you don't—you *can't* think that I will reveal it!"

He spread his hands. "Why not? Your cleverness would be greatly admired."

"You insult me," I said, but actually my feelings were hurt—deeply so, which was ridiculous, since this morning I had intended to do exactly that! "I sought to identify Corvus out of curiosity, not to show off. I shall keep your secret, Mr. McBrae."

He eyed me dubiously. "You will tell no one? Not even your husband or Lady Benson?"

"No one at all," I said stoutly. "Not the slightest hint shall pass my lips."

He still seemed uncertain, but at last let out a long breath. "Thank you. I appreciate your silence, my lady, for the caricatures are a source of necessary income for me."

"Then let us hope you remain anonymous." I supposed him to be one of those men who believe all females cannot help but wag their tongues—but I was used to keeping secrets.

"Tell me about the letters," he said.

First I needed to excuse myself as best I could. "They were all sealed with the highland cow, which is one reason I came to suspect you. And the postmarks at Lombard Street, which is not far from here, and also your black hair, like the drawing in which..." At the memory of that particular caricature, I couldn't go on. Instead, I blushed to the roots of my hair—not that I could see myself, but I could certainly feel it.

He didn't seem to notice; he'd gone to the drawing table to fetch a paper and pen. Perhaps to him scenes of naked buttocks, aroused members, and physically excited ladies are an everyday affair.

"I received the first letter shortly after the first caricature," I said. "I had never received such a missive before. It's not at all pleasant to get anonymous letters, especially with a black seal, but at first they merely puzzled me."

Fortunately, McBrae had another bottle of ink. He wrote *highland cow seal (black), Lombard Street postmark,* and the date when the first caricature was published. "What did the first letter say?"

"It doesn't really matter," I said. "None of them matter. I should simply ignore them."

"But you find it difficult to do so. It is often useful to discuss a problem with an impartial individual."

So I told him about all of them in turn—the contents of every letter and the dates I received them, as far as I could remember. It was a most unpleasant experience. Not that McBrae did anything to increase my discomfort. On the contrary, he merely wrote it all down.

"Did you tell anyone about the letters?"

"No," I said, and then, "Yes, I told my husband, because he happened to be there when I opened one of them—the one about being unworthy—but he advised me to pay no heed and destroy them immediately. He burned the one I showed him, but I kept the rest. No, that's not quite correct. I did burn one of the others, but I transcribed the contents onto another paper so I wouldn't forget what it said. And I lied about destroying them."

"Why?"

"Why did I keep them, or why did I lie?" I didn't want to answer either question.

"Both."

I chose the easier route. "I lied because my husband would have asked that very question." And, I realized with relief, I was under no obligation to give McBrae an answer, either. "He wouldn't have forbidden me to keep them, but he would have pulled a long face, and pursed his lips, and asked me for God's sake *why*, and very probably mentioned it to my brother, who would have told my mother..." Who would have attributed it to my tendency to madness, but I wasn't about to mention that.

He frowned. "Anonymous letters are not the sort of thing one discusses with one's mother. Surely your brother would know better than that. He might write to your father, perhaps."

"No, Julius considers Papa inept, which is frightfully unfair. He is merely indifferent to worldly matters. Julius can never hide anything from Mother, and she, fearing more scandal, would drag me back to Kent and—"

"And what?"

Do her best to lock me up. "Rant and rave about the reputation of the Medway earldom. Feed me more of that horrid invalid diet, and spread it about that I was too ill to have visitors."

"I fail to see how that would help. Going about in society, and ignoring the scandal if your correspondent made good his threats, makes far more sense."

"So I told her, but she disagrees. She dreads your caricatures."

"Good," he said.

Yes, perhaps from his point of view, but he wouldn't have to witness her reaction to the latest.

"Tell me, what is your deep, dark secret?" he asked.

My heart began to thud again. "What secret?"

"The one he claims to know. Everything about you, and so on."

"Nothing!" I spread my hands as if to fend off the truth. I cringed at the panic in my voice. "Nothing at all."

"Come now. You know my dark secret. Why not tell me yours?"

"I have a fairly tedious sort of life," I protested. "What is there to hide?"

"That's what I wonder. Not producing an heir for your husband is no scandal, merely a misfortune, and no cause for suicide that I can see."

"Not at all," I grumped. "Neither of us wishes to have children."

He raised his brows at this, but went on. "Putting up with his relationship with his mistress shows forbearance on your part, and since neither she nor you makes any secret of it, there's little cause for concern there, either. I thought you might feel slighted—hence the first caricature—but obviously you don't."

"Not at all. Albert and I have an amicable relationship, and Cynthia Benson is my dearest friend."

"So what, exactly, is your correspondent threatening to reveal?"

"It doesn't matter," I said loftily, which was stupid, because it indicated I knew the answer. I flapped a hand. "Whatever it is, it's all nonsense." For it *was* nonsense, I told myself. I'm not mad. I'm not even unbalanced. One little quirk, over which I have complete control…

Oh, very well, that's an exaggeration. I find it extremely difficult to control my tendency to check things over and over again, but what harm does it do? Why shouldn't I check things?

McBrae said nothing, merely watching me in the most unnerving way. "Whatever it is, it has upset you. And far worse, he—or she, for we are uncertain of the gender of your correspondent—seems to want you dead."

How horridly blunt. "Or locked away as a lunatic."

He shook his head. "Nowhere near as likely. In what way would someone benefit from your death?" he asked. "By suicide, no less."

"Someone who wants to destroy my family's reputation," I posited.

"Maybe so," he admitted. "That's a large field of players to choose from. Your mother probably has hordes of enemies. Your father, perhaps not, but what about one of your siblings?"

"I have no idea, but why make me the target?" Because I'm verging on mad, and therefore easy to destroy? Resolutely, I turned my mind away from my supposed affliction. "Perhaps one of my husband's political rivals."

"Much more likely. We have but to set our minds to it, and we'll find him." He rubbed his hands briskly together.

"We?"

"Of course. No one in your family is of the least use, so it is my privilege to help you."

"Thank you," I said doubtfully. "I appreciate your offer, but what can you possibly do?" I frowned. "Must you sound so pleased?"

"I enjoy solving puzzles," he said. "I also like snooping, eavesdropping, and mocking people's hypocrisy and folly—as you already know."

"Those are hardly classed as virtues," I retorted.

He grinned and poured me the last of the tea.

It is most embarrassing to be obliged to visit the necessary when visiting a gentleman. (I shouldn't have been alone with a gentleman in the first place, of course, but this was no amorous assignation.) When I suddenly realized that I'd best hurry home and invent a good excuse whilst doing so, I also noticed that my bladder was full to bursting. The prospect of jolting along in a hackney under these circumstances... Need I (ouch) say more?

"Might I use the necessary before I depart?" I asked primly.

He tsked. "The best I can do is a chamber pot, which is upstairs in my bedchamber." He paused, and I felt my face flaming again, as it was borne upon me, far too late, how very improper was my visit here.

A few minutes, while I told a dastard what I thought of him, was one thing.

Two full hours, eating like a pig, drinking gallons of tea, and chatting cozily was another entirely—for who would believe our time together was so very innocent?

And then the memory of those caricatures hit me with full force. McBrae found me physically attractive. Perhaps he truly lusted after me!

Oh, horrors!

"I'll bring it down." He left, and I took a deep breath, and another and another, and calmed myself. It wasn't the first time a gentleman had shown prurient interest in me, but I had never let it bother me, merely (if he happened to make an untoward suggestion) turning it off with a laugh and, if necessary, a set down.

How dreadful to think that while we sat and spoke together, while we discussed my predicament, McBrae might have been indulging in lustful thoughts. Perhaps he even anticipated putting those thoughts into action.

I must refuse his help, and do so *immediately*.

He returned with the chamber pot and politely retired. I took care of my business, donned my bonnet, and let myself into the vestibule where he awaited me.

"Thank you kindly, sir, for your assistance, but on second thought I feel it would be better were we to have no further contact." I nodded briskly and stalked to the door.

"My dear lady Rosamund," he said, "you are being ridiculous. Much as I would like to, I haven't the slightest intention of making improper advances to you."

Trust McBrae to understand and cut to the chase immediately. "Nevertheless," I retorted. "Pray open the door."

He sighed. "Very well, but you can't stop me from trying to find out who wrote those letters—which I shall do, I promise."

"Why?"

"For the reasons I listed earlier, and because I like you." He opened the door and indicated the hackney stand on the corner. Thank God, because otherwise he would have seen the glow of incipient tears in my eyes. Pathetic, I suppose, but how kind of him to like me.

Unless it was only a mask for lust. I hugged that thought like armor, even as I sighed with pleasure inside. Admiration is always welcome, and kindness even more so.

"I suggest you take a hack from here to a stationer's, which will serve as a reasonable excuse for the ink on your clothing, and from there a different hack to your home. Thus there is less likelihood that your meddlesome mother will find out where you have been."

This was excellent advice. Not surprising—he'd used similar shifts to keep his identity a secret—but it lent his activities a whole new dimension. Was he in the habit of indulging his lustful impulses with married women, and covering their tracks afterwards?

How sickening, I thought unhappily—although why should I care? I know what men are like. But I was saddened nevertheless.

Chapter Ten

I *f she hadn't seen the drawing, if she'd had no proof of my alias, would I have*
lied to her—or confessed? I suppose I shall never know.
—From the diary of Corvus

I did as McBrae suggested, stopping at Wilkes's. The new caricature was posted prominently in the shop window. As I requested a copy, I made a point of telling Mr. Wilkes that although I deprecated the unkindness to my dear mother, I rather enjoyed being portrayed as an angel. (If I had mistaken myself for a lunatic, so might others. I intended to quash that misconception.)

"It seems Corvus likes you, my lady," he said, and immediately paled at this impertinence.

I lifted one shoulder in a delicate, ladylike shrug, since no acceptable response came to mind. Imagine if I had blushingly agreed! I would look a fool. Nor did I wish to freeze the poor man out for his gaffe. "So amusing of him," I drawled, and changed the subject. "I should also like to purchase a sketchbook." Which was absurd, seeing as I never could learn how to draw, but he didn't know that. "And foolscap and some ink—preferably in a bottle that does *not* leak, unlike the one I almost purchased elsewhere a while ago." There, that more or less explained my stained pelisse. (Not that I owed him an explanation, but I rather enjoyed making up a story.)

By tucking the caricature in with the other paper, I hoped to smuggle it into the house unseen. I needn't have worried. I arrived home and opened the door upon a pall of silence. Stevenson greeted me with a dolorous expression and tried to relieve me of my packages.

"Never mind, Stevenson, I'm going up directly to change. As you can see, I spilled ink on my pelisse at the stationer's." I assumed a concerned expression. "I saw that horrid new caricature. How is my poor mother doing?"

"Very ill, my lady," he said. "I would not be exaggerating if I said she was prostrate."

"Dear, dear," I said. "I shan't disturb her, then." I hurried up the stairs, but had scarcely reached my bedchamber when my mother's voice broke the blessed silence.

"Rosie! Rosie, is that you? Come here this instant!" One would think, if she were truly prostrate, her voice might betray weakness, exhaustion, distress, et cetera, but she merely sounded enraged.

"In a minute, Mother."

"Immediately!" she cried, but I ducked into my bedchamber, secreted the caricature (temporarily) in a book, and turned to remove my pelisse—just as Albert came in.

I gaped at him in shock. He never enters my bedchamber. Thank God I had hidden the caricature first of all!

"I beg your pardon, Rosie, but your mother is in a desperate state. You must come to her this instant." He made a face. "Whatever happened to your pelisse?"

"I spilled ink on it at the stationer's. Mother would not wish to see me in disarray."

"I doubt she'll notice anything. I have never seen her so overset." He paced up and down, hands behind his back. "I gather you have seen Corvus' latest effort."

"Indeed I have." Swiftly, I removed my pelisse and sat at my dressing table to tidy my hair. "He was most unkind to Mother, and although I don't mind being portrayed as an angel, it certainly doesn't make up for the unkindness to her. Tell her I'll be right there."

A clear dismissal, but he didn't leave. I ached to check that the caricature was completely hidden, but I couldn't risk it.

"An intolerable insult," he said, and I was about to agree, for Mother couldn't be expected to shrug it off, when he added, "It makes you look ridiculous."

I slewed around. "Me?"

"I do understand that you wished to protect that ragged child, but a lady of status would never snatch a pauper from the hands of the beadle."

"I didn't snatch her," I huffed. "She wasn't even there at the time. Corvus put that in to create an effect. The drawing isn't supposed to be realistic, Albert. Mother and Lady Beddoes aren't old crones, and no one whipped the poor maidservant. He was merely trying to show how unkind and inconsiderate the well-bred are to their inferiors."

"A fallen woman!" he protested. "Hiding a bastard child!" Good God, he sounded like an overindulged matron, not a man of the world.

"She's not a fallen woman," I retorted. "Little Jenny is her sister."

He snorted, giving me a pitying look. "Not likely. Really, Rosie, despite being an innocent, even you know better than that."

I reddened, reminded of how I had made exactly the same assumption about Lucy. "It is equally possible for a woman of that age—early twenties, I judge—to have a much younger sister."

"If that is the case, why did she hide the child? A guilty act, if ever there was one."

"Because everyone would make the same horrid assumption you just did, and turn her away. Between starvation and hiding her sister, she made a logical choice."

"She should have continued in the profession in which she began," he retorted, adding immediately, "I beg your pardon. I should not mention anything so improper in your presence."

At first, I'd had no idea to which profession he referred, but this comment made it clear. I huffed. "I'm not a child, Albert."

He reverted to his habitual stance, that of politician. "Not that I wish to encourage such disgraceful activity, needless to say."

"Oh, stop it," I snapped. "You're as much of a hypocrite as the rest of your gender."

His face fell. I was immediately contrite. Usually I manage to avoid serious discussions with him. He calls me an innocent, but I sometimes wonder if he is even aware of the contradictions he espouses. Still, I am careful never to quarrel with him, as it serves no useful purpose.

I faced the mirror again. "I'm sorry, Albert. I didn't mean to upset you." I proceeded to put up my hair. "You're a good husband, and I truly appreciate your concern for me, and for my mother, too." *Now, please go away.*

"No matter, Rosie," he grumped. "I daresay you're overset, too." He waited impatiently while I finished pinning up my hair. I fumed, for I couldn't check anything with him hovering nearby.

At last he held the door open, and I had no choice but to accompany him.

"I intend to see that Corvus gets his comeuppance," he said. "Just you wait and see."

I hid a smile as I preceded him out of the room. He was in for a very long wait.

The aroma of burning pastilles greeted us as we entered my mother's bedchamber. I loathe pastilles. It was enough to make one choke.

Mother has several methods of showing displeasure, ranging from bitter silences to hissed tirades, from headaches and weakness to feigned desperation that is worthy of a stage-actress but utterly absurd on a well-bred woman.

I shouldn't say such things of my mother—I do know that. However, I wish to be sure you understand why I entered her room with the expectation of dealing with a combination of a tirade and some bodily ill or other. Tedious, upsetting even, but not so very difficult when one is accustomed.

No such luck. She lay propped by pillows, a quivering, tormented figure. All the color had washed from her face, paled to gray against the white of the pillowslip. Tear-tracks stood out starkly on her faded cheeks. One hand clutched a lace-edged handkerchief, whilst the other plucked at the sheet. This was no pose for effect. It was genuine distress.

I had seen Mother in such a state only once before: the day she suggested having me committed to an asylum.

It is painful to me to recount anything about that frightful day. I am ashamed to admit that I had lost control of myself. You already know that I often feel compelled to check something, and check it again, and then again. This compulsion was inconvenient, but it did not control me. It is difficult to give in completely to such an affliction with other people hovering about all the time; one feels such an idiot. So although I would often check my reticule several times to make sure I hadn't forgotten anything, I wouldn't let it delay the others for more than ten minutes or so.

It was late in my second season, and I had still not received a proposal of marriage of which my mother approved. What about my father's approval, you ask? Legally, his was what counted. I think if I had professed myself madly in love with one of my suitors, he would have given his consent. But I did not; I had not met a gentleman with whom I could contemplate physical intimacy with anything but disgust.

We spent the summer at home in Kent, and the good weather that year meant more outdoor occasions. Usually I love the warm months, because since the fireplaces are not used, I am freed from the obligation to check several times to make sure my bedchamber fire is safely contained.

Why should I check the fireplaces at all? Surely the servants are capable of taking care of such tasks. I have no answer for that. Perhaps I don't trust them to do so. Perhaps I am just an illogical fool. But I digress.

My affliction had become worse instead of better that year. I did my best to hide it, but Mother *notices* things. She chided me for behavior unbefitting a descendent of the house of Medway. For my thoughtlessness in delaying everyone else on various occasions. For my stupid attempts to bring attention to myself.

She couldn't have been further from the truth. I dreaded attention, and yet I couldn't help myself. I had to prepare my reticule for each occasion, and I had to check that it contained everything I needed, and then I had to check again. Logically, this made no sense. If I forgot my handkerchief or needed a comb or hairpins, Mother always had these items. I didn't need a sixpence or a shilling or any other money for that matter—our carriage always brought me home, and Mother had accounts with the *modiste* and the milliner and so on. In any event, I wasn't always quick enough with my checking, and Mother drove me out of the house in tears more than once.

Eventually I was reduced to carrying in my reticule only one handkerchief and my lucky penny, which Father gave me on my seventh birthday. I secreted it between the two layers of pasteboard in some reticules, and in a tiny secret pocket in others, so Mother didn't know it was there.

On one particular day, we were to attend an al fresco breakfast. One of the neighboring families had a visitor—the handsomest young man I had ever seen, of excellent birth and wealthy as well. After meeting him on several occasions, Mother felt that he was the ideal *parti* for me. I thought perhaps—just perhaps—I could stomach intimacy with such masculine perfection. She counseled me ceaselessly on what I must do to impress him, to draw his attention to me and me alone, to *captivate* him into asking me to marry him. On the other hand, I must not be seen as setting my cap at him, for such shifts were unbefitting a daughter of the house of Medway. As the daughter of an earl, I was a catch of the first order, et cetera, et cetera.

I didn't feel like much of a catch. I was dreadfully nervous, and terrified that some flaw in my behavior that would dash all my mother's hopes. My appearance, of course, was superlative; Mother and Mary Jane saw to that. My lucky penny was safely stowed in my reticule. Everything would be fine, I told myself.

But what if I didn't really have the lucky penny?

I emptied and refilled my reticule a dozen times, and although I put the penny into the pocket every single time, I felt compelled to check again and again. Mother was shrieking for me to hurry up, but I couldn't leave without my penny. Even though I knew it was there, I had to be *sure*.

"I put the penny in my reticule," I told myself. I counted to three—a lucky number—and said it again. I counted to three and said it again. A third time should do. "I put it in my—"

"Rosie, we'll be late!" Mother cried. (We were already fashionably late, so she feared being unacceptably so.) Come down *now*!"

Oh, no! I had to start all over. Feverishly, I dug into the reticule, fished the penny from the secret pocket, feverishly put it back in, but these things must be done properly, paying close attention, or how else could one know that the lucky penny was still there? "I put the penny in my reticule." No. "I put the *lucky* penny in my reticule." Not good enough. "I put the lucky penny that *Papa* gave me in my—"

I am sorry; I cannot go on any longer. The agony of it still moves me to tears. Suffice it to say that Mother found me performing this ritual and descended upon me in a fury, ripping my reticule open. She found the secret pocket and removed the penny.

"Enough of this folly!" she cried. "You are becoming progressively more unbalanced." She stalked toward the door. In desperation I grabbed her by her gown, tearing the lace trim, and wrested the penny from her hand.

"It's mine!" I cried. "Papa gave it to me."

"And I shall take it away again." She tried to pry my hand open, but I fended her off. She slapped me hard across the face. "Give it to me!"

"Never!" I shrieked. "I hate you!"

At this point, Julius appeared, drawn by our shrieking.

"Your sister is a lunatic!" Mother cried. "She believes in lucky pennies. She tore my gown."

"Rosie!" Julius roared. "What has come over you?" He whirled, to snap at the servants clustered in the corridor. "Be off, the lot of you."

Mother burst into loud, racking sobs. "She is just like Great-Aunt Edna! She must be put away before she brings eternal shame upon the House of Medway."

And then she fainted dead away.

Julius carried her to her bedchamber, where her maid revived her. When Papa came hurrying upstairs and exclaimed at Mother's deathlike pallor, Julian explained what little he knew (taking Mother's side, of course) and launched into a discourse about the relative merits of incarceration at Medway House or a private asylum at a distance. Imagine my terror!

I had to sacrifice my penny that day, in order to avoid such a ghastly fate. "Rosie is merely overset," Papa said. "Too much gadding about, I daresay. She doesn't really believe in lucky pennies, do you, Rosie?"

No, no, of course I didn't. I knew that my behavior made no sense. I shook my head and dropped the penny into his waiting hand. He tucked it into his pocket.

I dared not ask him for my penny back; he had saved me, but he would not be able to do so forever. I had to prove once and for all that I was completely sane, or risk the dreadful consequences.

"It would be best," Papa said, "if you could attend the al fresco party, Rosie. Are you well enough to do so?"

I took a deep breath and screwed my courage to the sticking point. "Certainly, Papa."

"Excellent." He put his arm around me and gave me a squeeze. "I'll take you. We'll let your poor mother rest."

If this was a ruse to get Mother up and moving, it didn't work. She uttered a shattered sob and turned her head away. Papa and I attended the al fresco breakfast. Despite my sadness, I rather enjoyed myself, it being much more pleasant without Mother hovering like a vulture. Even better, the handsome gentleman wasn't there. He had been called away due to a death in the family.

After Mother recovered, she decided I was unfit for marriage. Which suited me very well, and in spite of her incessant fussing, I began to look forward to social occasions. I became close friends with Cynthia, who was already Albert's mistress. It was she who suggested a marriage of form only—enabling me to get away from my overbearing mother and also avoid carnal relations. I met with Albert, and our frank discussion led to a proposal of marriage, which I readily accepted.

So there you have it. Generally, my affliction has been much less of a problem since my marriage, but it hasn't gone away. I don't suppose it ever will.

Although I crept into my father's bedchamber later and searched his coats, I didn't find my lucky penny. I still don't know where he put it—only that he didn't give it to Mother, for I overheard them quarreling one day a few weeks later. She wanted to force me to watch her throw the penny into the lake, where it would certainly sink below the mud and debris at the bottom and be well-nigh irretrievable. Father told her no, that would be unkind, and what I needed was compassion, not cruelty. My father is a dear, wonderful man.

I don't truly care anymore where my lucky penny might be. I am saddened by the loss, but I am probably better off without it.

To return to the current situation. The following morning, Mother had revived enough to sit up in bed. The instant I came to her room to enquire after her health, she launched into a lecture about the awful consequences of the caricature. The sacred House of Medway would be the butt of jests and sneers for months, nay years to come. She couldn't bear to stay in London any longer, to be pitied by her friends and sniggered at by her foes. She demanded that I accompany her.

I refused. "I quite understand why you wish to leave—Corvus treated you most unkindly—but I intend to stick it out here in London. I can hardly object to being portrayed as an angel."

"A lunatic," she retorted. "That's not a halo, it's a badly-drawn hat."

Although this had been my first impression, I now knew she was wrong. "What about the wings?"

"An incomprehensible jest," she snapped. "Corvus is a lowly, uneducated, disrespectful person of no account."

I clapped my mouth shut on the retort that he was neither lowly nor uneducated. He practically embodied disrespect, but that was part of his charm. "If he is of no account, then we should not let ourselves be disturbed by his drawings."

At this point Albert came in to pay his respects to Mother before leaving for his club. "Good day, Lady Medway. I hope your health is much improved."

"It won't be, as long as Rosie treats me so heartlessly. She doesn't care that I am practically at death's door." She fell back weakly upon the pillows, but she rather spoiled the effect by glaring at me. "Cruel, unnatural child!"

Albert turned a mournful eye upon me. "Truly, Rosie, how can you not feel for your dear mother in her affliction?"

"I *do* feel for her, and for Lady Beddoes as well. I would be upset, too, if Corvus depicted me as a crone."

Mother's glare deepened. "You should be upset by his vulgar attraction to you. The vile and disgusting implications of some of his drawings—" She covered her eyes with a dramatic gesture. "So *sickening.*"

"As you said, Mother, he is of no account. I simply ignore it."

"Most noble of you, Rosie dear," Albert said solemnly. "If I knew his identity, I would have him thrashed."

"I believe his interest in Rosie is the crux of the matter," Mother said. "How did he know about the dismissal of the wench next door? Or about the footman who fell down the stairs? I believe he watches Rosie to learn more about her, and the only way to get rid of him is to remove her from his proximity."

Albert bent a worried gaze upon me. "There is something in what your mother says."

My heart thudded into my throat. "There is not! Not all his drawings are about me."

"True, but you must admit that you feature in a great many of them. It is causing an undesirable amount of scandal. Out of sight, out of mind might solve the problem."

Surely he wouldn't take Mother's part! "I don't care about his drawings. I don't care about the scandal." I tried to control my voice, but it rose in panic anyway. "I shan't run away from London for such a stupid reason."

"There, do you see, Albert?" Mother cried. "She is unstable, and under such circumstances, it begins to show."

I clenched my fists. I longed to scream, to lash out at both of them and run from the room. Instead, I took a deep breath. "Corvus doesn't upset me, Mother. *You* do."

"Come now," she said. "You are my daughter. I love you dearly. I care for you."

What could I say to that? In her domineering way, she does love me.

"Mark my words," she said. "Sooner or later, you will lose what little composure you possess. Your affliction will take over, and Corvus will delight in revealing it to the world. Think of the damage to your family! To the Medway name!"

With superb composure (thus proving that I possess it in abundance), I refrained from retorting that the family and its precious name could go to hell, as she would have seen that as certain proof of instability (as well as language unbefitting a lady).

"Not to mention the Phipps name," she added with more than a touch of malice.

Albert frowned, and terror suffused me. By dint of a supreme effort, I managed a calm response. "Nonsense, Mother. If I were shown to be mad, it would have nothing to do with Albert." I was tempted to pursue that thought, reminding her that my affliction originated with her family and therefore any harm to the Medway name might be considered her fault, but that would be unkind and distress her even more.

I didn't want to distress her. I just wanted her to go away.

"But I am not mad. Albert and I have been married for over four years now, and not once have I shown a sign of unbalanced behavior." I scowled at him. "Isn't that so?"

"Yes, indeed. If your brother had not told me, I wouldn't have suspected a thing."

"Precisely," I said, tamping down my renewed resentment at Julius' perfidy. "My mother is panicking for no reason. I have handled the recent gossip with humor and grace, just as a lady should."

"True as well." He nodded briskly. "Don't worry, Lady Medway. Rosie will do just fine here with me."

With that he left, and I breathed a tentative sigh of relief—but I couldn't help fearing that my mother would succeed in making him change his mind.

Lady Beddoes came to call, enraged and blaming everything on me for having attracted Corvus' attention—as if I had done it on purpose! Mother defended me, despite the fact that she'd said much the same of me only a day earlier. On the other hand, she harangued Albert ceaselessly, trying to convince him to send me home to Kent.

I spent my days in the usual round of social engagements, pretending nothing was wrong. I believe I acquitted myself well (honor and grace, et cetera). My acquaintances commiserated insincerely; I simpered my thanks, telling everyone that Mother was wounded to the soul by Corvus' cruelty.

"Very proper," Albert approved, not catching the irony at all. Nor did Mother's friends. Fleetingly, I thought of McBrae, who would not only understand but find a way to mock such a histrionic statement.

Worst of all was Mrs. Brill, who informed me that my mother had always been weak-minded, and that she hoped the *on dit* that I too was on the verge of a hysterical decline, due to Corvus' prints, was untrue. I controlled myself easily, more due to anger than any other emotion. How dare she insult my mother!

Politely, I advised her to be careful what she said and did, for one never knew when Corvus might be listening. It would serve her right, I said, to be made the subject of one of his prints.

She laughed maliciously. "Did you by any chance receive a well-deserved letter in the post?"

My heart battered my chest, but the revolting eagerness of her lizard gaze gave me courage. "I beg your pardon?" I drawled.

Her tongue flicked out. "You'll see." She walked away.

Was she my horrid correspondent, seeking to frighten me into losing my mind? Had she originated the gossip, or merely spread it? At least I now knew what people were saying about me. What if Mother went out into society again and heard it, too?

I couldn't prevent that, and as before, my hands were tied. I could not hire a boy to watch where her mail was posted while I was still so closely watched myself.

I hardly slept, spending wakeful hours each night plotting how to escape before Mother and Albert could bundle me into what I saw as the coach of doom. Strangely enough, I found myself imagining a daring flight across London to Gilroy McBrae.

Which only went to show how disturbed I was. I couldn't possibly take refuge with a gentleman I scarcely knew, unrelated to me—particularly one who had lustful thoughts about me—but in my imagination, with McBrae I was absolutely safe.

That, I knew, was merely the fantasy of a frightened woman, whereas the fact was my husband's persistence in refusing to give me up. A few days later, after denying all morning callers, Mother returned to Kent.

"How did you convince her to go away?" I asked my husband.

"I didn't do much," he said modestly. "I remained opposed to her wishes, and eventually she got bored with moping about in bed."

I suppose I shouldn't have been surprised. Staying in London was no fun when she couldn't bring herself to accept any invitations or even show her face out of doors. Lady Beddoes proved far more mettlesome than my mother. Much as I despise her for her treatment of Lucy, she kept her usual engagements as if nothing had happened.

"Don't tire yourself gadding about town," Albert added. "In that respect, your mother was correct. You are somewhat fragile—subject to needless worry and fright, I believe—and therefore must take extra care of yourself."

I took instant offense. "I am *not* fragile, if people, my mother and brother in particular, leave me be."

"Tsk," Albert said. "Look in the mirror, Rosie. You are exhausted, and I fear for your health."

He was right about my haggard appearance, but that was due to lack of sleep. With my mother safely out of the way, I anticipated a return to peaceful slumber. I decided to take Albert's advice for one day at least, and therefore made a trip to Hatchard's for a romantic novel with which to while away an evening at home. I arrived home to find that a letter had arrived by the afternoon post.

No, it wasn't the anonymous sort. It came from the matron of the Home for Indigent Female Orphans, thanking me and stating that a mistress had been hired to read to the orphans, so she need no longer trespass on my valuable time—but monetary contributions would always be welcome.

Was this the letter Mrs. Brill had warned me of? It was certainly her doing. Most likely, she had convinced the matron that I was in poor health, and this letter was that lady's tactful way of dispensing with me. A month earlier, it would have annoyed me most awfully, but at the moment I hardly cared. In any event, my muse had deserted me.

Did this mean Mrs. Brill *wasn't* the anonymous letter writer? Yes, most likely it did. I burned the matron's letter without hesitation and buried myself in the romantic novel.

The next morning, another of those horrid letters arrived. One good night's sleep, and then this! I ripped it open, muttering curses under my breath.

YOU WERE WISE NOT TO GO TO KENT. A QUICK DEATH IS PREFERABLE TO A SLOW, LINGERING ONE.

Dismay washed over me. After several days without an anonymous letter, I'd begun to believe the torment was also over.

"What's wrong, Rosie?" Albert had lingered over breakfast—God knows why, as he never does so—but I was too upset to hide my feelings.

"It's another of those stupid anonymous letters." I tossed it across the table to him.

Albert read it, then read it again, his scowl deepening. "What the devil is this supposed to mean?" When I didn't answer, he transferred his scowl to me. "Have you received others, since the one you showed me?"

I sighed. "Yes, several."

"Why didn't you tell me?"

"Because I didn't want to upset you." I shrugged. "They're all nonsense. They say things like how worthless I am, and how I would be better off dead."

"Good Lord!" Albert banged the table with his fist. "Something must be done!" Yes, I know that phrase usually means less than nothing from the mouth of a politician, but this was my dear husband, who in this instance felt genuine concern.

"Such as what? I have no idea who is sending them or why. I admit to being a little unnerved each time I receive one, but that soon changes to annoyance." I retrieved the disgusting missive, tore it into several pieces, and tossed them onto the table.

"You have no idea who might have written them?"

"No. All I know is that he—or she—seems to want me dead, possibly by my own hand. But why? I don't have any enemies, as far as I know."

"It seems you have *one*." His brow wrinkled in concern.

"Perhaps not. I thought they might be written by one of Mother's enemies, such as that horrid Mrs. Brill, or by someone who hates Julius. But what if they are written by one of *your* enemies instead? As a politician, you cannot help but have plenty."

He made an astonished face. "Not that kind, Rosie! My sort of enemy hires a caricaturist to mock my policies." He frowned. "What if someone hired Corvus to mock me by way of you!"

"No," I scoffed, and then, realizing I sounded far too certain, I added, "No one knows who he is, so how could anyone hire him? But it is an unfortunate fact that were I to commit suicide, it would reflect badly on you."

"Indeed it would!" he said, appalled. "Good God, Rosie! What shall we do?"

I poured myself a second cup of coffee. "Nothing. I have no intention of doing any such thing, so you needn't fret."

He pouted. "I can't help but fret, Rosie. I wish you had gone to Kent."

"But I didn't, and I shan't," I said. "Believe me, I would be far more suicidal there than I ever could be in London."

"You are stubborn to the point of folly," he said. "However, I don't have time to argue right now. If you receive any more of these foul communications, you must tell me at once."

"Very well," I said, but of course I wouldn't. When he left the room, I retrieved the pieces of the letter and hid them in my bedchamber with the rest. And made a copy in code, of course. Two copies, actually.

The next day's letter read as follows:

IMAGINE CORVUS' GLEE WHEN YOUR INSANITY IS REVEALED! BECOME THE LAUGHINGSTOCK OF LONDON, OR END IT ALL NOW. THE CHOICE IS YOURS.

At first, I was inclined to scoff. I no longer feared that Corvus would seek to harm me.

No...unfortunately, that was not quite true. When one is plagued by incessant worry, one begins to see the world as a hostile place. What if McBrae had lied to me about helping? Or, if not, what if learning of my affliction proved too enticing for him to resist?

I shut away this ghastly notion. I had to assume he stood my friend—or at the very least, not my foe. Sadly, I recalled my rejection of his assistance. I was on my own; I must follow what few slim clues I possessed. Anyone could start a damaging rumor, and every letter in London seemed to pass through Lombard Street. The highland cow seal had led me nowhere.

Sighing, I copied the letter in code, secreted the original with the others, and sat down to make a list of those gentlemen who might have a grudge against either Albert or Julius—particularly those with a connection to Scotland (since one was unlikely to find a seal with a highland cow in England). I hid it in several places before settling upon my reticule. If I had it with me, I knew for sure that no one else would find it.

Of course, that meant checking my reticule over and over again before I went out that evening. I would far rather have remained at home, as the occasion was a ball hosted in Almack's Rooms by Sir Rodolph Cart, one of Albert's political cronies, and his wife Melissa, both of whom I disliked. However, Albert's dithering about whether I should attend made me determined to do so.

"Are you absolutely certain, Rosie?" he asked. "I cannot have any gossip about your odd behavior."

"Why should anyone gossip? I have never behaved oddly in public."

"What about when you chased all over London after that beggar child?"

"She was my responsibility," I retorted. "My attempt to improve the prospects of an unfortunate girl." I suffered a twinge of conscience at this statement, but recall that I was speaking with a politician, not a confessor. My whole intent was to justify myself. "An effort in which Mother and Mrs. Cropp unjustly interfered. Ladies are supposed to behave charitably, not to persecute the less fortunate."

"Nor to make a spectacle of themselves," he said peevishly. "Charity is all very well, but what about the day you came home with ink all over your pelisse?"

"An accident," she said. "There's nothing odd about that."

"Perhaps not of itself, but you went to the shops without even a footman to accompany you. And that was not the first time you did so."

I refrained from rolling my eyes. "The footman wouldn't have prevented the mishap with the ink."

"Not only that, you took a common hackney, when you should have ordered the carriage."

"Mother had taken the carriage," I retorted, beginning to be seriously annoyed. He seemed to *want* to find fault with me!

"Your mother is no longer here. Henceforth, you will take the carriage and a footman at all times."

"I will not!" I said, but he looked so mulish that I gave in partway. Clearly, this whole affair had affected him adversely, for he had never ordered me about in the past. "Fine, I'll take Maurice if it makes you happy, but I refuse to order the carriage for a short distance. Walking is much healthier and more practical." Maurice would be typically morose about it, but he would have no choice.

"Very well," Albert said grumpily, "but I am still uncertain whether you should attend this evening's dinner. What if the dastard who wrote those letters has begun to spread the word that you are mentally unsound?"

What indeed? I ignored a shudder of dread and said, "Then I must be out and about, at balls and other entertainments, to show the world that the gossip is nonsense." I let out an exasperated breath. "Albert, don't you see that hiding at home is the worst way to counter such rumors? I don't know why you're making such a fuss. Such gossip will harm my family more than you, for if worse comes to worst, it will come out that my Great-Aunt Edna was mad."

He threw up his hands and conceded. Our second quarrel in only a few days, after four comfortable years together. What a shame!

Despite my brave words, my stomach was a knot of anxiety when we set out for the ball.

I rather like Almack's. So few London homes have substantial ballrooms that it is common practice to hold large entertainments there. One knows one's way about: the retiring rooms, for example, and the back entrance past the service area, where one may sneak out to get some air, and so on. Judging by the state of my nerves, I would need more air than usual.

Lady Cart greeted us with a simper and kissed the air by my cheek. "Dearest Rosamund. How *do* you do?" She has small, dark eyes, rather like some maliciously inquisitive bird.

"Dearest Melissa," I countered. "So kind of you to inquire. What a delightful ball!"

That bright gaze widened. "But how goes dear Lady Medway?" she exclaimed, as if to deprecate my delight in anything at the moment.

"It was quite frightful for my poor darling mother, but country air will revive her."

"That horrid Corvus." She gave a moue of distaste entirely at odds with the gleam in her eyes. "I don't know *what* I should do if he were to caricature me."

"But surely he could find nothing unkind to say about you, Melissa," I simpered and prepared to move on. A footman swanned past, deftly carrying a tray with wine. There was something familiar in his bearing. I blinked, wondering, as he served one of the guests. A tuft of black hair peeked from beneath his wig.

The footman from Lady Baffleton's ball? I chuckled; it seemed Lady Danby's attempts to punish him had proven ineffectual.

"I dare swear he would find reason to admire me," Lady Cart said, moving her curves in a sinuous way. "But whatever he might do, I shouldn't let it overset my mind."

That jolted me back to reality. I raised supercilious brows. "My mother had every reason to become distraught."

"Of course, of course, darling," Melissa cooed. "And so did you."

"Me? Why? One can scarcely complain about being portrayed as an angel." *Which you would never be.* What, I wondered unkindly, would Corvus make of Lady Cart?

"Distraught on your mother's behalf," Albert said, and steered me into the ballroom. "You see?" he hissed. "It's already happening."

"I could hardly fail to notice," I snapped back. "However, I acquitted myself perfectly well."

"Then why were you laughing?"

Hell and damnation! Excuse my language, but dare I no longer chuckle at a private joke without being thought odd? I couldn't tell him about the footman, or he might feel it his duty to tattle to Lady Danby. "I was contemplating how Corvus might choose to caricature Lady Cart. She is horrid, and I refuse to let her bother me."

"Then I shall have to be bothered on your behalf," he said.

Whatever did he mean by that? Fortunately, I spied Miss Tubbs and took refuge with her—which says a lot for my uneasy state of mind. A gossip is scarcely a safe haven, for she had doubtless heard the latest and meant to quiz me.

"Should I feel flattered or saddened?" I asked her, once the polite preliminaries were over.

"About what?"

"About being demoted from the object of carnal fantasies to a mere angel of mercy."

"A very pretty angel," Miss Tubbs said dryly, and I felt myself blush in response, which made her laugh. She felt she had scored a point.

"Oh, very well," I laughed. "Perhaps I *am* flattered, at least by the attention. But I expect he'll find another subject, as my life is frightfully humdrum most of the time."

"Aren't you afraid of what he'll draw next?"

"Not at all," I said, which was more or less true, as I trusted him. More or less. And he would do well to trust me, come to think of it. Not that I had the slightest intention of betraying him, but he couldn't know my mind any more than I could know his.

I sighed. Sad to say, I rather longed for a sight of McBrae. A brief word or two, as if that could reassure me that all would be well.

"Are you sure? " She peered anxiously at me. "You don't look well, dear. Quite peaked, as a matter of fact."

"I didn't sleep well whilst Mother was so ill," I said. "I haven't had much time to make up for it."

"Is that all?" she asked. "Mr. Phipps seems worried that you are as upset as she, merely putting a brave face on it."

"He told you that?"

"No, I haven't spoken to him. I got it from Lady Danby, who got it from her son, who got it from another M.P."

I felt my fists clench and forced them to relax. "Albert is a fussy old woman,"

I said. "I shall have a word with him about this."

A gentleman came up then to ask me to dance, and I gladly consented. He chatted cheerfully without once mentioning Corvus or madness. But soon the dance was over, and I found myself running a gauntlet of prying females who all seemed to believe I was on the verge of a decline, or worse. How I longed for my dearest Cynthia, or even Lady Danby's blunt companionship.

At last I excused myself to go to the ladies' retiring room, where I fended off a few more insincere inquiries after my health. After casting a furtive glance about to ensure that no one was watching, I escaped to the back door.

Cool darkness enveloped me. I leaned back against the bracing cold of the wall and gulped in huge lungsful of malodorous London air. I tried to sort through the chaos of my thoughts. One: my correspondent had carried out his threat. Two: I had made no progress at all toward uncovering his identity. Three: I was unfortunately at the mercy of Albert and his needless fears. It is a travesty of justice that a husband has absolute rights over his wife, and yet what could I do to stop him, if he chose to bundle me back to Kent?

Only my dear father could control my mother and brother. Once in Kent, I would be unable to write to him, for Mother and Julius would have my mail intercepted. Even if I managed to send a letter, they might confiscate the response. I had nowhere to go, no one to turn to...

The door beside me slipped open. I squeaked in alarm.

"Shh!" The door shut quickly, but I sensed the dim form of a man beside me. "Don't be alarmed, it's only me."

"McBrae?" I gasped. Oh, what a blessed relief.

"The same," he said, passing me and fetching up on the other side.

"I didn't know you were at the ball," I said.

"I wasn't invited. I'm not acquainted with any of Lady Cart's set."

"And yet here you are," I said.

"Because I thought you might need to talk to someone who doesn't fear you are delicate, on the verge of a decline, bordering on insane, or any of the other idiotic gossip that is going about—with, I may say, no justification whatsoever."

"Thank you," I said miserably. "My correspondent has made good his threat, and my stupid husband is making the situation worse by fretting about me and blurting out his worries to anyone who will listen."

"Indeed," McBrae said. "I wonder why?"

"He fears it will reflect badly on him. It's unlike him to babble like this. As a politician, he usually knows when to keep his mouth shut. He has become impervious to logic and commonsense."

"Just the sort of man we need in government," McBrae said, and I laughed and felt better, and suddenly had an idea. "Oh! Perhaps it's because of Cynthia. Lady Benson, you know. He's worried for her as well, and although he doesn't discuss it with me, I can tell that he is dithering about what to do."

"About what?"

"She is expecting a baby."

"Ah," he said.

"I hope to persuade him to let me go away with her, seeing as the Continent is out of the question. That way, he can get rid of both his embarrassing wife and embarrassing mistress at the same time."

McBrae said nothing, and a horrid thought occurred to me.

"Oh, *please* don't put Lady Benson in a caricature," I said. "She is distressed enough as is, poor dear." Not that she showed it, mind you. I rarely saw her nowadays, but when we happened to bump into one another, she was as calm and composed as always.

"I won't." After a silence, during which I pondered asking him to swear upon his honor, he added, "Don't worry, I'm not even tempted. I have a much better idea in mind."

Believe me, I *was* tempted—to ask what he meant to draw.

He spoke before I could do so. "We don't have much time," he said, his voice urgent now. "Someone is sure to come looking for you. First of all, don't let the gossip distress you. Remember that I am on your side."

"Thank you," I said again, although I couldn't see in what way that would help me.

"I won't let anything dreadful happen to you."

I huffed. "It's very kind of you to say, but I don't see how that's possible, particularly if Albert bundles me off to Kent." Miraculously, my voice didn't wobble.

"You'd be surprised at what I can do." He sounded completely sure of himself.

"But why should you?" I cried, and then the obvious reason occurred to me. "I shan't become your mistress, no matter what."

"Shhh! I shan't ask you to." Now he sounded insulted.

"I beg your pardon, but—"

"I like you, and I like being helpful. Surely that's reason enough. Have you any ideas about who the letter-writer might be?"

Thankful for the change of subject, I dug into my reticule. "I wrote a list of possible enemies of both Albert and my brother Julius. You may as well have it, as I can't think how to get any further than that." I was about to hand it to him, but hesitated. "An asterisk denotes a connection to Scotland." Pause. "Because of the seal." In a small voice, I added, "No offense meant."

"None taken." Our hands touched briefly as he palmed the list.

I also told him about Mrs. Brill and the letter from the matron, and how my hands were tied about doing any investigating of my own. "My husband says I must take a footman with me wherever I go."

"I've often pondered caricaturing Mrs. Brill," he mused.

"Oh yes, please do," I said. "As a lizard."

He chuckled, and the next instant the door shot open. "Rosie, are you out here? It's pitch black and cold as the devil."

I clapped a hand to my chest and scurried forward. "Albert, don't frighten me like that. It was stifling in the ballroom. I came out for some fresh air."

"All alone? In the dark?" (Thank heavens he hadn't noticed McBrae.) He fussed all the way back to the ballroom. I had had enough. It was early yet, but all I wanted was to go home.

Grumpily, he agreed to take me, not because he wanted to stay longer at the ball, but because he preferred to go directly to Cynthia. I told him he should take a hackney. I would be perfectly fine without him—safe in our coach, protected by our coachman and footman, but he insisted, complaining all the while.

I'd had enough of him, enough of doing without Cynthia, enough of wondering what he meant to do. "Have you made any arrangements for her yet?" I demanded.

He started, scowled, and glared at me—or at least I assume that's what he did, for it was dark in the coach. "About what?"

"Don't be coy, Albert. She's going to have a baby! *Your* baby, and therefore your responsibility."

After a dark pause: "She *told* you?" He sounded furious and entirely unlike himself. "I *commanded* her not to."

So horrid, as if she were a mere servant. "No, she didn't tell me—I guessed. She was vomiting. And crotchety, which is unlike her. And her breasts have grown, too. It was obvious. I repeat, have you made any arrangements? Poor thing, she's worried sick." At least, I assumed she was. I *hated* not being able to visit her.

"I am in the process of doing so," he said stiffly.

"Good," I said, not quite sure I believed him. Politicians are adept at claiming progress where there is less than none. "Tell me what you have planned. You won't send her too far away, I hope."

"No farther than absolutely necessary," he said. "It's—it's unconfirmed so far. I'd rather not discuss it until I have concluded my arrangements."

Which most likely meant he had no plan at all. "The situation is not going to take care of itself, Albert."

"Did I say it was?" he snapped. "Cynthia seems to think she can handle everything, but that is absurd."

Actually, it wasn't, but he wanted to see himself as her savior, despite the fact that he was the cause of her predicament.

"I don't want to hear another word about this," he said. "And don't you dare tell anyone else."

Heavens, how grim and determined and, once again, unlike his usual. "I'm not indiscreet, Albert. I've known for a while, and not one word has passed my lips until tonight." Which, strictly speaking, was true. I wasn't about to admit to having told McBrae less than half an hour ago. "Very well, Albert dear, but if your plan doesn't work, I have an idea. What if Cynthia and I were to travel together to someplace where neither of us is known? The wilds of Ireland, perhaps. She could give birth there, and we could return in a year or two."

"Two years?" His voice cracked. "I can't do without her for that long!"

"I know you'll miss her, Albert, but think of her reputation. She means to keep the baby, you know."

He was silent. Surely he didn't want her to foster it out! He dislikes children, but how devastating for a mother to have to give up her baby to strangers. I cannot for the life of me understand why society turns a blind eye to fornication, while condemning the likely result. Surely the opposite should be the rule: condemn fornication but welcome all innocent children, regardless of the circumstances of their birth.

"In order to do so, she must stay away long enough that no one knows for sure that she is its mother," I said.

"I am aware of the difficulties," Albert said stiffly. "I intend to make it possible for her to keep it."

"How?" I demanded. "She will have to go away, and going away with me makes perfect sense. Thanks to Corvus' horrid print about us, it will never occur to people that it's because she is *enceinte*."

"Thereby making me look as if I were cuckolded by a *woman*? You must be mad!"

That shut me up, as that word usually does.

"I shudder to think what Corvus would do with that," he added in a voice of utter horror.

The coach pulled up before our front door. "Who cares what Corvus does?" I cried. "Maybe you should think of someone else besides yourself. Think of *her* feelings, *her* reputation, instead of yours."

Which was unfair of me, I realized at once. I was selfish too. I wanted to leave Town for my own sake just as much as Cynthia's.

Chapter Eleven

M *y fantasies are most entertaining—and regrettably childish: riding to Kent, sweeping her onto my saddle bow, and galloping into the sunset. Unfortunately for their fulfillment, she is still in London, while I haunt the halls of power searching for an explanation of the obvious.*

—*From the diary of Corvus*

I slept fitfully, my mind leaping, awake or asleep, from one worry to another. At last morning arrived. I rang for Mary Jane and climbed thankfully out of bed.

Mary Jane bustled into my bedchamber. "Good morning, my lady. Oh, what's wrong?"

Everything. "Nothing," I said.

Her face creased with concern. "You don't look well, my lady."

"I slept poorly," I told her, and at her dubious expression, I added, "Don't fuss, for heaven's sake. I've had enough of that from Mr. Phipps to last a lifetime."

"He's worried for your health, my lady, and what with all the gossip going around..."

Even the servants were talking about me! Not that this is anything new—servants always discuss their betters, but this time I feared the gossip. "What are they saying?" I asked, dreading the reply.

"That you are suffering from melancholia, or perhaps mania, or perhaps both. That there is reason to believe you may do yourself harm."

My heart sank. In the space of one day, everyone in London thought I was mad and on the verge of committing suicide.

"There is worse," she said. "They wonder if you really *did* push the footman down the stairs."

"What?" I shrieked.

"I know you didn't, but…" Her eyes filled with tears. "I'm ever so frightened, my lady."

I had to take control immediately. "Who, precisely, suggested that?"

Her lip trembled. "Mrs. Cropp."

I am not a violent person, but I would gladly have strangled my house-keeper then and there. "You mustn't let what she says upset you, Mary Jane. She dislikes me, as you very well know."

"Yes, my lady, but I can't help but hear her when we're all in the servants' hall, and when it's about you, they want to know what I have to say."

"I trust that you stand up for me?"

"Yes, indeed I do, my lady, but I can't say it helps much. You know what Mrs. Cropp is like."

She eyed me, clearly worried—because of the effect the gossip had on me, or because she feared that perhaps I truly was mad?

At last she said, "Perhaps a soothing tisane this morning instead of your cup of chocolate?"

"I don't need soothing," I retorted. Which wasn't true, but a tisane wouldn't help. First of all, I would have a word with Albert about Mrs. Cropp. "Is Mr. Phipps home?"

"No, my lady. He breakfasted early and left."

So that would have to wait until later.

I had no appetite for my usual hearty breakfast, but worry about the future made me force down a scrambled egg. The post arrived as I was buttering my second slice of toast.

DECISIONS, DECISIONS. POISON? A KITCHEN KNIFE? A NOOSE, HANGING FROM THE DRAWING ROOM CHANDELIER?

I am ashamed to say that I almost threw up my breakfast. Only the most determined self-control kept it down. Once I was sure I would not disgrace myself, I swallowed the rest of my coffee and forced myself to think.

What should I do now? Showing the letter to Albert wouldn't help. Keeping the dratted things hadn't done any good, either. I stowed it in my reticule for the moment. Then I took it out and reread it, put it back, and checked it again. I should let McBrae know the contents, but if I tried sending a letter from here, Stevenson would doubtless notice to whom I directed it, and he might feel honor bound to tell Albert.

Suddenly, I had an excellent notion—I would visit Cynthia. I was tired of pretending to be estranged. I longed for the comfort of a close friend. I could write the letter there—no, two letters, one to McBrae and the other to my father—and post them myself.

How annoying that I was obliged to bring Maurice with me! But now was not the time to flout Albert. I even considered ordering the carriage, but it wouldn't do to keep the horses waiting in the street for heaven knew how long, while I visited Cynthia. Maurice seemed even more morose than usual, but he dutifully got us a hackney and clung on behind. When we arrived at Cynthia's, he climbed down from his perch and knocked on the door.

Fortunately, I had a premonition of what was to come. I clambered down from the coach without the steps—which is awkward, but needs must—and hurried after him.

Astonishingly, the door was answered by Sir Roderick Frockmartin, a look of utter fury on his face. His hat was on his head, his gloves in his hand, so evidently he was on his way out. I had expected the maid to try to deny me again. Sir Roderick—particularly the way he was glaring at me—was far, far worse.

I had no choice but to tackle him. "I am here to see Cynthia, whether you like it or not. How dare you forbid her to see me?"

"I did no such thing." He stood back to let me pass. I signed to Maurice to pay the jarvey and stormed into the house. Instead of leaving, Sir Roderick closed the door.

I scowled up at his proud, angry face. "Mrs. Delabole said you did."

His lips twisted into a sneer. "So Cynthia told me, and I assured her it was no such thing. If I wished to keep you away from her, I would find a more effective method than complaining to Mrs. Delabole. I expect she thought a command from me would carry more weight with you, but it is clear that you care for nobody but yourself."

My mouth dropped open from shock. He had never been so rude to me before.

"You should be ashamed. If you really cared for Cynthia, you would lure your husband back to your bed." He slapped his gloves against his hand.

"That is none of your business! It is between Albert and me and Cynthia, and has nothing whatsoever to do with you!"

"It has everything to do with me." He opened the door and left.

Whatever did he mean by that? I spied Mrs. Delabole at the head of the stairs, loathing in her old, rheumy eyes. She'd doubtless heard the whole conversation.

It is no very pleasant thing to be the object of hatred, but I did not intend to let it disturb me—at least for now. I had come to see my dear friend, and see her I would. I marched up the stairs and stalked past Mrs. Delabole to Cynthia's room.

She was seated on her daybed, embroidery in hand. "Rosie!" she said, setting the stitchery down. "How kind of you to call." She gestured languidly at her elderly companion, who had appeared in the doorway. "Go away, Mrs. Delabole. I have had enough of both you and Sir Roderick this morning."

"Humph," the old lady said, but she closed the door and left.

"What has upset Sir Roderick so?" I asked. "He looked furious, and he was horridly rude to me."

"He says Albert is useless, so he has taken it upon himself to plan my future. I told him he could do no such thing, and he left in a rage." She shrugged. "He's right about Albert, though—absolutely hopeless."

"I don't know what's got into him lately. He has become quite stupid." I paused, but ploughed forward. "Did he tell you the latest gossip about me?"

She cast her eyes heavenward. "Yes, people think you are suffering from a suicidal form of madness. It's utterly absurd. You're the strongest, most reasonable person I know, and so I told him."

"Thank you." I didn't feel strong, and I knew very well that I had an unreasonable streak, but any encouragement helped buoy me up.

She gazed at me, a slight frowning marring her features. "Please promise you won't kill yourself."

"I promise. I would far rather kill whoever it is that spread the rumor about."

"I daresay, but don't repeat that aloud. Everyone is saying you pushed that footman down the stairs."

How, I wondered, had the gossip spread so fast? I'd assumed Mrs. Cropp had made up the rumor about the footman—for I had heard no suspicion of it last night at the ball. Nor had McBrae, or if so, he hadn't mentioned it. Perhaps he'd been sparing me...although I doubted he was the mollycoddling sort.

"Albert wants you to go away to Kent until the rumors die down," she said.

"I know he does, and I refused. I suggested that you and I should go away together, and he almost had a fit at the notion of being cuckolded by a woman." A smile flickered across her face, and I frowned. "That's why you seemed amused, when I suggested it earlier."

"Yes, darling. I couldn't help imagining the scene."

I laughed. "As interpreted by Corvus?"

She chuckled. "Precisely."

"I wish we could leave together," I said wistfully.

"Yes, darling, so do I, but I have a far better plan—one that will be best for everyone. The baby and I will be fine, and Albert will be content."

"What plan?" I asked.

"I shan't tell you, for I'm still not sure how it will work out. In a few more days, I'll know."

She refused to discuss the subject further and rang for tea. Soon she was yawning, saying that nowadays she needed to nap every afternoon.

"Go ahead, dearest," I said, "but that reminds me, I must write a couple of letters, and I only remembered after I left the house. May I use your desk? It won't take but a minute or two, and I can put them in the post on the way home."

I bade her sleep well and settled myself in the little room upstairs where she keeps her accounts. I cut two quarter sheets of foolscap and set to work.

First I wrote to Papa. I couldn't afford to sound panicky, but nor did I wish to underestimate the danger in which I stood. I begged him to travel to Kent to calm my poor mother. I explained that a letter to her would not suffice, for as a consequence of some foolish rumors, she had become increasingly irrational about my so-called condition, the Medway reputation, et cetera, and that I feared she would convince Julius and Albert to constrain me against my will. That contrary to what she imagined, I was doing perfectly well and that he need not worry about me—but that I longed to see him soon.

The letter to McBrae proved much easier to write.

Today's letter suggested a choice between poison, a knife, and a noose. I shall of course ignore it, but thought you should know.

Also, the latest on dit *says that Corvus was right about who pushed the footman down the stairs. I'm confused as to where that rumor began. I didn't hear it last night, but rather from my maid this morning. Did you hear it yesterday? No, you mustn't write to answer me. I'm merely wondering.*

I didn't sign it, for there was no need. Also, I felt uneasy about doing so. I didn't want to risk anyone learning of the connection between him and me, if the letter happened to go astray. Not that there was the slightest hint of impropriety, but you know by now (if you didn't already) that society seeks out the most salacious explanation.

Satisfied with both missives—or as satisfied as I could be under such trying circumstances—I prepared to seal them. I cleaned Cynthia's seal and began heating the wax, but no! I couldn't use her seal, for it is distinctive, and the letter could be traced back to her.

Not that I expected anyone to do such a thing, but I was as jumpy as a cat, and what if McBrae started wondering about the seal? Most likely, I would have no opportunity to explain where I'd written the letter.

I rummaged through the drawers of her desk, hoping she might have wafers instead, or perhaps another seal. I went through the top drawer once again. Such a jumble of items: pens in need of sharpening, pencils ditto, a penknife, bits of wax, both red and black. (My mother believes that a messy drawer means a messy mind. Since her maid takes care of all tidying in her chambers, I will make no further comment. Nor will I discuss my own desk drawer.) I was about to ring for the housekeeper, who was more likely to use wafers than her mistress, when I found a seal at the very back of the drawer.

I turned the seal over and shot to my feet, knocking over the chair. It was the highland cow! Dizziness assailed me. I gripped the desk, reeling with the shock.

Cynthia, my dearest friend in the world, wanted me dead?

Battling nausea for the second time that day, I sank to the carpet and buried my face in my hands. I don't know how long I sat thus—perhaps only a minute or two—but footsteps on the staircase brought me to my senses.

Was it Cynthia? Horror swarmed up, but commonsense took over. No, she was in her bedchamber, close by. One of the servants?

Trembling, I righted the chair and took my seat again. No one disturbed me, and the footsteps descended once more. I had folded the letter to McBrae, ready for a seal. Now I re-opened it to tell him the dreadful news, and dipped the pen in the inkwell.

My hand shook violently, spotting the foolscap with ink. I laid it down and took long, deep breaths. I couldn't write the ghastly words yet. I must leave here immediately. What if Cynthia woke? How could I face her?

I understood her motivation all too well. If I were dead, Albert could marry her, and she could stay in London and keep her baby. I even felt a little sorry for her—but much sorrier for myself.

I had to find someplace else to finish my letter. I stowed the two missives in my reticule and tidied the desk, replacing the seal with the highland cow where I had found it.

I tiptoed down the stairs, desperately hoping Cynthia would not wake, for I knew I would be unable to hide my distress. The same maid who had tried to refuse me entry was in the drawing room with a duster. I sent her to fetch Maurice, which gave me a minute to gather my thoughts and decide where to go.

Not back home, for I would have to leave again to mail my letters. Nor could I use my own seal. I would have to purchase a new one. I marched to a hackney stand, Maurice puffing behind me. "Mr. Charles, Stationers, in the Strand," I told the jarvey.

Why all the way to the Strand, you ask? There were several stationers closer to home, but Mr. Charles might let me sit at the same table in the back, where I had gone through the seals before—and so he did. I ordered Maurice to await me at the front door, and when we were out of earshot, I asked Mr. Charles for pen, ink, sand, et cetera, as well as a selection of seals and some red wax. If he wondered why I chose to write a letter in his shop, he was far too polite to ask.

I had had plenty of opportunity during the long hackney ride to compose the damning words to add to my letter. Even after all this time to compose myself, my hand shook as I added a single sentence.

P.S. I just found the highland cow in the desk of my dearest friend.

I couldn't think of what more to say. I felt obliged to tell McBrae, but I didn't expect him to do anything—for what *could* he do?

And what was *I* to do? Tell Albert that his mistress had sent those dreadful letters? My entire being revolted at the thought. I brushed away a tear.

"Lady Rosamund."

I started, almost dropping the seal. A middle-aged, sandy-haired man stood before me, cap in hand. It was Hamish, the servant of McBrae.

He bowed. "My lady, I, ah..."

"Yes, Hamish?"

"Is there any way in which I might serve you?"

Needless to say, I was taken aback. He'd been frightfully rude to me the first time we met.

"Master Gil scolded me good and proper," he said. "Seems it's you that needs protecting, not him."

"He is very kind to me," I said faintly. How much had McBrae told Hamish? Could I trust him?

He seemed genuinely contrite, but I was a poor judge of character, as I unhappily acknowledged to myself.

"If you don't mind me sayin' so, my lady, you dinna look well."

I huffed a tiny laugh—I hate to admit it, but I was on the verge of hysteria. "No, I'm not at all well, Hamish." He seemed like a gift from the gods. If

Albert questioned Maurice about where we'd been and why—which I was certain he would do—I could easily explain sending a letter to my father, but not to McBrae. You may judge my confusion of mind, in that it didn't occur to me until later that I could simply lie, saying I had written to one of my sisters, or my godmother, or a friend.

How horrid to have to lie, though. I far prefer plain dealing. Or secrets of which no one knows to ask.

"Might I ask you to carry a letter to Mr. McBrae? It's nothing improper, I promise you." Explaining myself to a servant—yet another sign of my extreme agitation.

"Aye, my lady. I know that now."

"Thank you," I said gratefully. I warmed the wax and chose a seal with a rose on it, trite but appropriate. He took the letter and told me not to 'fash' myself—how quaint of him—and that his master would take care of everything.

Which almost had me in tears again, for what could McBrae possibly do?

I sealed and directed the letter to my father and posted it myself on the way home.

Chapter Twelve

*S*he is innocent, courageous, and in grave danger. It is my bloody awful
duty to save her. I hope to God she won't see me as a knight in shining
armor.
Or do I? Perhaps I should satirize myself.
   —From the diary of Corvus

Fortunately, I had no engagements that evening. I would have felt obliged
to show a brave face—but looking at myself in the mirror, I knew that
was impossible, and the worse I appeared, the more people would talk. I
spent many wakeful hours that night trying to put the blame on someone
else—Mrs. Delabole, for example, or Sir Roderick, both of whom hated me
and also had plenty of opportunity to use that seal. Sir Roderick's statement
that he would find a better way to get rid of me took on sinister implications.

But only briefly, for my death wouldn't help him get Cynthia for himself,
and I didn't see how Mrs. Delabole could have sent letters day after day
when she could scarcely walk to the corner of the street. Well…perhaps by a
maid or footman, but surely the servants would have gossiped, and…

No, I was fooling myself. Neither of them knew of my affliction unless by
way of very recent gossip, as far as I was aware.

I couldn't even blame the letters on Mrs. Brill anymore.

I was obliged to accept the fact that Cynthia wanted me dead. Albert must
have told her about my so-called instability, and she had found a way to use
it to her advantage. Her insistence that we should seem estranged made
perfect sense now. Even the most hardened murderer—which Cynthia was

not—must find it taxing to pretend friendship whilst plotting to drive one's victim to suicide.

I sat gloomily eating breakfast the following morning—alone, thank God, so I could indulge my misery over several cups of coffee—when Lady Danby dropped by. It was far too early for morning callers, but when Stevenson came to ask if I was at home, I motioned to him to let her in. She liked me and might spread some positive news about me.

"How are you, Rosamund?" she said, hurrying into the room with a rolled up sheet of paper. "Ignoring the gossip, I hope."

"Certainly." I stood to embrace her. "It becomes more absurd with each passing day. I am appalled that people are idiotic enough to believe it."

"This should turn the tide a little." She unrolled the paper, and I moved cups and dishes to hold the corners down.

Oh, dear. I cut short a laugh—because it was funny, but also not at all.

Corvus had drawn a group of ladies—all too recognizable, alas—vying to be caricatured by himself. They displayed their bosoms, their legs, and their bums, and quarreled over whom Corvus would like best. All their less appealing features were magnified—such as hook noses, big mouths, ears that stuck out, crooked teeth, and so on. Miss Tubbs is indeed thin, but in the drawing, she was scrawny as a stick. Melissa Cart, whose comments at Almack's had probably inspired the caricature, had rucked her gown up almost to the apex of her thighs. Her tongue hung out, long and dripping like a dog's!

Meanwhile, a group of gentlemen peered from the doorway, one of them commenting (crudely, I think), that he always judged a trollop by her quim, whatever that was. I had a fair idea, but I didn't wish to discuss such an unsavory subject with Lady Danby.

And I couldn't ask Cynthia.

Pain washed over me anew, but I thrust it away. "Poor Miss Tubbs. No wonder she didn't rush over here, hoping to beat you to it."

"Corvus is a dreadful man," Lady Danby said, "but one cannot deny that he often hits the bull's-eye. However, I am still annoyed with him over that drawing of me chasing the footman, which made no sense whatsoever."

"I don't think he's dreadful," I said. "He is doing his best to make people aware of the evils of society."

"And what did I do that was so very evil?" she demanded.

I shrugged. "You assumed that a footman, who had accidentally jostled me, was answerable to you. I made it plain that I didn't mind—and he wasn't even your servant."

"In other words, I'm a busybody," she said. "Either that, or a lascivious old lady. How dare he!"

"No, I don't think he meant that. The suggestion of lasciviousness is because people enjoy it, but what he tried to point out is that many ladies—and gentlemen too, I assume—believe servants are their inferiors, and therefore unworthy of kindness and understanding."

"Because they *are* inferior, and must do as they are told or risk the consequences."

"So we have been taught, but I'm not so sure anymore," I said.

"My dear child, what has come over you? I discounted all the rumors, but that does sound rather mad."

That shook me, but I persevered. "They may be inferior as to social status, wealth, and education, but they are also people like us, some intelligent, some stupid, some capable and hardworking, some morally upright, some not. I believe Corvus is trying to say that they deserve far more respect than they get. What about the maid dismissed so unkindly by Lady Beddoes?"

"Tsk." Lady Danby shook her head. "Immoral, deceitful servants must be got rid of. Give them an inch, and they'll take a league."

"Surely we can afford to give them a league or two," I said, trying to pass it off with a bit of a jest. I didn't need another friend turning against me. "Would you care for some coffee?"

Lady Danby nodded an assent, but as I passed her the cup, I noticed her peering intently at me. Did she truly fear that I was insane?

She frowned. "You seem to understand a great deal about Corvus' caricatures."

Was that all? I hoped my slump of relief was not too obvious. "I am portrayed in several. I couldn't help but spend some time thinking about them."

"Humph," she said. "He is a cruel man."

"He certainly can be," I temporized, for although this was true, he now seemed the embodiment of kindness to me. On the other hand, his interest in me might be due to lust. We all act for selfish reasons, don't we? Even altruism is a way of feeling good, proud, pleased with oneself, and so on.

"Think of your poor mother," she said. "How she suffers from his cruelty!"

And how Lucy would have suffered—for her very survival, and that of Jenny, had been at stake until McBrae stepped in and found her a new employer.

But this was a battle I would never win—or maybe I was too cowardly to pursue the matter. "I should buy something pretty to cheer Mother up," I said. "Would you like to come shopping with me today?"

She agreed, and somehow I managed to check my reticule only three times before we left. The last anonymous letter was still tucked in the bottom, but I didn't have the energy, or perhaps the courage, to hide it in my bedchamber, for that would mean checking it over and over while Lady Danby waited and wondered if something was wrong. I checked my reticule once more, nonchalantly I hope, in her coach. (Thank heavens, I had no need to drag Maurice along, for Lady Danby's footman accompanied us.) We went to her *modiste* and mine, and to a milliner's, and I found some pretty rosettes to send to Mother.

I can't say I enjoyed myself, but if I'd been alone, it would have been far worse. With Lady Danby lending me countenance, people couldn't come right out and accuse me of madness or murder. And yet, how mortifying for me, the daughter of an earl, to be obliged to another lady for a degree of acceptance by my peers! Fortunately, everyone was gossiping about the latest print, which helped divert a little of the attention from me. We encountered none of the ladies featured in it—hardly a surprise.

"They are all at home, licking their wounds," I said to Lady Danby, who laughed. I am ashamed to admit that I felt quite superior for venturing out despite every caricature, even the worst ones.

My comeuppance was waiting when I reached home. For the second time, an anonymous letter had arrived by the afternoon post.

YOUR HUSBAND MEANS TO SEND YOU TO KENT TOMORROW. THIS IS YOUR LAST CHANCE TO AVOID A LINGERING DECLINE AND A MISERABLE DEATH. AN OVERLY LARGE DOSE OF LAUDANUM SHOULD DO THE TRICK.

"Is something amiss, my lady?"

I started, to find that I was still standing just inside the front door, clutching the letter, while the butler watched me with grave concern. I shook away the frantic thoughts coursing through my mind. "Not at all, Stevenson. Have tea brought to my bedchamber."

I stumbled upstairs. I refused to let myself think about how my dear Cynthia could have written such dreadful words. For some reason, the fact that I knew it was she made it far, far worse. Did Albert truly intend to send me to Kent, or was this merely a bluff on Cynthia's part?

She hadn't bluffed before. The last time she'd threatened me in one of the letters, she'd carried it out. How little we know of those we love! Albert must have told her his plans, and she thought to force me to kill myself tonight.

One of the maids arrived with a tea tray. I drank two bracing cups and did my best to dispel my anger, for powerful emotions are not conducive to rational thought.

Surprisingly, little of my fury was directed at Cynthia. She was a pregnant woman, fearing for the future of her child, and while I naturally do not condone tormenting one's friend until she takes poison, I have heard it said that a mother can become a tigress when her child is at stake. (Why does it seem that my mother's tigress emerges only to harm me?)

Most of my anger was directed at my husband. I don't think he is particularly intelligent, but a clever politician such as he should be capable of soothing and calming his paramour with a trumped-up plan until he comes up with a good one. He manages to convince voters, other MPs, various government leaders, and I daresay even the Prince Regent, of all sorts of nonsense.

I had to escape—to run away to my father, the only person who might take my part. But if I hired a coach and left London, Albert would guess where I had gone. He would pursue me, and I didn't think I had enough money at my disposal for a headlong flight to the North of England. And although Papa would do his best to protect me, my husband had the right to do with me as he chose.

Yes, it's a horrid, unjust law that gives a man such power over his wife. He already has physical ascendancy, which is bad enough. Not that I had ever feared physical brutality from Albert, but he would have to exercise it to get me into a coach for Kent.

I had one other option—to take refuge with McBrae. I think, in my desperation, I was even willing to become his mistress, if he would keep me safe from Albert forever.

Yes, I know that sounds hysterical, particularly considering my repugnance of carnal passions, but it was a fair description of my state of mind. Once I calmed down, I realized that Papa could bring a great deal of pressure to bear upon Albert, politically speaking. He would most likely ask Albert to leave me safely in the North with him.

So I need not beg McBrae for anything but a brief period of concealment, and perhaps assistance with reaching my father. Imagine my relief!

I dashed off a note to him, relating the contents of the latest letter, and explaining that I might find myself obliged to ask him for help. That was all I dared say. I felt watched and hounded from all sides, and what if Albert or Maurice or even Mary Jane saw the note! Perhaps I was not thinking rationally; I don't really know. In any event, I sealed the note (after rereading it a dozen times) and left the house in a rush, before Maurice could try to accompany me. I hastened to the confectionery, where I bought some barley water drops (even youngish ladies need them from time to time), and paid the confectioner's boy to deliver the letter for me.

That settled, I hurried home and upstairs again, where I locked my door, for Mary Jane mustn't see what I was doing. I hid the offensive letter with the others—I didn't waste my time putting it in code—and packed a small valise with a few necessities, a nightdress, and two changes of clothing. It was frightfully difficult choosing what to take, for that is not nearly enough for a lady of fashion! Ordinarily, I am obliged to change my clothes at least three times a day, but it was all I could carry.

I went through my dressing table for every banknote and coin in my possession, stowing some in my reticule and the rest in the valise and in an old-fashioned pocket, which would fit under my wool traveling gown. I was supposed to go to the theater that evening, but instead I would plead a headache. Albert was to dine with some of his political cronies.

Once he was safely out of the way, I would don my gown, pelisse, hat, gloves, and half-boots, as well as a long, dark, hooded cloak suitable for all sorts of weather, and sneak out the front door. Hopefully, it was safe to take a hackney alone after dark.

I put the valise behind the clothes press and unlocked the door just before Mary Jane came upstairs—thank heavens, for I didn't want her wondering why I had locked it. Long-time servants think they have the right to know everything, and Mary Jane is not above asking prying questions.

Especially when she is infected with the same senseless worry as everyone else. "Are you well, my lady? I just returned from Rundell and Bridge." She'd gone there to pick up my diamond ear drops, which had been sent for cleaning. "Mr. Stevenson and the kitchen maid both expressed concern."

You see what I mean? Much as I appreciate such dedication on the part of my servants, it was the last thing I needed now. I was just about to retort that I was perfectly well when I recalled my plan. "It's nothing, just a headache," I said, pinching the bridge of my nose.

"Tsk." She put the ear drops in my jewelry box and began to bustle about, picking up my hat and gloves and eyeing the rosettes with approval.

"They're for my mother," I said. "A token of my affection."

She sniffed. "A pity, for they would suit you well." There we disagreed, and well she knew it. "Shall I send them to Medway? Or perhaps wait until Lord Derwent is next in Town."

That was reassuring—seemingly, she wasn't in on the secret of my imminent removal to Kent. Nevertheless, I watched her narrowly. "Send them, I suppose. I'll write a short note to accompany them." No sign of guilt showed on her features...but perhaps Albert feared she would warn me, and therefore had told her nothing. He wouldn't care if she were forced to pack in a rush.

I wouldn't need much clothing while locked up at Medway. Or in an asylum.

Fear washed through me, and I shuddered.

"Oh, my poor lady. You truly are unwell. Shall I undress you and put you to bed?"

"No!" I put up a hand to fend her off. I had already packed my nightdress, and besides that, what if she noticed that some other clothing was missing? "I shall just lie down for a while."

"Perhaps a tisane would help. I'll ring for—"

"I don't need a tisane," I said. "I need quiet and darkness. You may tidy up later." I let her close the curtains and then shooed her out of the room.

The next several hours were the longest of my life (so far at least, for who knows what the future will bring?). Now that I had made up my mind, I was desperate to leave. I locked the door again. I opened the curtains and wrote a note to the friends with whom I was to attend the theater, pleading the *migraine*. I checked the contents of my valise. I counted and re-counted and re-stowed my money.

I chose some jewelry to bring along. Perhaps McBrae would pawn it for me, to provide more funds for my journey. To make room for a necklace and bracelet in my reticule, I sewed some of the coins, as well as my diamond drops, into the hem of my cloak. (I wish I could take the credit for this excellent hiding place, but I had read about it in a romantic novel.)

I was about to pick the stitches open to make sure the diamond drops were truly safe in the hem when, providentially, my stomach rumbled. Relieved to have an excuse to stop checking, I rang for some dinner. I had to take a firm stand with Mary Jane, who wanted to feed me that horrid invalid diet.

"Just because I have a headache doesn't mean I'm not hungry," I said, handing her the note for Maurice to deliver. "You're becoming as bad as my mother! Don't come back unless I ring for you."

This offended her so much that she left again without a word. Cook sent up a fine wedge of pork pie, with sorrel and onions, bread and butter, and a cup of small beer. For once, I would have appreciated something stronger.

Soon after I finished eating and sent the tray away, my nerve began to fail me.

At last, Albert knocked at the door, and when I bade him enter, he tiptoed in, peering at me. "How are you, Rosie? Unwell, I hear."

"Nothing but a migraine. I'll sleep it off and be right as rain in the morning."

"Excellent!" he said heartily. "It was lonely downstairs, dining without you."

What nonsense, since we seldom dine together. He was trying to pretend that all was well, the sneaky dastard! And then I realized that he was dressed in his old pantaloons and smoking jacket. "I—I thought you were dining out!"

"Cancelled at the last moment," he said. "Tomlinson has the grippe, so I'll be taking care of some work at home tonight. There's always plenty on the desk of an M.P., you know." He gave a falsely hearty laugh.

Damnation! I had counted on his absence. If one of the servants caught me leaving, they could do nothing about it. But if Albert caught me...

For the first time since my teen years, I wished I had a gun. Papa let me learn how to shoot a pistol, which is quite unusual for a lady, but he wouldn't give me one of my own. Not that I wanted to shoot Albert or anyone else for that matter, but 1) I absolutely *had* to escape, and 2) I dreaded crossing London at night on my own, even in a hackney.

But fretting didn't help. I stowed a penknife—the only weapon I possessed—in the pocket of my cloak. I dressed in my traveling gown and settled myself to wait until Albert either went to sleep or left to visit my treacherous best friend.

I was frightened and tired—too tired, believe it or not, to check anything again. I even thought about bringing—or burning—the anonymous letters, but I hadn't the energy to decide. Darkness fell, and gradually the house quieted. Obedient or offended, Mary Jane left me alone. Footsteps of servants came and went. Albert's went by. I waited. Would he stay or go to visit Cynthia?

Five minutes later, he passed again. He thudded down the first flight of stairs, and his footsteps faded. I opened my door and listened. Several seconds later, the front door opened and shut.

I locked myself in my bedchamber again, donned my half-boots and pelisse, and had just fastened my cloak when the creak of a board alerted me. Had Mary Jane come to check on me? Or…

An ominous sound came from across the room…that of a key turning in my lock! Albert must have returned. He was locking me in!

I leapt up and stormed over to the door. "Unlock it this instant, you—"

The door opened, and McBrae slipped in. "Hush!" He closed the door softly and locked it again.

I gaped at him, speechless. Belatedly, I remembered that *I* had locked the door earlier. That click of the turning key had been McBrae *unlocking* it with another key, to come in. My only excuse for such a muddled mind is extreme uneasiness and fatigue—unacceptable for a daughter of the House of Medway, et cetera, but so it was.

Still, how dare he barge into my bedchamber? "What the *devil* do you think you're doing?" I hissed.

Unfazed by my unladylike language, he said, "Helping you. Isn't that what you want?" He glanced about the room, pointedly took in the valise ready by the door, my bonnet and gloves on the bed. "You were planning to escape tonight."

"What choice did I have? How did you get into my house? Where did you get a key to my bedchamber?"

"Does it matter?" he said impatiently. Yes, it did, but what he said next distracted me. "Listen to me, Lady Rosamund. That letter is a trap. If you leave this house tonight, you'll be dead by morning, an apparent suicide. In the Thames, most likely."

So blunt and calm about it. Pride made me respond with composure. "How can you possibly know that?"

"Anyone who is well acquainted with you knows you would never kill yourself. Therefore, you must be made to *appear* to have done so."

I tried to digest this, but I couldn't see *how*. Cynthia couldn't *murder* me. She couldn't overpower me if she tried. As for her venturing out at night to do so, the mind boggled.

Oh, Lord, had she *hired* someone? God, oh, God, it just kept getting worse.

"I have no choice but the risk the trap." I meant to sound determined, but when he shook his head, I had to struggle to control my voice. "You don't understand. If I stay here, I'll be packed off to—to…" My voice caught, suspended by fear.

His arms came around me, so warm and comforting and safe. "No, you won't, lass. Leave it to me." Damn the man for sounding so certain. So strong.

"But what will you *do*?" I whispered into his coat. He said nothing, and with a sigh I pushed myself free. "You're as bad as Albert, talking about making plans but never revealing what you'll actually *do*." Why must men keep secrets from women? Cynthia mightn't have hatched a plot to kill me if Albert had made a reasonable arrangement for her future.

She'd at least had a valid reason for not telling me her plans.

"I've made arrangements for your departure," McBrae said. "Hamish will arrive early tomorrow morning with a message and a coach and four, saying your father is desperately ill and needs you to come to him immediately. It's a more practical method of escape."

I let out a long breath. "Yes. You're right. It's much better." In fact, it was brilliant. "Albert can hardly object to that. He can't even oblige me to go to Kent first, for I would lose too much time."

"I have to go now." He unfastened my cloak and eased it gently off my shoulders. "Lock your door again when I leave, and pretend to sleep."

I stifled a hysterical laugh.

"Don't make a sound, and don't let anyone in. I mean it—no one at all, not even someone you trust. I believe you're safe here, but just in case, no creeping to the kitchen for food. All will be well come morning."

What can I say? I believed him. "Thank you," I whispered.

Was that a rueful smile in the flickering candlelight? He nodded, and before I knew what he was about, he swooped in and kissed me.

And then he was gone.

For a while I stood there, my fingers pressed to my lips.

I had never been kissed before. I had always imagined it to be an unpleasant experience. Instead, I felt…astonished. More than that—exhilarated! And by only a brief, firm pressure of his lips on mine!

Soon I came to my senses. An interesting experience, no doubt, colored by my desperation and his dashing appearance at the last moment, but that kiss would never be repeated. I locked the door and began to unpack the valise, so that all would appear as usual when Mary Jane rushed to pack for me in the morning.

I shall spare you the exhausting details of that night. Suffice it to say that I soon lost confidence in McBrae's plan and decided to flee on my own if Hamish did not appear by dawn. If he did arrive, I could unpack quickly and leave no sign of what I had done, couldn't I?

No, not really. I am no hand at folding gowns, so if I tried to replace the gowns in the clothes press, Mary Jane would know I had taken them out. Which I might easily do, but I would leave them for her to put back. So I left them out.

At some point during that horrid night, I showed enough commonsense to remove the anonymous letters from the book on knot gardens and burn them. I think I realized, at that moment, that I did not intend to return. I would never feel safe here again.

What a pity I couldn't offer to give Albert a divorce. Unfortunately, it takes an Act of Parliament to get one, and the required grounds are absurd. Non-consummation, for example, requires proof that the husband is impotent. (Here I was rolling my eyes again.) Also, after four years, it was probably a bit late for that reason. Adultery on the wife's part is the usual grounds, which I would contemplate only if the alternative was death—as I had done briefly earlier, and rejected with relief.

(How absurd that a wife cannot divorce her husband for the same reason. I would gladly have done so for Cynthia's sake.)

At last I lay on my bed, fully clothed and too tired even to fret. I must have slept, for it was past dawn when I started awake to the sound of footsteps, doors opening and closing, and startled voices.

I glanced at the clock on my mantelpiece: past six o'clock. Was Albert planning to spirit me away before I had a chance to realize what was going on?

Surely McBrae would have thought of that possibility. Could it be Hamish, come to fetch me? Heart thudding, I crept to my door.

"No," Mrs. Cropp wailed loudly from below. "Lord have mercy, no!"

Heavens, whatever was going on? I had never heard Mrs. Cropp wail in all of my life. She certainly wouldn't lament my imminent departure, as we heartily dislike one another. In fact, she would probably rejoice if I were committed to an asylum, horrid woman.

I unlocked my door and peered out just as Mary Jane reached the landing. "Oh, my lady. It's the most dreadful news." She burst into tears.

"What is it?" I put an arm around her and drew her into my bedchamber.

"Oh, my lady! The master's dead!"

Chapter Thirteen

O f all the ghastly surprises I could have imagined, this was the last. I may sound calm now, reflecting on that dreadful day, but tears sprang to my eyes at her words. Mostly shock, I assume, but I did have some affection for my husband. He had been kind and generous to me, and our recent falling-out was nothing compared to the years of amity.

Stevenson, poor man, was pale and drawn, but he held himself together better than the other servants. "It seems, my lady," he said in a low, throbbing voice, "that Mr. Phipps was struck down by a coach whilst crossing the street."

That didn't sound like Albert. Usually, such accidents happen to drunkards, children, and dogs. Albert is far too canny a politician to let the malt get above the water, so to speak (a vulgar phrase, but I simply don't care).

Was too canny, I should say. It takes a while to become accustomed to the loss of a spouse, even when the marriage was an arrangement for our mutual convenience.

"Where? And when?" I asked, dabbing at my eyes with a handkerchief. Visions assailed me of Albert bleeding to death in the dusty street.

"It's most distressing, my lady," Stevenson said. "The master would say it was unsuitable for your ears."

"Nonsense." I spied a stranger hovering by the door, clutching his hat uneasily. A constable, if I wasn't mistaken. I beckoned him over. "Come here, my good man. Did you see it happen?"

"No, missus, I mean milady, but the watchman called me to the scene of the accident. It weren't far from here, milady—Oxford Street. By what the coachman says, Mr. Phipps run into the street like he were chased by the devil. Coachman hauled on the reins, but there was no stopping them horses quick enough. Mr. Phipps went right under them hooves. The watchman sent for a doctor, but only as a formality like, for Mr. Phipps were already dead."

"He died quickly, then," I sighed. Poor Albert! "That's a mercy."

"Aye," the constable said. "Very sorry, my lady."

And yet, how utterly strange. Who would chase Albert? A footpad, if it was not yet light? "Did the coachman see who was pursuing my husband?"

"Not as far as I could tell, my lady, but he was mortal upset. Couldn't hardly talk."

"I see." I pondered. "Unfortunate man, of course he is shocked. I should like to speak to him, please."

The constable gave me a pained frown, as if such a request astonished him. "Aye, my lady," he said hesitantly, "if you're certain."

"Why wouldn't I be?"

"The master would say it was improper for a lady to involve herself in such an unsavory matter," Stevenson said, a catch in his voice.

"Nonsense," I said again. "It was Mr. Phipps who sent me to the magistrate when the footman fell down the stairs." I dabbed at my eyes again. "Send for the coachman, please, and Stevenson, kindly inform Sir Edwin Walters of this tragedy." My voice trembled on this last word. Poor Albert, with his high and mighty ambitions, cut down in the prime of life.

Next a mournful procession came slowly up the street. Well, the only mournful-looking people were the two men carrying the hurdle upon which the body of my husband lay, covered by a cloth. The rest were the usual gawkers, even at this ungodly hour.

Except for one man—a sandy-haired Scot watching from across the street. Hamish widened his eyes and opened his hands in a mute question.

I closed my eyes and shook my head ever so slightly. I would not be going anywhere today. When I opened them again, he was gone.

Mary Jane tried to bustle me away from the door, but I set her gently aside. "Let me see him. I must be certain that it is he."

"I can identify him, my lady," Stevenson said, but he looked far paler than I felt, so I insisted. Perhaps I should have heeded my servants, for the sight of my dear husband, his head battered by hooves, made me horridly ill. I turned away and allowed Mary Jane to guide me upstairs.

Sir Edwin arrived, exclaiming, looking extremely put out. The tragic manner of Albert's death, he said, would be referred to the coroner, with whom Sir Edwin intended to have a word. "These coachmen are all the same. They drive too fast, and they're drunk half the time." He patted my hand. "We'll make an example of this one, shall we?"

As if punishing the coachman would make me feel better! "But we don't know anything about him. If anyone is to blame, it is whoever chased Albert into the path of the horses."

Sir Edwin tutted. "I daresay, Lady Rosamund, but you must leave it to the authorities to decide who is at fault."

The coachman arrived, along with his master, a blustering Cit. Stevenson took immediate offense at the Cit's attitude and tried to fob him off, saying I was unable to speak to anyone at the moment.

Protective servants can be so annoying. Fortunately, I heard him from the drawing room, where I was taking tea with brandy and feeding Sir Edwin the last of Cook's macaroons. (There weren't many; I suspect the staff, in a state of shock and seeking comfort, had indulged themselves.)

"Usher them in here, Stevenson," I called, so he had no choice. The Cit stomped in, objecting that there was no need to question Johnson, who never drove too fast—and then spied the magistrate.

"Sir Edwin!" he cried. "Thank God you're here. You'll see that justice is done." The coachman hovered in the doorway, twisting his cap in his hands.

Sir Edwin stood and bowed politely—exactly the opposite of what I expected. "Lady Rosamund, allow me to introduce Mr. Bixley, owner of one of our largest breweries and a staunch supporter of law and order."

Ah, money does talk, doesn't it? Cit though Bixley might be, Sir Edwin preferred not to offend him.

I assumed a pathetic hauteur of the sort at which my mother excels. "How kind of you to come, Mr. Bixley."

He bowed. "Such a tragedy, Lady Rosamund. My condolences, but I assure you, my man was not to blame, but rather the villain who chased your unfortunate husband into the street."

"Just what I was saying," Sir Edwin put in.

"My man never drives too fast," Mr. Bixley said. "He's been with me for years, and not a single mishap."

"I would not dream of blaming your coachman." I dabbed at my eyes, although they were mostly dry by then. "It was kind of you to accompany him, but quite unnecessary. I merely wished to hear his account of the accident."

"Surely not," Sir Edwin said, shocked. "Such a tale is not for the ears of a delicate lady."

"For my own peace of mind, I wish to know exactly what happened and perhaps understand why." I beckoned to the coachman. "Do come in, my good man."

"Yes, yes, Johnson, come in and tell Lady Rosamund," Bixley said.

The coachman approached, pulling his forelock. "He come out of nowhere, milady. One minute the street was clear, and the next he run directly in front of my pair."

"Was my husband running from someone?" I asked. "A footpad, perhaps?"

"Hard to say, milady. It weren't quite light, and afore I had a moment to think, Mr. Phipps were directly in the path of my horses, and 'twas all I could do to keep them from bolting. I do believe someone turned and run t'other way, but I didn't catch but a glimpse."

"Aye," said Mr. Bixley. "I saw him, too, but not to identify him. Medium height, maybe. Wearing a long, dark coat or cloak, looked like. But as Johnson says, it happened quickly, and dawn was just breaking. This time of year, I make a point of reaching my brewery by first light."

I sighed. "It must have been a thief, for I can't imagine anyone else chasing Mr. Phipps about at daybreak, or anytime for that matter." It seemed I would never know the answer. "Thank you so much for your trouble. Would you care to stay for tea, Mr. Bixley?"

Needless to say, the brewery owner was deeply gratified at this invitation, but he declined politely, citing business to attend to. I indicated to the hovering Stevenson to usher them out again, and endured a lecture from Sir Edwin on what Albert would have wanted me to do and say.

Which did not include inviting a Cit to tea. "He's a mushroom, my lady—not your sort at all!"

I suppose that depends on what one's sort is. I was beginning to wonder if I had been born into entirely the wrong stratum of society—although there are hypocrites of all kinds, aren't there?

"I shudder to think what your dear mother would say," Sir Edwin pronounced.

Ugh! That reminded me that Mother and Julius would no doubt descend upon me in short order. Mother would bustle about, ordering mourning clothes, which hopefully would keep her too busy to worry about my sanity or lack thereof.

Lady Beddoes soon came over from next door, all a-flutter, and before long Lady Danby and Miss Tubbs arrived. It is fascinating how quickly word spreads and how visitors conglomerate. Ordinarily, these ladies would be scarcely out of bed at this time of day.

Other ladies arrived. Over and over, I related what I knew of the fatal accident. It didn't become any easier with the telling. I had to keep dabbing tears from my eyes, but Mary Jane kept me supplied with dry handkerchiefs. Most of the ladies wanted to blame that poor hapless coachman, some even demanding that I lay charges against him. Fortunately, Cook had launched into a flurry of baking, so I was able to distract them with sweet cakes and tea.

When a moment arose, Lady Danby took me aside. "Lady Benson must be devastated," she said. "I believe she truly loved Albert. I thought to see her here. Have you written her?"

"I have not had a moment to do so." This was a lie. Cynthia's reaction to this appalling accident had occurred to me, but I was not at all in charity with her. To tell the unpleasant truth, I cared not one whit about her feelings. I was not sure I could face her with equanimity, much less sympathy. "And I cannot possibly leave here. Lady Danby, would you mind calling on her to see how she does?"

She is a kind-hearted lady, so of course she agreed, and returned later to report that Cynthia was prostrate with shock. "She has not your fortitude, my dear," Lady Danby told me.

No, Cynthia had plenty, but she was upset because Albert's death had ruined her plans. Now she would have to start all over. (But at least her new plans needn't involve killing me.) She was probably staying in bed to avoid anyone else guessing she was *enceinte.*

At least I need not fear receiving any more anonymous letters.

I wrote to my father by express post. I was obliged to write to Mother and Julius as well, although I would far rather have ignored them. They arrived late the following day. I believe they would have caused a great deal of trouble for Mr. Bixley and his coachman, if the coroner had not already brought in a verdict of accidental death.

Needless to say, Mother and Julius did their best to persuade me to come home, but Albert's death put me in possession of a great deal of money and, more important, the freedom to do as I chose. My father arrived just in time for the funeral. He invited me to come live with him, if I chose. I declined a permanent move—I know he values his solitude—but I promised to come visit him as soon as I could get away from London. (And Mother and Julius couldn't do a thing to prevent it!)

Albert was an important man, so the funeral was impressive (not that I attended; ladies usually do not, and a number of my dear friends came to keep me company on that dismal day). Afterwards, mourners gathered for a cold collation. So many guests were expected to pay their respects that I was obliged to hire two temporary footmen and have most of the refreshments catered. Even the Prince Regent stopped by for a few moments.

His Highness astonished me by tutting and saying, "He was to have a barony, you know." At my obvious surprise, he frowned. "Didn't he tell you?"

I simpered and sighed, as the Prince seemed ready to take offense. "He hinted of a delightful surprise." I wished I could weep on cue like a stage-actress. "So that was it! Dear, dear man, no wonder he seemed so pleased.

Alas, this makes his death doubly tragic!"

Not that I give a pig's tail for baronies (how could I, as the daughter of an earl?), but elevation to the peerage would have meant a great deal to Albert, and my response seemed to placate the Prince.

McBrae also appeared briefly, underdressed as usual. "My condolences, Lady Rosamund." His eyes, as they met mine, were both speculative and rueful.

Recalling the kiss of that fateful night, I felt myself coloring up. To cover my confusion, I murmured one of the usual platitudes.

"If I may be of service in any way, do not hesitate to let me know." He passed on to mingle amongst the guests.

"In what possible way could that nobody serve you?" my mother demanded. "I don't know why he came. He was scarcely acquainted with Albert."

"He was merely being polite," I lied. I knew full well he was here to see me. Fortunately, I didn't need any assistance at the moment, for he was a most unsettling man.

It was a long, taxing affair, not only because death and funerals are exhausting, but because people had not yet forgotten the gossip that I might be unbalanced. I ignored the sideways glances—some kindly, some uneasy, some horridly sly—but that sort of stoicism is most wearing.

There was one amusing moment, when I caught sight of a particular footman sidling his way through the guests. I only saw him from behind, but suddenly I knew it was the selfsame man who had jostled me weeks earlier. Apparently he was still finding regular work. I wondered if I should hire him—I still had only one permanent footman, Maurice—but one of the guests distracted me, and I forgot to look for him again.

After the funeral, Cynthia wrote, begging me to call on her as soon as possible. Since Albert was gone, she need not consider his plans, whatever they might have been. She intended to leave Town in the near future, but had decided not to risk deciding on a final destination because word might get out. Now that Albert was no longer with us, did I wish to reconsider my suggestion that we travel together?

This seemed a strange request from someone who only a few short days ago had planned my demise. And then it struck me, as I pondered the note, that her handwriting bore absolutely no resemblance to that of my anonymous correspondent. Admittedly, those letters had been written in all capitals, but shouldn't there be some similarity?

A creeping uncertainty came over me. I had burned the originals, so how could I compare?

Fortunately, in my exhaustion that night, my obsession with checking things had failed me. I had forgotten to burn the one letter that still remained in my reticule.

I took it out and examined it. Just as I had thought—the *essence* of the writing was much different. It is hard to explain precisely what I mean. I am no handwriting expert, but would Cynthia be able to disguise her writing so very well? Perhaps. Perhaps not.

Or could she have hired someone to write the letters? That seemed foolish beyond words, and...

I suppose you have guessed already. You probably knew the truth pages and pages ago, for you are an impartial observer.

I did not want to believe the appalling notion that swept over me. I had already been carried away once, by the assumption that Cynthia was the culprit. I trod my slow way up to Albert's study. It didn't take long to go through enough of his correspondence to confirm my suspicion.

Albert's capital letters resembled those in the anonymous missives much more closely. And he was a calculating sort of person. He was skilled at devising strategies to make people do as he wished. That was why he had such a successful political career.

I fell into a chair, overwhelmed, struggling to gather my thoughts. Memories crowded my mind: Albert insisting that I remain in Town despite my mother and brother, despite the increasingly damaging gossip...no, *because* of the gossip *he* had spread not only amongst the ton, but amongst his cronies who ordinarily had nothing to do with me. My death would do him very little harm, for he would blame my tragic insanity on my mother's family—nothing to do with him.

It all made sense. He was about to become a peer. As a peer, he would need an heir. He could have forced me to bear one, I suppose, but he preferred to avoid conflict, and I would certainly have put up a fuss. Not only that, he loved Cynthia, who was already expecting a child. With me out of the way, he would be free to marry her.

He had regular access to her house and therefore to the highland cow seal.

No wonder he hadn't come up with a plan for Cynthia's future—for he already had another one for mine.

And now he was dead instead.

I burst into tears. I wept all over his desk, and Mary Jane found me there, apparently inconsolable. I put up with her well-meaning attempts to comfort me, pulled myself together, and went to visit Cynthia.

We hugged and consoled one another, although naturally I didn't say why I needed consoling. She assumed we both grieved for Albert—which we did, in our own far different ways.

On the way over, I had done some thinking. I don't believe he killed the footman, for pushing a man down the stairs is a frightfully uncertain way of committing murder. What if the poor man hadn't even been hurt? But that accident, coupled with Corvus' first drawing of me, gave Albert the idea of how to get rid of me. Or so I surmised. I would never know for sure.

"Yes, I'll come with you," I said. "We'll go visit my father, and decide where to go from there."

And so it was settled. I returned home full of plans for departure, the first of which was to get rid of Mrs. Cropp. Luckily for her, she had received a small bequest from Albert, so she wasn't exactly destitute. I couldn't in all conscience give her a letter of reference, but she's not a stupid woman. I expect she will write to my mother, explaining that I forgot to give her a reference before leaving Town, and therefore asking her to kindly provide one instead.

Stevenson received a bequest as well, but he was happy to stay on with a skeleton staff. In the meantime, he took on the task of making travel arrangements for Cynthia and me.

"How did this cloak get behind the clothes press?" Mary Jane asked the next day. "I'm sure I put it with your winter clothing." She brushed dust off it and laid it on the bed. "You'll certainly need it Up There, my lady. Brrr!" She was not happy with the prospect of remaining in the North for an unspecified length of time. "Luckily, it's a dark wool and therefore suitable for mourning."

She went on muttering, while I tried to remember what had happened that fateful night. Had I left the cloak on the clothes press? I supposed I must have…

Oh, drat! Next thing, she would ask where were my diamond eardrops. I had sewn them into the hem of the cloak. How in heaven's name would I explain that?

Not that I owed her an explanation, you understand, but she would think it a sign of madness. A suspicion, once it enters someone's mind, never quite goes away. I had been doing my very best to show no sign of my affliction, hoping for a fresh start. Yes, as a widow, I had control of my life once more, but control can be wrested away by a determined male relative. If Mary Jane became worried about me…

I picked up the cloak, threw it around my shoulders, and paraded back and forth before the mirror. "It's lovely and warm, perfect for long, snowy winters," I said, trying to decide how to get rid of her—or alternatively, to leave the room with the cloak wrapped around me. Which would look eccentric, considering it was summertime.

Surely an earl's daughter should have the right to seem eccentric.

But not mad, alas. My recently-acquired control of my life and fortune was conditioned upon maintaining the appearance of sanity.

"My lady?"

Startled out of my dark thoughts, I turned to Mary Jane. "What?"

"Your diamond drops." They sparkled in the palm of her hand. "I'm not sure that you'll need them Up There, but one never knows, and they would be unexceptionable after your strict period of mourning."

"Yes," I managed, despite the whirling chaos in my mind. "Let's bring them."

I went into my boudoir, still wearing the dratted cloak. I examined the hem. There were no coins and no gaps in the stitching, which was as pristine and perfect as the day I purchased the cloak. (My *modiste* uses only the most competent seamstresses.)

But I had made a few gaps in the hem…hadn't I? And inserted both some coins and the eardrops, and stitched the hem again—but far more sloppily. Hadn't I?

Yes, you may say, for you have read this tale. But when one has an affliction such as mine, one can easily doubt oneself. What had I done, and what had I only *thought* of doing?

And yet, I remembered checking the hem once, twice, maybe more. No matter how frightened and fatigued I had been that night, I knew perfectly well what I had done.

I returned to my bedchamber, tossed the cloak on the bed, and opened the drawer of my dressing table. At the back were a number of coins which I had certainly not put there recently. I went down to the empty drawing room, where I could think in peace.

Not that my thoughts were peaceful—precisely the opposite. I remembered wearing the cloak. I remembered McBrae gently unfastening it and dropping it over his arm.

And kissing me in that dim room…and immediately slipping out the door. With my cloak—earrings, coins, and all.

How had he returned them? By subterfuge, obviously, and the answer soon came to me. That footman… Weeks earlier, I had wondered if perhaps the footman at Lady Baffleton's was Corvus himself. Once I knew Corvus and McBrae were one and the same, I dismissed that theory—or rather, I forgot it. What if my guess was correct? That raven-haired footman, whom I'd seen only from behind, was at Lady Cart's ball at Almack's. So was McBrae. He was in my house the day of the funeral, and again, briefly, so was McBrae. What if, acting as a footman, he had slipped up the back stairs and restored my cloak and its contents? It was entirely possible. If he could sneak about my house at midnight, he could certainly do it in the midst of a horde of servants and guests.

But…why not just bring them to me openly?

CHAPTER THIRTEEN

***

And so, the last part of the mystery was solved. I believe Albert intended to lie in wait for me, perhaps to immobilize me and drop me in the river, as McBrae suggested. Albert encountered McBrae instead—disguised by the hooded cloak he took from my bedchamber. I cannot say what happened next, but in semi-darkness, a cloak and a long, dark coat may look much alike.

Cynthia and I left London the following day.

If I had not found her diamond earrings in the hem of the cloak, I wouldn't have returned it to her. Will she realize that it was gone, and if so, will she remember how and when it disappeared? She was overwrought that night, but she is an intelligent woman with a stronger mind than most.

It is only a matter of time.

—From the diary of Corvus

About the Author

Rumor has it that Barbara Monajem is descended from English aristocrats. If one keeps to verifiable claims, however, her ancestors include London shopkeepers and hardy Canadian pioneers. As far as personal attributes go, she suffers from an annoying tendency to check and recheck anything and everything, usually for no good reason. Hopefully all this helps to explain her decision to write from the point of view of a compulsive English lady with a lot to learn about how the other ninety-nine percent lived in 1811 or so.

As for qualifications, Barbara is the author of over twenty historical romances and a few mysteries, for which she has won several awards. On the other hand, she has no artistic talent and therefore is really stretching it to write about an artist who draws wickedly good caricatures. But she's doing it anyway, because he's irresistible. To her, anyway. Not so much to the aristocratic lady. Or at least not yet.